DARKENED SOUL

C. G. BLAINE

*For Grandma Smitty and Henry.
Lose one; gain another.*

ONE

CHAZ

One of the glaring misrepresentations of creation surrounds women being brought into existence. Eves weren't some afterthought, plucked from the ribs of Adams to keep them from screwing the livestock. And yes, plurals because every remix of creation included a pair. Women were always a part of the plan, coming from the same dust, given the same flesh and free will as men. They just figured out better ways to use both.

And I, for one, am damn glad they did.

Especially when the short skirt and legs that have been keeping my attention from across the bar pass by me. I swivel my stool, and her eyes linger on mine before they dart to the hallway in the back.

It only takes a glance at Kai to know he's not going anywhere. The blonde who dragged him over to the booth earlier has more of her ass on him than the seat. The kid might only be twenty-three, but between his constant thrill-seeking and the ability to talk the panties off anything that moves, I can say without a doubt, he'll go down as my favorite charge.

By the time my new friend looks at me again, I'm finishing my beer and standing up to follow.

"What's your name?" she asks, her nails digging into my scalp.

It's the first thing she says to me after dragging me into the ladies' room. We wasted no time in getting past the pleasantries of her tugging open the button of my jeans and me pressing her up against the tiled wall.

I chuckle at her sudden interest. "Does it matter at this point?"

She slips her fingers into the waistbands of my jeans and boxer briefs and nudges them down. Her eyes drop to my cock, lip dragging between her teeth before she looks up again. "Only if you want me to moan it."

She wraps her hand around my shaft and gives an upstroke, squeezing right as she reaches the head, causing me to hiss. Then she swipes her thumb over the tip, gaze still on mine when she sucks the pre-cum off her skin.

Holy hell, this chick. I almost stop hiking up her skirt to continue down this road—*almost*. "You can cry out whatever you want, gorgeous. Sex god or badger."

She laughs, looping her arms around my neck as I hoist her up by the backs of the legs. They lock around my waist, her head shaking. "I'm not calling you—oh fuck."

Her head falls back against the wall when I pinch her clit through the fabric, and a sweet whimper escapes. I slip under the edge and drag back through her bare pussy to circle her entrance.

"So fucking wet for me already." I sink a finger inside her easily, and after a pump, I add a second.

She tightens, both her thighs and cunt as she starts to ride my fingers. I watch them slide in and out of her, glistening with her arousal. Fucking mesmerizing.

Short on time, I withdraw and grab the condom I tossed on the sink. The second I roll it down my shaft, her heels dig into my ass, lining herself up for me.

"Fucking wet and no patience."

"None," she says. "Now fuck me."

Since I have none either, I drive into her all at once. Her amber eyes roll back, lips parted on a gasp, but then she's there with me again by the next thrust. Our mouths connect, tongues colliding. She tastes like that cinnamon shit some tool sent her a shot of earlier.

With my next stroke, she moans out the sexiest sound, and curiosity wins out.

"Chaz," I say.

She smiles against my lips, her lashes fluttering. "I'm Nyx."

I pull away enough to see the rest of her face. "Like the goddess."

"Uh-huh," she answers, her head lulling back again.

Her throat stretches out, displaying flawless skin. I kiss and lick her neck, gripping her thigh while I fuck her harder. We say very little of anything intelligible for a while. Each flex of my hips, she meets—hands, mouths, and teeth everywhere.

"Yes." Nyx's back arches off the wall. "Faster, Chaz."

My name is fucking magic from her mouth. I groan and hitch her leg higher, angling to pound deeper. She starts clawing at the back of my neck, and feeling her lose rhythm, I rub her slick clit with my thumb.

"That's right, gorgeous. Choke my cock while this pretty pussy comes."

She cries out, and I fucking let her, not caring if the entire bar hears her. I increase pressure on her clit for more. Her cunt's like a vice. When it spasms around my cock, I couldn't hold back if I wanted to. I slam into her a few more times and then come hard enough my vision fades. I groan into her neck, my dick still pulsing as I lazily slide in and out of her.

Her skin smells fantastic, and I breathe her in for a second, pushing deep one last time. It earns me a satisfied hum, fingers stroking the back of my hair.

While I lower her feet to the floor, my lips catch hers, and it occurs to me how ass-backward the entire exchange has been. Even for me, a bar bathroom without a word from a girl I don't know is a little much. Not that I'm complaining. Fuck, after this, I might need to consider the idea more often.

Nyx straightens her skirt before I flip the lock on the door. I flash her a grin and let her lead the way out. It gives me another view of the ass that made me follow her in here in the first place.

She's already past the end of the hall when Kai rounds the corner with his arm draped around the sexy blonde. I step out of the way as they pass me and glance back to catch his smirk. He pushes open the door across from the one I just exited and guides her in. At least I had the decency to screw in the ladies', which not only smelled like fucking roses, but also looked like it'd been cleaned within the last century.

I hesitate at the end of the hallway to watch the door close behind them, still uneasy about my charge being in a public restroom. Then again, I'd worry about my sanity if I *wasn't* concerned after the whole demons-tried-to-kidnap-a-Nephilim bullshit from the beginning of summer. Three months isn't quite long enough to get over nearly losing your eternity. Give me a solid four at least.

"Hey." Nyx reappears and tugs on my arm. "Buy me a drink?"

I raise an eyebrow at her. "After that? You should be buying me one."

Her eyes roll, but she smiles. She really is gorgeous, raven hair and melty amber eyes, with a spark of sin radiating from her.

I already planned on buying her a beer. Call me a romantic, but I thought it would be *before* I was inside her. After I flag down the bartender for drinks, we head outside to the patio where a tall wooden fence blocks the street. Most of the time, my lap ends up as the chair when I bring someone back here, but she lands on the picnic bench next to me. Still not complaining. It'll make bailing the second Kai's ready to leave all the easier.

Only when Nyx turns to face me—batting her long lashes and denting her lower lip between her teeth—I know we won't make it that long. Her eyes lower, and she's going to ruin this in three … two … one…

"You want to get out of here?" She twists at the neck of her beer bottle. "Or maybe you can call me sometime? We can fuck in a restaurant coatroom. Compare and contrast." She laughs out the last few words and peeks up again.

I half-smile, really wishing she hadn't just said any of that.

Luckily, my charge rarely takes long to seal the deal. The adrenaline starts pumping through Kai, giving me the first hint of divine light. The slow burn unfurls in my chest before creeping down my arms. No matter how long my punishment on Earth lasts, the return of the light never disappoints.

"You don't want me to call you," I say, setting down my beer.

Her eyebrows pull together, and she goes back to watching her hands. "I'm pretty sure I do. I mean, you did refer to yourself as a sex god and then only made me come once, but—"

The heat hits my hands, spiking through my fingers until the tips burn. I skim them over her cool cheeks and cradle her face between my palms. The light leaves them and warms her skin beneath.

"You don't want me to call you," I tell her, softening my voice to barely above a whisper. "You don't want me to take you home or walk you to your car."

Nyx's body relaxes as she brings her hands to hang from my wrists, melty amber eyes gazing up at me. "I don't?"

I shake my head. "You don't want anything from me. In fact, you're going to go inside, buy yourself another drink, and not care if you ever see me again."

She nods, slowly at first, but then surer of herself as the light seeps in, my words becoming a reality. When I let my hands fall away, she blinks a few times before glancing around. Her attention returns to me, and she forces a smile.

"I'm going to get another beer." She stands and holds out a hand like she's worried I might offer to go with her. "I'll be back."

The door slams behind her, and I take a swig of my drink, thankful as fuck she won't be. Nothing against her. She was one of the more tolerable mortals. It's just that I'm at my quota. Two Nephilim to keep alive so my soul doesn't become a permanent fixture outside those heavenly gates. And it will take more than a set of pouty red lips and a perfect ass to distract me.

A hell of a lot more.

Even if my dick gives off the impression of being easier to sway.

TWO

CHAZ

Sometimes, existence stays the same for so long, I forget how fast everything can go from la-di-da to all-out fucked. Then, out of nowhere, all hell breaks loose—sometimes literally. Demons surface, my brother loses his shit. Two brothers, if you count the one ready to give up his immortality to spend eternity with his charge. And, I mean, no offense to Cassannah, but I do.

While all that crazy might have died down, I still have to deal with the lingering possibility that the one being who has a massive hard-on for killing me may or may not have the sole object in existence necessary to pull it off. Which means a constant waiting for everything to go to hell again.

I snag the amulet off the kitchen counter, tossing the chain over my head on my way out the door. I stick it down the collar of my shirt before I cross the hall and walk into what might as well be my second apartment. The new living arrangements required a serious downgrade from a badass condo to a one-bedroom with terrible plumbing. But I've subscribed to the policy that the closer my charges, the better.

Avery spares a flick of her gaze before returning to her book, curled up on one end of the couch in the living room. "Hey," she says, distracted. She tugs at the blonde strands stacked on top of her head, tightening the knot, and slides the black frames up her nose. "Kai's in the shower."

No shit. I could hear the pipes whining from my apartment.

I plop down beside her, and she pulls her socked feet back, tucking them underneath her. I flip on the TV while she reads, the silence between us very much our norm. If Kai earns the award for being my favorite charge, his twin sister deserves accolades for being my lowest maintenance. She was eight before my powers kicked on because of a true threat of danger—a drunk driver when she was riding her bike home from the library. No hazardous habits or even fun ones, so adrenaline responses with her stay minimum. Most days.

"Has he introduced you yet?" She absentmindedly weaves the black cord of her locket through her fingers.

Kai has one too, only dangling from his are their father's dog tags—killed by an IED when they were kids. The twins have worn their necklaces constantly over the past year. Not that they have the choice. I cast protection spells on them to ward off demon powers and other bullshit and used the light to "*suggest*" they leave them on permanently. It allows for a longer leash with them, and with two to juggle, every inch of breathing room helps.

I tap the end of the remote on my chin, deciding on a movie to stream. "Who am I meeting?"

Her baby blues pop up. "Whoever he's seeing."

The book snaps shut, and she tosses it to the floor, readjusting to sit on her knees. Boring or not, gossiping about her brother always lights a fire in her. If only she knew about half of his extracurriculars. Underground boxing rings, street racing—whatever he can find to keep the adrenaline pumping.

"He broke out the Armani cologne he bathes in whenever he has a steady fling," she says.

The chick thing doesn't shock me. Kai's been lying low lately. Lots of stops at a coffee shop and an apartment complex several blocks from here. Surefire signs he's found a new fixation.

He settles down now and then with a girl he's ready to give the world to, then he gets bored out of his mind in about a month and triumphantly returns to a one-ride-only philosophy. But since his trip to the men's room with the blonde a few weeks ago, most bursts of light from him come late at night when he's alone—or when the pipes moan a warning that he's in the shower. So, he's not screwing whoever he's supposedly screwing, which *is* surprising.

Avery checks behind me as the floorboards creak in the hallway. Kai struts out in the nicest pair of jeans he owns and a shirt he fucking stole from me. He pushes his hair back, a few shades darker than his sister's, so it sticks up in the front. I'll be the first to admit, my line of Nephilim has been nothing short of exceptional in the looks department.

"Get lost in my closet?" I ask as he stops at the end of the couch.

"Jealous it looks sexier on me?"

I snort, shaking my head. Kid's cocky as shit. Another trait passed down through their line. It serves as a reminder that running through those veins is angel blood—half of it anyway, undiluted by the generations between him and my original Nephilim.

Kai shoves his phone and keys in his pocket, backing toward the door. "I've got to run a quick errand, but I want you here when I get back."

I wave him off. He wants me to ask why, but as long as it isn't anything that makes my job harder, I don't care. He's barely out the door when I bite back a grin, having found the perfect movie. There's a reason I only watch TV at their apartment, and she's sitting right next to me.

"Another horror movie?" Avery hugs a throw pillow to her chest, pouting as she sinks into the cushions beside me. "You should see a therapist or something. You get *way* too much pleasure out of making me squirm."

"Squirm, scream, panic. I'd be thrilled if you developed an anxiety disorder."

I throw her a wink, and she rolls her eyes.

We settle in for an hour and a half of jump scares. With each one, the light floods through me. I stretch out my fingers, feeling the power ready and waiting. Her heart pounds, and her palms sweat, and I'm loving every fucking second of it.

"What's that?" Avery shoots up on the couch, looking away from the screen.

A surge of light has me scanning the shadows, but the chance of real danger lurking inside the apartment is minimal. I have this place spelled to shit against demons and even other angels—a bag of crystals that block either from entering, other than me. I stashed the blocker bag behind a vase in a kitchen cupboard Kai and Avery never use with another one hidden in an air vent as backup.

"Oh my God." She latches on to my arm. "Did you hear that?"

I pause the movie because I did hear something. A muffled *thud, thud, thud.* Then comes a whiny voice in the hallway, equivalent to what I can only describe as road rash to the soul.

"Chazaqiel!"

Fucking. A.

I groan, hitting play, and then I toss Avery the remote. "I'll be back in a minute."

"Where are you going?" she asks, claws still sinking in until I shake her off.

"I forgot my phone."

And to spell the entire apartment complex.

I open the door and close it again without a sound, and then I prop against it to watch the universe's most irritating heavenly parole officer bang on my door across the hall. Straight blonde hair hangs to her waist, the black skirt tight on her hips and curving over her ass. Lydia curses under her breath, bringing a phone to her cheek. If I listen hard enough, I can hear the vibrations from mine on the kitchen counter.

My apartment's spelled too, stopping her from dropping in whenever she wants. Given the set of her jaw when she turns to the side, she's not impressed with my no-uninvited-guests policy. I give her a few more seconds to hit peak annoyance and then straighten up.

"The angel you're calling doesn't want to deal with your shit right now." I cross my arms when she spins. "Fuck off until next millennium at the beep."

She scowls, lowering the phone. "You're such a—"

"Beep," I say, stepping around her to unlock my apartment.

She huffs in the doorway, unable to cross the threshold. "Using divinity blocking spells makes me think the three of you left are hiding something from me."

"We are." I grab the bag hidden in my cupboard and pick one of the crystals out to deactivate the spell. When I turn around, Lydia's in the archway that leads to the living room. I set the bag and crystal on the counter, and on my way through, I duck down to her ear. "Our shit from you."

"I'm sure Cass reported to you about Samyaza?"

I stop, stiffening at the name. Samy—my brother, the leader of the original Watchers. Samy, Cass, Rosdan, and I were brought into existence together. As angels, that was *our* beginning, but our beginning ties to *the* beginning. The beginning of everything. The divine light that shaped the cosmos is the same energy, the same substance used to create us. But by coming into existence together, the four of us share a deeper bond. We're family, so when one of us goes the fuck off the rails, it's a jagged cut—infected from the start.

Not that I'll give Lydia the pleasure of knowing any of that.

"I think he mentioned something," I say, feigning indifference.

She narrows her eyes, suspicious of any bullshit out of my mouth.

Fair, because it is all bullshit. I know every detail about what happened with Samy. Far more than the scraps she's pieced together. I also know the Demon of Destruction cracked open the Abyss, so he could get the Dimming Blade—the only thing that can wipe an angel from existence—but *she* doesn't know anything about that.

And I'm not going to be the one to tell her.

"Why are you here, Lydia?" I ask. "Is this another sad attempt to get with me? Because I hate to burst your bubble, but—"

"Please stop talking." She holds up a hand, her cheeks brightening. "I would give up my eternity to forget that night." She drops her arm and sighs. "Since none of The Fallen have been checking in once a century as required, I'm conducting random drop-ins. So, report on your charges."

The Fallen. Our punishment as Watchers shines as a prime example of how fast everything can go to shit. Twenty of us were sent to Earth to oversee mankind. None of us expected to find such a shitshow when we got here, humans starving and struggling to survive. Sure, my brothers and I *technically* went against God's plan by deciding to help them. Still, I stand by the fact that they would have learned how to predict the weather and plant a fucking seed anyway. Except, while we were busy teaching them how not to die like dumbasses, a bunch of the other Watchers created a race of angel-human hybrids—the Nephilim—which led to a fucking bloodbath.

Was it a disaster? Yes. So much so that God opened the Abyss, bringing on a flood that scratched out creation so a new one could begin.

Did the thirteen assholes who couldn't keep it in their pants deserve to be punished? Probably. They weren't remorseful for the part they'd played, even after they were turned human and told their souls would rot outside of Heaven's gates for eternity after they died.

Should those of us who were only guilty of being *too nice* have been banished from Heaven until we redeemed ourselves? Hell no. But we were, and I've been tied to one of the seven Nephilim bloodlines saved by God for our punishment ever since. Their powers on lockdown, mine only available when one's in danger—or when they experience a spike of adrenaline, my favorite loophole. I've kept all my charges safe until they died of natural causes, self-sacrifice, or an act of God. And now, I'm down to the last two. Then I'll finally be able to go the fuck home, where I belong, with the divine light pulsing through my veins—a true angel and not this sad excuse of a babysitter.

"Kai and Avery Benson," I tell Lydia.

She stares at me, expecting more, and when I don't provide, she rolls her eyes. "You guys make me drag every single word out of you. What happened to the other charge you had last time?"

"Their mother, Rachel Benson, died of cancer just shy of a decade ago."

The same type as her father and his grandmother and her brothers before that. The cancer had been skipping a generation until then. Now, it seems to hit all my charges, the last one before she turned forty. After she died, Kai and Avery were raised by their paternal grandparents, who are currently enjoying retirement in Arizona.

"Avery," Lydia says, a hint of disdain rolling off her tongue. "Do I have to worry about you screwing her like Kasdaye and his little—"

"Hannah. And can you blame him?" I add with a smirk. "She's hot."

Lydia's always had a thing for Cass, and her nostrils flare at the mention of Hannah Kelley, his final charge and *love of his existence*—his words. The connection we share with a charge is strong, and Kelley's cool and all, but the sacrifice to be with a mortal is our immortality. To ask to become human and give up the light we've been fighting to get back this entire time.

"Whatever." She clips her tone, trying to regain control even though she's never had the upper hand. "Just keep your ass in line, and remember, I'll be back soon."

"I'll be waiting, gorgeous." I gesture to the door. "Now, why don't you go bother Rosdan? Give him a chance to turn you down."

She levels me with a glare. "Screw you, Chazaqiel."

"Been there, done"—she's gone before I finish—"that."

I sigh, returning to the kitchen. The crystal goes back in the bag, the bag back in the cupboard, and my ass back across the hall. When I throw the door open without warning, the light that was dulling reignites as Avery jumps.

She groans, realizing it's just me. "You suck."

I chuckle and crash down on the cushions beside her. Maybe I get the Cassannah attraction a little. The light feels incredible on its own. Throw in direct contact with the source and sex, and you have one hell of a combination. A chance at combustion under the right circumstances.

I end up watching Avery instead of the movie, tracing the soft curves of her face and then lower, my mind playing with the possibility.

After a while, she flinches at something on the screen and covers her eyes. The heat inside me churns and thrashes around along with the beat of her heart.

As she lowers her hands, she glances over. "If you plan on messing with me again, don't."

I shake my head, sliding closer. I've never thought about Avery as anything but a charge until recently, but I won't lie, I've been wondering.

Her eyes dart between mine when I lean in. "Chaz…"

"Yeah, Aves?" I brush my fingertips up her jaw, and her eyelids fall halfway closed at the contact. I move my other hand to where her pulse throbs in her neck so that it beats against my palm, and she swallows as my mouth hovers in front of hers.

"Fuck it."

And my lips are on her.

She sucks in a breath, her face cradled in my hands while I toe the hell out of this line. I don't even know what I'm expecting—sparks or fucking fireworks or some revelation I'll never recover from. A transformation, me and her different than before, savage and ripping at each other to get more.

But it's just Avery. Smooth skin that smells like her body wash and a mouth I could spend some time on. Nothing existence-altering though.

Our lips are still mashed together when hers turn up, and I chuckle, still kissing her.

I keep a hand on each side of her face, pulling back. "Want to pretend this never happened?"

She nods, smiling, but when she tries to sit back, I hold her there until her cheeks warm under my touch and her eyes look lost in mine.

We have quite a few years left before I'll need to drop out of their lives, so they don't realize I'm not aging with them.

I'd rather not spend it in some awkward dance with her.

"I came back in here, and we watched the movie," I tell her. "No weird kiss or anything other than a normal Chaz and Aves movie night, okay?"

I get another nod, another smile, and I let her go. She slumps back on the cushions, turning to the screen, and after a few seconds, she curls up next to me and rests her head on my shoulder. Roughing up her hair, I relax more than I have in a while.

It would be fucking fantastic if the feeling could last. If, after the shitstorm and the vague threat from Lydia, I could at least make it to the credits without the door flying open.

I jerk my head to the side as Kai strolls in, giving us a grin before he glances over his shoulder.

Then she walks through the door.

Pouty lips. Perfect ass.

Our eyes connect, hers widening when he hauls her to his side.

His hand splays out over her stomach, his mouth pressing a kiss to her temple. "Guys, this is Nyx."

Fuck.

When Kai introduces us, she sticks out her hand and puts on a sham of a smile.

"Chaz," she repeats. Her mouth forms around my name the way it did when she moaned with my cock buried inside her.

With that image front and center, I slip my hand into hers. "Nyx." Then, for kicks, I tug her closer and kiss her cheek. "Like the goddess," I whisper.

I pay little attention through the rest of the intros. They met at the coffee shop where she works, and she burned his macchiato or some shit. He's been there every day since but only orders water. Blah, blah, Avery thinks the story is adorable and drags Nyx into the living room, insisting they stay for the rest of the movie.

That means the four of us are tucked in together on the couch. Me, the charge I just kissed, the chick I fucked in the back of a bar, and my other charge, who considers me a brother and is now dating the previously mentioned couch occupant.

Lovely.

A few jolts from Avery in, I tip my head back on the cushions, maneuvering around her head to see Nyx on her other side.

Even in profile, lit with the blue light from the screen, I catch the tension in her face, down her neck, and into her shoulders.

When she looks over, I don't even pretend I'm not watching her. She acted like she didn't know me, like my hands hadn't been all over her, in more places than Kai's—unless he's figured out a way to have sex without triggering adrenaline. Her indifference shouldn't bother me, but Avery's overreaction to the movie cranks the furnace on my irritation. The light fuels my own overreaction to the woman I'm now in a stare-down with over the back of the couch.

Kai's arm slides around her. She licks her lips, and my jaw ticks when she turns to him.

"You said there's water in the fridge?" she asks. Kai starts to stand up, but she pats his leg. "I got it."

She sure as shit does.

I wait for her to disappear behind the wall blocking the kitchen, and I stretch, purposely knocking my elbow into Avery's head. She whips toward me, lips pursed.

"Beer?" I ask.

I get a curt nod.

As I get to my feet, Avery's attention drifts back to the screen where, in about thirty seconds, the possessed-looking kid will start freaking out like he's … possessed. Movie-type possession, that is. The darkness never really alters appearances that much; it just takes over and extinguishes the soul.

Kai kicks at my foot as I pass. "See if Nyx needs help."

I sure as shit will.

When I round the corner, she's pulling a pitcher of water out of the refrigerator. She turns around, slamming straight into my chest just as Avery screams from the other room.

Perfect timing, Aves.

Light floods through me, and my hands catch her face. She looks up as I tilt her head back, the heat pouring from my palms.

"Why are you here?" I ask softly.

Her eyes soften to honey-colored pools, the pitcher resting against my chest. "Kai wanted to watch a movie," she answers, almost robotically.

Divine light—the most potent truth serum in existence. But I still follow up. "How did you meet him?"

"A coffee shop. But I'd seen him before at the bar where I met you."

I should let her go, stop interrogating her. Except part of me wants to push further and find the right question to reveal that she's really here to see me. Fuck, because having her be some nut, hunting me down and getting with my charge to get to me, is better than a random second encounter?

"You aren't here to see me?"

Her head shifts from side to side. "No. I didn't want to see you again."

Words I planted in her head somehow manage to fucking spear me. Shit. She's really dating Kai.

I feel the power start to fade and brush my thumbs over her cheeks. "You won't remember this conversation."

When I let her go, I back up a few steps.

Nyx blinks out of the daze and notices me standing near the door. All the tension returns to her. "Glasses?"

I point to the cupboard, crossing my arms while she pulls out a glass. She fills it, returns the pitcher to the fridge, and turns around in front of me. Her teeth work her lip to the point that I think it might bleed before I move around her to the refrigerator.

"He doesn't need to know," I say, grabbing three beers. "Actually, I'd prefer Kai doesn't know how I really met his girlfriend."

"I'm not..." She's still facing away from me, but she turns over her shoulder. "We're still feeling things out."

An interesting distinction she felt the need to throw out there, and like a complete asshole, I smile. "Well, by all means then"—I slam shut the fridge and pass her without another glance—"feel away."

I hand off beer bottles on my way back to my end of the cushions. I twist off my top and land it on the coffee table in front of me with a *tink*, propping my feet up next to it.

Nyx comes back a minute later, no glass. Kai's arm goes around her, and Avery inches closer to me as the creepy music picks up on the screen. She's hiding her face in my shirtsleeve, all of me burning hot when I feel eyes on me from down the couch. I bite back another smile and hold Avery to my side.

Lydia clearly pinned her concerns on the wrong Nephilim causing trouble. Because this is setting up to go all kinds of wrong.

THREE

CHAZ

"Make her forget you fucked her," Cass commands. "Tell her the first time you met was at the apartment. And suggest she never see your charge again, too. Don't screw around with this mortal soap-opera bullshit."

I laugh into the phone. Leave it to Cass to jump straight to the nuclear option. But he's not wrong. A little light and a smooth suggestion, and Nyx disappears. Things could go back to normal, and I wouldn't need to hang back like I have been the past few days. It would also mean the texts from Avery would stop.

Messages have been popping up while I bounce between following her to lectures and watching Kai from across the street as he becomes a piece of furniture in the coffee shop. Avery has dissected every aspect of what she could coax out of her brother about his new obsession, and she likes to share with the class.

Nyx Lamore. A twenty-three-year-old barista, only able to afford her first-floor one-bedroom, thanks to a small inheritance from an aunt she never met. She also has a twin sister but doesn't talk about her, and her parents died years ago too. Kismet, according to Kai. Bullshit, according to Chaz.

I flop back on my bed, turning the palm stone over in my hand. The flat, polished crystal works like a crystal ball, except two-sided with each side tied to a charge's soul, giving me a quick way of summoning their image. I spend longer on Avery as she's crossing the street on the way to her car after her last class of the day. Mostly to avoid watching Kai across the hall with Nyx. She's splattered with paint for some fucking reason.

The phone vibrates against my cheek, and I pull it away to check the screen.

"Why's your charge texting me?" I ask.

Then I see *what* Hannah sent and roll my eyes at the morality police.

You will NOT make a woman forget she slept with you.

"Unless it's life or death," she adds, shouting from somewhere near Cass. "And being annoyed is neither."

Fucking Kelley.

But again, point made.

"At least get her away from you and your charge." Most of the edge has left Cass's tone. I'm still not used to the effect she has on him. Who knew all it would take to soothe my brother's forever-tortured soul was a fiery redhead who doesn't put up with his shit?

I toss the palm stone into the air and catch it. Maybe I shouldn't do anything. I wouldn't if this were just some random chick my charge brought home. They're a fling, and soon enough, the whole Nyx storm will blow over—with or without my suggestive influence.

Kai doesn't even like coffee.

My phone vibrates again. I turn my head to check the screen, lit up with a message from *Cursed One.*

Call me. Now.

Our other brother must be feeling left out.

Anytime I start to bitch about any part of my existence, I only need a text from Rosdan to settle me down. The dude hasn't caught a break in … well, ever. While twins have been a rarity in my line, Ros deals with them regularly. This last go-round, triplets.

I sigh, letting the stone fall onto my chest. It slides off onto the mattress when I sit up. "Well, you two have been shit for help. Remind Kelley I'm here if she ever wants to—"

"Fuck off," Cass says. "Deal with your charge before it blows up in your face."

He hangs up, and I chuckle, calling Rosdan. I've made it to the living room by the time he answers—or before he starts making demands.

"Let me in," he says, followed by a click.

And he's the polite one.

I redirect to the kitchen and disengage the spell. "It's open," I shout, setting my phone on the counter.

Rosdan charges in, flying right past me.

"Great to see you too, dude," I say, shutting the door behind him.

"Sorry. Mark's at the gym—new kickboxing class. I waited for his heart rate to get up so I could drop, and I don't have much time." When I turn around, he's holding out his hand with a wild look in his dark eyes. "Amulet."

Another attempt to get Samy's amulet working. It's essentially been nothing but dead weight the past few months, but Ros is determined to find a spell so we can use the power stockpiled inside.

I pull at the chain to bring it out from under my shirt and then drag it over my head while I give him a once-over. "I take back the *great* part. You look like shit."

Dark circles under his eyes, hair a mess like he's been pulling at it—sure signs of a stressed-out Ros.

He practically jerks the amulet out of my hand. "It'd better be this one. I'm running out of scrolls."

"Maybe Samy cast an original."

"Fuck, I hope not. I'll still be trying to figure it out when the triplets go to college." He holds the amulet to his chest and chants the spell. Nothing happens, so he shakes the crystal—which houses enough divine light to blow up the moon—like it's a remote with dying batteries and tries again.

Not even a spark.

"Shit." He shoves the amulet back at me, tugging at the back of his hair. "I really thought I had it."

"I know, buddy." I pat him on the back, walking him toward the door. "You'll get it next time."

He stops and scowls at me. "You're such an asshole."

Then he drops out of my apartment, leaving my hand suspended in the air when he goes. I leave the amulet on the counter by my phone and grab the crystal to reengage the spell when someone knocks.

"Still good," I call, setting the crystal down again.

The knocking continues, and I shake my head. Rosdan's erratic episodes always put me in a good mood.

I head for the door, grinning as I let him back in. "You couldn't possibly have another spell—"

I cut off, my decent mood crumbling. My grip on the wood tightens while Nyx blinks up at me.

"Hey." Her wet hair drips on the carpet, nothing but a white towel covering her. The corner tucked in the front dips the terry cloth down to show her cleavage.

Fucking hell. I assumed the whining pipes meant Kai was in the shower.

She holds the top of the towel with both hands. "The hot water cut out on me, and Kai said I could finish my shower over here?"

I should say no and send her back across, but then the elevator dings down the hall, and she gives me a pleading look.

Shit.

I back out of the way, so she can rush inside.

"Thank you," she calls over her shoulder.

I follow her. As she pads across my living room, my gaze stays on her bare feet—the safest place to look right now even if the black paint on her toes is sexy enough to give anyone a foot fetish. She turns around in the doorway, waiting for me when I make it past her legs.

"A coworker took me to one of those places where you drink wine and paint." She stretches out her arm, splattered with a rainbow along with a swipe of blue on her neck. "She got tipsy and overzealous with the acrylics."

"Good to know," I say, not sure why I should care.

"I just didn't want you to think I randomly bathe at people's apartments in the middle of the day or anything."

The *or anything* sounds like it carries more weight, and my lips twitch, fighting off a smirk. "Got it."

A non-acrylic pink paints her cheeks as she reaffirms her hold on the towel. "Will your shower work for more than a few minutes?"

I nod. When I moved in, I waited until Avery was panicking over a screwup in her school schedule and suggested the landlord fix a few things. The shitty plumbing was number one on the list. Otherwise, anytime the apartment above or below me used any water, my shower ran cold. Probably the reason Nyx is about to climb into mine.

Once she scampers off, I decide to head across the hall and tell Kai to ask before sending wet and naked chicks to my apartment. But as I turn, the water kicks on, and I glance at the bathroom door—cracked ajar. I forgot to warn her to turn the handle so it would latch without springing open, not a repair priority since I live alone. Even less of one right now.

Steam rolls out of the shower as she drops the towel. Raven hair cascades down to the middle of her back, and the bare curves of her ass are even sexier than I imagined.

My hands flex at the memory of touching her. At how she would feel with her skin slick from the humidity. By the time she turns for the shower, I'm hard. Standing in the middle of my damn living room.

It takes a lot to look away. To pay attention to the heat now flooding through my chest. But then, I couldn't give a fuck about Nyx because everything inside of me pulses *Avery*.

It's instant. All my thoughts are on her face, her light pounding through me. And the floor drops out from under me, the world around me shifting until solid concrete catches under my feet.

I search the abandoned sidewalk, locking on to the blonde hair disappearing around a corner. I drop again to the corner rather than walking, and when I step out, I sense the guy before I see him through the front window of the grocery store that Avery's heading toward, cliché black ski mask over his face.

What will happen plays out in my head. He'll grab the money in the cash drawer—the clerk standing there, frozen—and then he'll shout a vague threat, backing to the automatic doors before he turns and runs straight into the completely innocent blonde who holds my eternity in her heartbeat.

I take off at a dead sprint. The guy stuffs the cash into his coat with one hand, the other waving the gun. He's only a single step backward when I slam into Avery from behind, launching us into another store's darkened entryway. Everything falls away but her. And then the ground returns under me, and the two of us are standing on the top level of a parking garage with nothing else but a lonely white Escalade.

The light starts to fade with her no longer in danger, but it picks right back up as she frantically glances around, confused about where she is and how.

She spins to face me, and my hands fly to her cheeks.

"Shh," I tell her when she whimpers, panic swimming in her eyes. "You're okay." She calms, vision glazing slightly, and I continue, "You changed your mind about going to the store. It wasn't such a bad day after all, and you haven't smoked in weeks. Why start again?"

The light starts to fade as she nods.

"Head to your car and go home. You won't remember seeing me or talking to me." Before I lose all the light, I let go of her and drop back to my apartment, landing in the same spot I was standing in a few minutes ago.

I grab the palm stone from my pocket, flipping to Avery's side. She's just coming out of the daze, her head swiveling side to side until she finds the elevator. I watch for her to slip the keys into her ignition, and then I collapse into my recliner, listening to the water from the shower.

Avery is safe. Nyx is naked. And as fucked as it sounds, I'm still hard.

Darkened Soul

The next day, Kai plants himself at the coffee shop with his laptop again. In high school, he interned for a tech company and scored a job with them right after graduation. Perfect for him since he can work when and where he wants. He mostly dicks around and then works a week straight to meet a deadline.

Since he's immobile, I decide to stick close to Avery. It has nothing to do with Nyx or how I keep undressing her in my head each time she walks past the glass storefront.

Aves works at a daycare a few days a week after her classes. By the time she finishes her shift, it's already dark. She parks her car under a lamp in the lot and keeps a hand on the pepper spray in her purse, senses peeled for any creeps she might encounter on her way into the building. A Watcher's dream come true.

I give her a head start before I follow inside. Running into each other in the lobby might lead to a conversation about work in the elevator. They think I sell life insurance—not the most creative cover, but boring enough that they rarely feign interest. Which is good because I know shit about it.

I've barely walked into my apartment when my phone vibrates. I toss my keys on the counter and fish out my phone to check the message from Kai.

Chinese. Get your ass over here.

Wednesdays are the one night of the week he stays in without question. Kai and Avery usually drag me over to their place or else show up at my door, barging in when I answer. Not my preference, given the hidden compartment in my closet chock-full of scrolls, vials of Nephilim blood, and other shit that might land me on a few lists.

Rather than waltz my way into another awkward night, I pull out the palm stone. I turn to Kai's side and focus on his face to avoid any unwanted visuals—something all Fallen have learned the hard way at some point or another. Once his image appears in the crystal, I slowly pull back to reveal more of his surroundings. I scan for Nyx, but I only see the twins, sorting through paper bags and carryout containers.

Before heading over, I jump in the shower. I'm getting dressed when my phone lights up with another text from *Cursed One*. I swipe my phone off the bed and read through the spell he sent. I grab the amulet from the nightstand and clasp it while I chant the words. Unsurprisingly, nothing happens. Our brother was smart. He wouldn't have used anything easily figured out to access the power.

I put it on, hiding it in my shirt. Call me a sentimental bastard, but I still can't stomach throwing it in the closet with the rest of my mystical stash. As I walk into the twins' apartment, I'm texting Rosdan to keep searching. When I look up, my eyes land on Nyx.

She's on the couch, her back against the arm and her legs draped over Kai with Avery on the other end. *Damn it.* I should have rechecked the palm stone. I blame Ros, getting his Cursed One juju all over me via text message.

"About time," Kai says as I cross in front of the TV to a shitty papasan chair. The wicker creaks under me, and I'll count myself lucky if it holds for the next few minutes until I leave.

Kai tosses me a set of chopsticks, but I throw them right back.

"I already ate," I say, glancing at my phone.

I haven't, and I'm starving, but it's almost eight, which means—

"Shit." Avery drops her chopsticks into the container before setting it on the end table. She grabs her laptop out of her bag on the floor and then rushes into the hall that leads to their bedrooms.

Weekly video chat with their grandparents for the save.

Kai's not far behind, sliding out from under Nyx's legs. He rounds the couch and leans over the back to plant a kiss on the top of her head. "Be back in a few."

She nods. "Take your time."

We both watch him until he disappears too.

A few seconds later, Avery says, "Hi, Grandpa," and Kai shuts the door, muffling her voice.

I've already stood by the time Nyx turns her head around, and I feel her tracking me through the living room.

"Really?" she says. "You'd rather leave than be alone with me for five minutes?"

I stop a few feet from the end of the couch. "Who said I was leaving?"

I was, but now that she called me out, I veer into the kitchen. When I come back with a beer, I take Avery's seat and pull her carton of dumplings onto my lap.

"Oh." Nyx twists at the gold earring wrapping around her cartilage. "Sorry. I thought you—"

"Weren't mature enough to treat meaningless sex like exactly that?" I open a set of chopsticks and add, "Trust me, it will take more than you to get rid of me."

She drops her hand and presses her lips together, glancing at the closed door like Kai will burst out and save her. Serves her right. I could be across the hall already instead of swimming in awkward silence.

"So," she says after a minute.

Oh, fuck me. I should have just left.

"How did you and Kai meet?" She smiles, tight-lipped and forced as hell. "He said you've been friends for a while but didn't give me any details."

"Skydiving."

"You're one of those people too, huh?"

I look up, dumpling suspended halfway to my mouth, and a hint of her real smile appears.

"Ready to throw yourself out of a plane or off a cliff like you have a death wish," she says.

I snort. "Not exactly."

It's more like, I was sick of constantly trying to differentiate between real danger and the kid's adrenaline. I needed a way to keep closer tabs before I went insane—or even worse, before I missed something. Now, I can be right there with him, enjoying the rush of light while we casually fall from ten thousand feet.

Nyx waits until I'm done chewing and readjusts, bringing a knee up to her chest. "Explain it to me then because I don't understand why Kai does it." One more glance over her shoulder. "What's the appeal?"

"It has nothing to do with wanting to die. The exact opposite, actually. The thrill makes him feel alive."

Kai's done the same math I have, noticed the pattern emerging in his lineage. He thinks he'll die young and plans to do all the living he can before it happens. Even as an immortal, I get it. If I thought I would lose the light forever, I would be doing whatever I could to drown in it. To feel it in every space of my being for as long as I could before it was gone.

She studies me for a second. "But not you?"

I shrug, less interested in the conversation now than thirty seconds ago. The next question she asks, I'll fake a phone call. But instead, she stares at the couch cushion between us. "I guess that's the difference between Kai and me."

I should leave it, but the word tumbles out of my mouth. "What?"

"I'm not so worried about feeling alive as much as I am interested in surviving." She looks up. "You know?"

My jaw clenches as I nod, dropping my attention back to the container in my hand. Surviving. What my entire time on Earth has been in a sense. Just getting through each day, snailing my way toward what I really want.

Nyx averts her gaze fast when I look up, but not fast enough for me to not notice she was still staring at me. She scans the room, pretending I didn't catch her. I rest my head on the cushion, my face turned to see her. It doesn't take long at all for her eyes to return to me, and they stay fixed on mine.

Ninety percent of us knowing each other has been just this. Watching each other. From across the bar, from down the couch. She leans to the side, her cheek against the fabric. Fuck, I need to leave. Haul my ass across the hall and stop imagining take two with her.

Maybe Nyx comes to the same conclusion because when a faded laugh reaches us, she jerks her head up. She checks the door before swinging her feet off the couch.

"Tell Kai I needed to go?" she asks, slipping on her shoes.

She doesn't wait for my answer, beelining for the door. Unlike her, I make no attempt to stop her. In fact, I've just made the decision to lie low until this chick vacates Kai's life. Back to shadow mode. While I'm at it, I need to get laid. Preferably by a woman who can keep her damn eyes to herself.

FOUR

CHAZ

"I have got to get rid of Nyx."

Kai lets himself in while I fucking sing the "Hallelujah" chorus inside. Once he's rifled through my cupboards for chips and grabbed us beers, he falls onto my sofa. I crack open my can and throw back the footrest on the recliner. His announcement is unsurprising since he's creeping up on the three-week mark of no sex.

He leans forward, hanging his head between his shoulders. "You can fucking tell just by looking at me that I haven't gotten any, huh?"

"Yeah, you'll have to explain that one to me."

Kai slumps back, sipping his beer and staring off at nothing. "She said she's sick of meaningless sex and she wants something real."

I raise my eyebrows at him. "That sounds like the opposite of everything you want."

He shrugs. "It is. But she's so hot, dude. You know she'd be a phenomenal fuck. Maybe I should just hold out a little longer."

Before I can encourage him to lose her number, he snaps his head up, digging in his pocket for his phone. "Shit." He stares at the screen, and I get a flash of warmth in my chest. "There's a fight tomorrow night. At the Border Heights Hotel."

Underground boxing. Not my favorite of his activities, but I figure I can work it to my advantage.

"So, kick some ass in the ring, and then we'll go celebrate by ending your dry spell."

The smile spreads across his face in record time.

Fuck. Yes. My charge is back.

The first sign of warmth hits my chest as we cross the dark parking lot. We take the service entrance into the hotel. The light stays at a steady stream and then spikes with Kai's first step over the threshold. Adrenaline runs high on fight nights and not just in him. The air buzzes, everyone in the room on another frequency. It also means a cramped space with sweaty mortals with just as much alcohol seeping out of their pores and a fifty-fifty shot at someone puking near me.

"I love this," Kai says, bouncing around. He shakes out his hands to redirect his energy. "The feeling right before a fight. Nothing better."

I nod and slap him on the back, more energy flowing through me. This is why I haven't put the suggestion kibosh on boxing. I'm just as addicted to the high. It also helps that the kid has yet to take a hit in ten fights. I have a feeling the first time a fist connects with his jaw and knocks his ass out cold, I'll change my fucking tune.

We're almost to the stairwell that leads to the basement when he slows down, checking his phone.

"Hold up." He turns back the way we just came, and as I look, the door at the end swings open.

In walk two burly dudes. One holds out his arm to keep the door open for someone.

And I sense her before she passes him.

"Are you fucking kidding?" I say.

He just shrugs. "She's fucking hot, and I'm so close." He holds up his finger and thumb, showing me just how fucking close, before he saunters down the hall toward Nyx.

I shake my head, bringing my hands to the back of my neck. My reaction isn't only to the fact that I can't avoid this woman, even when I try, but also to her outfit in general. A short black leather skirt and a tight white tank top. The clicks of her knee-high boots echo through the hallway.

Once she's in reach, Kai pulls her to him, his hands running over her. His lips brush hers, then they move up her jaw. Our eyes meet as his mouth reaches her ear. She half-smiles at whatever he said and looks away from me to him, and my jaw clenches.

As they walk toward me, I glare at them both. "You plan on taking her in the ring with you?"

He waves me off, ushering her into the stairwell. "She'll be fine with you."

They disappear down the steps, and I follow, inwardly cursing myself for not locking him and Aves in a room somewhere. Again.

Kai ducks into a hallway, leaving Nyx with me at the base of the stairs.

I flip him off when he glances back and shouts, "Take care of her for me."

"That bad of a request?" she asks.

I look down at her as she's staring up at me. Melty. Fucking. Eyes.

"Not an easy one. You're barely wearing clothes and about to be in a room full of dudes riding high on hormones."

Shouting fills the stairwell when I push the metal door open.

Nyx walks through but stops just inside. Her gaze drifts over the sea of unwashed men spread in front of us and then down at her bare legs, and she crosses her arms over the peek of skin between her top and skirt. "Oh."

Fantastic. Now, she has me feeling bad when she's the one making my existence more difficult.

"You look fine," I bite out. "I just wish Kai had told you to throw on a sack so I wouldn't have to spend the night threatening every asshole who looks at you."

Her eyes return to me. "Every single one?"

I shrug. "Everyone who isn't me."

Because I don't know when to fucking quit, I add a wink.

She licks her lips to suppress a smile. "I'll just have to keep you in line myself then."

With her feelings no longer hurt, I press a hand to the small of her back, guiding her into the crowd. She latches on to my arm and plasters herself to my side to dodge people. It takes no time at all for the first set of bushy eyebrows to rise, the owner's head following us.

In the center of the room, a chalk outline serves as a ring with a wall of muscle surrounding it to keep anyone from joining in on the fights. We push our way as far forward as we can before the bodies become so compact that I'd have to physically remove them to get us closer. I'm usually right at the front, but Nyx won't stand a chance up there.

I stand with my arms crossed as they announce the fighters for the first round. Kai's will come later when the room's drunk and rowdy. Nyx cranes her neck, trying to find an opening to see the two shirtless guys being escorted toward the center. It's only the second time I've seen her with her hair up, the back of her neck and shoulders bare. I swipe my fingers over the faded tattoo at the base of her neck without thinking—a ring created by a serpent swallowing its own tail. She stills at my touch, and I hang my head so my mouth hovers near her ear.

"Your tattoo," I say above the shouting.

She turns her head to see me. "It's the Ouroboros."

I resist rolling my eyes. "I know."

Depending on who you ask and in what century, the symbol represents fertility, the life-death cycle, rebirth. The *correct* meaning, though, is the original one. Immortality.

"But what are the lines?" I trace the ring before following one of the four vertical and wavy marks, inked overtop. It feels familiar—her skin under mine, but also the lines themselves. The spacing and staggered formation. I've seen them somewhere I just can't pinpoint when in the past several thousand years.

Before Nyx can answer, someone shoves in front of her. She shifts into me, and my other hand catches her waist to balance her. More people scramble and cram into the space in the seconds before the fight starts. A swarm of locusts with us in the middle.

Her back to my chest, ass against my crotch, our eyes locked. I should let go, except the warmth inside from the light rivals the heat coming from her. Both intoxicating.

Next thing I know, my fingers are sweeping again. This time, they glide over the exposed skin below the hem of her tank, skimming across her stomach. She tenses for a second but then spreads her hand over mine, resting her cheek on my chest. She stares up at me with her lips parted. The shouting turns to white noise as I bring my hand from her neck to her chin. I'm about to dip down when my angel senses tingle.

My head snaps up, the light inside of me sending my attention straight to the man on the far side of the makeshift ring. He's leaning against the wall with his arms and ankles crossed, leering at me. While he looks like an asshole wearing a suit in a place like this, it's not the outward appearance I give a shit about. It's the darkness swimming beneath the surface. Flowing through him like the light does me.

Fucking demon.

After a second, his attention averts to the fight. I resist the urge to drop straight to Kai. The demon doesn't seem all that interested in me, so there's no fucking chance I'm pointing a giant neon sign at my charge. Most demons want nothing to do with Nephilim. Not even the upper-level ones, which this douche obviously is with his suit and styled black hair. Abaddon was the exception, and that asshole only tried to snag one for another sad—and failed—attempt at taking me out. For the Demon of Destruction, he's shit at his job.

I scan the rest of the crowd for any other darkness, only half-aware Nyx is still standing in front of me. I'm not even touching her anymore. Like I said, my dick might act like it's easily swayed, but strip everything away, and only three things remain. Charge. Light. Home. The fucking mantra of my existence.

"I have to go," I tell her, not even looking down.

"What? You can't leave me here." She tries to grab my arm when I walk away, but I shake her off. "Chaz," she calls. She says something else, but the fight is starting and her voice blends with the others.

I look straight ahead until I reach the exit, then I check over my shoulder. The demon hasn't moved an inch, his focus still on the fighters. I relax, confident he's not after anything that's mine. Uppers thrive on seedy shit, so I shouldn't be surprised to finally run into one at a place like this.

I'm about to turn back when a pissed off woman breaks through the horde of dudes. I pretend not to notice her and push out the door. Kai's still my priority. With all of these humans around, I can't just drop to get away from her, so she easily catches up.

"Hey," Nyx says once we reach the stairwell.

"Hi," I deadpan, but I don't look at her.

She follows me into the hallway Kai went down earlier. They've held fights here a few times, and the fighters hole up in the out-of-commission break room toward the end. Even if he's not on the Upper's radar, I want him as far away as possible.

She marches fast to keep up with me. "What happened back there, it was—"

"Nothing happened." I spin before we reach the only open door in the hallway.

Nyx barely stops short of running into me. Her mouth's open, undoubtedly ready to argue, but my palms are already glowing by the time they cup her cheeks. She takes a quick intake of air, and I realize she thinks I'm going to kiss her. Not at all my plan. Until she grabs the front of my shirt like she wants me to.

And then I fucking lose my mind.

I step into her, the light cutting off from my hands as my lips crush hers. The moment crashes over me, her pulling at me to get closer and every molecule of me wanting to give her exactly that. But as rapid as the onset of my insanity, I recover from it just as fast.

My mouth leaves hers—her face already warm and a dreamy look in her eyes when they flutter open.

"Nothing happened," I tell her, my voice calm. "I asked about your tattoo, a guy pushed you into me, and I caught you so you wouldn't end up on the dirty floor."

She nods. "Thank you."

I half-smile. "The crowd was getting rough, so we came down here to find Kai. We didn't talk or even look at each other." I pause, letting her mind fill with new memories. "Now, we're going to get him and leave because you aren't feeling well."

"I don't want to be here," she says.

"Let's get out of here then." I release her, not even waiting for her to come out of the daze to turn around.

Charge. Light. Home.

Not mortal-chick anything.

The room is rowdier tonight. More drunk guys and yelling, and for whatever fucking reason, Nyx insists on being closer to the ring. It feels familiar from the get-go. The hotel, her tiny skirt, how she looks over her shoulder to see me. Dark lashes fan over her molten eyes, my hand on the back of her neck.

"The Ouroboros," she says.

This time, when she falls back into me, I don't hesitate to tip her chin up. I graze my lips over hers and then nudge her face to the side, my mouth moving down. My tongue drags over her neck. I taste the salt on her skin, feel her palm sliding up the front of my thigh.

A groan escapes when I rip my mouth away from her. The demon watches from across the room, his red glare staying on me this time. I should get Kai, but Nyx feels exactly like I remembered.

I lower my attention back to her before I turn us around. We push through the men, their gazes raking over her. Once we clear the crowd, I let her go. She glances over her shoulder to make sure I'm following her to the stairwell. And fuck me, I am.

The cool air hits us when she rushes through the door. By the time it bangs shut, I have her in the shadows under the stairs, pushing her back up the wall.

"Fuck, I want you," I rasp, my palms on her ass.

Her legs wrap around my waist, and she pulls my mouth to hers. Our tongues are already tangled when our lips collide, teeth clashing right after. She tastes like sin, forbidden. I thrust forward, my erection rubbing against her clit, and she moans the sweetest fucking sound. She's not Kai's—never was. She's never let him touch her like this. Feel her like this.

Nyx is mine.

My lips stay on hers while I look over at Kai. Blood pools around him on the floor, darkness seeping out of his chest where the demon hit him with a fireball. The shadows swirl around him, and I can't feel the light anymore. All that's left is her, overwhelming my senses, pumping through my veins.

Nyx moans, rolling her hips, and I grind against her again.

"You should get that," she mumbles into my mouth.

It only takes a second for me to figure out what she means, but I'm not finished claiming her yet. One of my hands creeps up her shirt, pushing her bra out of the way. As I cup her breast, her heart races. It matches the faint pounding that keeps trying to interrupt.

"Chaz," she says. Then, after a few more seconds, "Chazaqiel."

The sound of my full name makes me pull back to see her. "Sorry, gorgeous. I need to answer the fucking door."

I wake up in my living room. No Nyx. No concrete steps overhead. The only thing that is the same between the dream and reality is my raging hard-on. I'm still on the couch, where I crashed after a drunk Kai stumbled back to his apartment and passed out.

The knocking grows louder as I rub the heels of my hands into my eye sockets and maneuver through my dark apartment. Dark because it's two in the goddamn morning.

Skipping the door, I head straight to my kitchen. I flip on a light and pull the blocker bag out of the cupboard, so I can take out a crystal and disengage the heavenly security system.

"It's open," I say.

Rosdan blows in. This time, he at least shuts the door. Without a word, I hand him the amulet. Then I crash back down on the couch, because I really prefer my brother *not* notice my cock tenting my sweatpants right now.

"How are you here?" I ask, adjusting.

"I scared the shit out of Mark and then suggested he use the treadmill until I get back." He studies the amulet, running his fingers along the edge of the gold back casing. "I was helping Alistair with his homework the other day."

Ros thought it would be a brilliant idea to nanny for his charges. A ten-year-old with a Cass obsession and two-year-old triplets—two boys and a girl.

"He's working on a report," he says. *"The Sword in the Stone."*

"You tell him it's all bullshit?"

I get a sideways glance for that.

Little about the stories humans have passed around about the sword is how it really went down. Hell, it wasn't even in England, like most people think. Some hermit in Italy looked out his window at the right moment and caught an angel all lit up with his wings spread. It was Michael—a complete dick, by the way, who wouldn't protect a human if his existence depended on it. The guy marked the spot with a sword. Funny thing about an angel drop spot, the light affects the ground. So, the sword stayed, unmovable, until a Nephilim wandered by and yanked it out. Nephilim blood. Never know when it will come in handy.

"I don't have to remind you whose Nephilim pulled the sword," Ros says.

Samy.

I don't say it out loud, but we've been playing Finish the Thought long enough that Ros raises his eyebrows like I did.

"He always had a thing for it," he says. "Even the bullshit version. So, what if…"

I nod. "He made the spell so it can only be cast under certain conditions."

"One of the last scrolls had a spell I'd never seen before. It looks like he somehow infused our powers into the amulet over the years, and then something to do with intentions. It might be another dead end, but this feels right."

"Chant away then, brother."

Ros closes his eyes, his words barely audible as his lips move.

The crystal starts to glow.

Nothing more than a quick spark, but more than we've ever gotten before.

His eyes fly open, catching the last of the show before the amulet powers down again. He drops to the floor, landing on his back and raising his arms in the air. "Fuck yes. You're not such hot shit now, are you, Samy?"

"I hate to bring down the taunting party, but the spell didn't work."

"Not completely, but it's a start. From what I can tell, it's like training it to respond to us. The more we cast with the right intentions, the stronger the power it releases."

"And what's the right intention?"

Rosdan climbs off the floor and tosses me the amulet. "No idea. I just tried to channel Samy."

I catch the chain as Ros drops out of my living room. Only then, he reappears a second later.

"You good?" he asks.

"Why wouldn't I be?"

He cocks his head to the side, studying me. "Cass said you called him for advice about your charge."

"So?" I stand up and head to the kitchen for a beer.

"No one in their right mind would ask Cass for help with their charge."

I snort. He's got me there. When I close the fridge, he's still staring at me from the archway.

"You figured out the whole wanting-to-bang-your-charge's-girlfriend problem then?"

"All solved and wrapped up with a bow." I crack open my can and lean back on the counter.

He smirks and nods. "So, the groaning before you answered and the hard dick are—"

Before he finishes, I toss the crystal back in the blocker bag, and he involuntarily drops out of my apartment. While I sip my beer, I stare at the amulet in my hand. But instead of thinking about how close we are to unlocking it, I'm picturing Kai in a pool of blood. Thinking about what it felt like not to sense the light from him anymore. Even if it was just in a dream.

The half-assed approach at avoiding Nyx isn't working. I can't keep my eyes, hands, *or* my mind to myself. If I want to steer clear of Cass's nuclear option, I'll have to take it up a notch until Kai moves on.

I'll need to disappear.

Luckily, I'm one of The Fallen. A Watcher. Being invisible is what we fucking do.

FIVE

NYX

"Miss Lamore."

I ignore the nurse chasing me through the entryway, not in the mood to deal. Not that I ever am, but today is definitely not the day.

"Miss Lamore," she tries again.

"Sorry, I'm running late." I don't slow down to throw out the excuse over my shoulder.

She catches up with me as I descend the porch steps. "We need to discuss the changes to your grandmother's medications."

"Not a doctor," I say, crossing the yard.

I'm almost to my car when she rushes in front of me. I consider going through her but huff out a breath and cross my arms. She beat me fair and square. I'll give her thirty seconds.

Once she's convinced I won't bolt, she tugs at her white cardigan to recompose herself. "Thank you. Now, as you know, the disease has progressed far faster than the doctors..."

And here's where I tune her out. This is why I visit at night. Her nurses let me come and go without forcing updates, which are pointless anyway. Ninety-eight-year-olds don't suddenly make miraculous recoveries. Their bodies fail them, their minds, until they stop talking and recognizing you.

I twist around to see the front of the house while she talks about test results and scans. My eyes scale the two-story Victorian I bought when we moved to Colorado a few months ago. It really is quaint. Smack dab in the middle of nowhere with a tattered porch and a bench swing hanging from chains. A rusted tricycle sits next to the banister at one end. I wonder who left it there. If, when they climbed off after riding up and down the wooden beams, they had any idea they would never get back on.

I doubt it. We rarely recognize those types of moments as they're happening, only after we realize we're missing something—or someone. That's when last times become important. When they're already gone.

Guessing we're somewhere around the half-minute mark, I face the nurse straight on. She's talking about morphine when I hold up my hand to stop her.

"With all due respect," I say, "I don't have time. Do what needs to be done to keep her alive. Those were her directives, and it's what all of you are being paid to do."

She lifts her arms, only to drop them again in exasperation. "That's what I'm trying to tell you, Miss Lamore. There's nothing more we *can* do for her."

"Well"—I crowd her toward the car until she's forced to sidestep out of the way—"I really don't have time for this then."

She shakes her head as I jerk the door open.

"And with all due respect to you," she says from behind me with no respect at all, "that woman deserves more than a weekly drop-by from someone who can't show the least bit of compassion when she's dying."

I bite the inside of my cheek until the metallic tang touches my tongue and close my eyes. She has no clue what she's talking about, but it isn't worth the energy. Let her think I'm cold and uncaring, that the last two words out of her mouth weren't a vise grip on my heart. I won't waste time trying to prove otherwise when *I* can still do something to help her.

Once the door to the farmhouse slams, I breathe deep and exhale slowly, hoping when the air slides out of me, it takes the bullshit with it. I'm still gripping the doorframe when I notice the piece of paper stuck under my wiper blade.

Wind blows the chimes hanging from a tree beside the house, the rest of the yard eerily quiet while I retrieve the note. I climb in the car before reading it. It has a phone number scribbled in the middle. My eyes roll at the familiar handwriting, and I pop open the center console. I grab the cell phone from underneath a pile of napkins and dial the number, irritated and he hasn't even answered yet.

"My goddess," Hex says.

"Why are you leaving me notes?" I look around in case he's lurking.

"You wouldn't give me your number." He pauses, and I hear the smirk as he adds, "But now, I have it and can hear your voice anytime I like."

Still not seeing him anywhere, I turn the key in the ignition. If he hasn't made his presence known by now, he's long gone.

"Is there a point to this call?"

Dirt kicks up behind my car as I fly down the long driveway. I glance at the phone vibrating in my cupholder. Seeing a message from Kai, I almost smile—*almost* because I'm still talking to the ex from hell, but Kai's name on the screen is a welcome relief. He went MIA on me for a few days but resurfaced last night, texting to explain he'd been buried in work and promising to make it up to me.

I had panicked when he stopped calling and didn't come by the coffee shop, thinking he'd finally gotten sick of taking it slow. Not that I could blame him if he had bailed. I've made him wait for weeks even though Chaz was inside me without knowing my name. To be fair, the bathroom sex was a one-off. Fantasy fulfillment fueled by nerves, liquid courage, and a cut jaw and chin dimple I never saw coming.

"I'm just checking in," Hex says. "On you. On Nyla."

The way he tacks my sister's name on so casually at the end reminds me of all the reasons I loathe him.

"Fuck you," I bite at him. "You don't get to say her name. Not after what you did."

He sighs dramatically, like he does. "Oh, Nyxie. One day, you'll forgive me for all that, you know."

"Not in this life."

"Well, here's to the next one then. And hey!" His tone turns mocking for the last two syllables. "We might not even have to wait very long to find out if you can't get your shit together."

"That sounds like a threat," I say, turning onto the highway.

"Did it now? Because it was meant as a warning." Hex drops his voice low, the real reason for the call finally on the surface. "It's time to quit screwing around, love. Get him in the open and alone. And soon. I might be a heartless bastard, but at least I'd feel *a little* bad about killing you. Boss man, though, is on a completely different level, and if you don't deliver, you can bet—"

The rest of the wager is lost to the wind when I throw the burner phone out the window. I don't need Hex to remind me what's at stake, and I sure as hell don't need him to tell me I'm out of time.

The nurse already did both.

SIX

CHAZ

> *Last-minute convention out of town*, I text
> Kai. *Gone a few days at least.*

> *No worries, bro. We'll do something stupid when you get
> back to celebrate our reunion.*

I snort at his text. Our reunion would come a hell of a lot
faster if he'd end things with Nyx already.

Of course, he hasn't exactly been *seeing* her either. A deadline
had him locked in his room with his laptop for the past four days.
He did little but code. Avery convinced him to eat a few times, but
even then, he kept typing away on his keyboard while he chewed.
He stopped all outside contact too, reading texts but not
responding. Which meant I could text him every day, asking him
to hang out to keep up appearances without worrying about him
taking me up on the offer.

He finished in the middle of the night and texted me saying
he was alive. I waited until now to answer since, after sending a
few more texts, he crashed for fourteen hours. So did I until Avery
got up and went to her classes. With him working twenty hours a
day, I'd follow her all day and then keep tabs on him most of the
night. Probably not necessary, but I've felt an even stronger need
to watch him closely since the dream. I guess the guilt of letting
dream-Kai die carried over, too—and lasted a lot longer than the
hard-on.

I'm in my car outside the daycare, watching him through the palm stone while Avery works. Right after he answers me, he calls someone. I use the incantation to hear, so I know what to expect from my night. Now that he's free from his corporate chains, he'll be itching to do something stupid *before* I get back from my fake trip.

"Tell me you have a race tonight," he says. A few seconds later, he grins. "Bowie, I never want kids, but if I ever get a dog, I'm naming him after you."

So, racing it is. I'm about to hit the mystical mute again, but then he dials someone else. He tosses his phone on the bed, leaving it on speaker. And then Nyx answers. Four days of no sightings or erased moments in hallways or dreams. The last probably because of the lack of sleep, but still. Just like that, she's back. Her voice fills my car, crawls into my ears, implants in my brain.

"We still on for tonight?" he asks, dragging off the shirt he's worn for three days straight.

"Still on," she says.

Great. They already made plans. She must have been his other messages last night or earlier when he woke up and immediately reached for his phone.

"I'll pick you up around nine. The first race starts at ten."

"You're sure we can't do something sane?" Nyx sounds unimpressed with the night's festivities. "I mean, if this is our official first date as a couple, shouldn't we do something in which the boyfriend doesn't chance wrecking and dying?"

Fucking what? What's with this couple shit? Nyx is supposed to be on her way out, not digging herself further in. And how the hell did they go from not talking for days to dating in a few text messages?

I blow out a breath, resting my head on the back of the seat.

"Trust me, sexy, I'm not going anywhere." Kai drags a towel out of the laundry basket of clean clothes on his floor. "We'll hit the track for a quick race and then come back here. You're still staying, right?"

Now, they apparently have sleepovers.

I wait for her response, white-knuckling the steering wheel.

"Yeah," she says, her voice higher than normal. "I can't wait."

DARKENED SOUL

I stop listening. I quit watching for a while too. I need to take advantage while I can because, in a few hours, I won't have any choice but to watch them. Together.

Then later, I'll feel them.

I hover behind a collapsing metal shed, ducked in a shadow with the hood of my sweatshirt pulled up. We've been here often enough that I know the layout and can stalk around without being seen. I won't call it a racetrack. It's a field with something that resembles a dirt track in the middle. Broken bleachers on one side even though most people sit on the hoods of their cars. A few dilapidated buildings are scattered around, adding to the charm.

Just like at the hotel, with Kai's first step out of his car, an inkling of light appears dead center in my chest. Kai runs around to shut Nyx's door and hooks his arm around her. They dodge a piece of farm equipment and then disappear behind one of the buildings.

Once they have a solid head start, I pull out the amulet. Ever since the breakthrough last week, I can't stop messing with it. Sometimes, I get a burst of energy, sometimes not, but I have no idea what makes the difference. My own personal sword in the stone—the bullshit version anyway.

Am I worthy, Samy?

When I cast the spell, I get enough of a light boost to drop to the corner Kai and Nyx walked around. Works when I'm too lazy to walk a hundred feet—check.

Thirty seconds later, I'm trailing them through the cars parked farther out in the field. They stop to chat with someone selling beer out of a cooler. Nyx shakes her head, holding on to Kai's arm and nervously looking around. Not quite her cup of tea, if I had to guess. Seriously, why the fuck are they still seeing each other?

The way the tight black jeans undoubtedly hug the curves of her ass is hidden beneath the bottom of a baggy top. And that only shows her collarbone and from her elbow down. Still sexy as fuck, but at least she's mostly covered. Kai must have warned her about the asshats out here. Probably worse than the ones on fight night. Drinking in the middle of nowhere really brings out the creep in some people.

They make their way over to the car Kai will drive—the owner loves the money he makes from betting on the races but is terrified to drive himself. I watch through the palm stone rather than step out of the shadows, staying away from the tall light pole on this end of the track. A matching one illuminates the other end to keep at least most of the place visible. The last thing they want is some drunk chick wandering off, tripping in a hole, and getting left out here all night.

Since Kai can't keep tabs on Nyx and drive, he'll need to find a babysitter. Oh, the prospects. He nods at a stocky guy who used to drive. Rex? Or Ned? Who am I kidding? I don't fucking care.

Ned slaps Kai on the back and scans Nyx. When he pauses on her well-covered tits, I consider dropping in and laying him out. A quick punch, wipe a few memories, and then we can all go about our night. I catch her grasping on to Kai with her other hand. He turns to her with a smile and tucks her hair back.

I know I'm supposed to be invisible and not caring and shit, but I flip on the sound.

"One race, and then we'll get the hell out of here. Go on a real first date instead of some field."

She nods, smiling. "You're sure I can't talk you into leaving now?" Her hand slides from his arm to his stomach and then up his chest. "You can take advantage of some of those boyfriend privileges."

He groans at her suggestion and kisses her. Not a cutesy peck this time. He's kissing her the way I've kissed her, his hands roaming over her where mine have been. For someone who doesn't care, I sure am ready to tear my own charge's lips off his face. A man can live without lips. I shove the stone in my pocket, a tic developing in my jaw. There's not a chance in hell I'll watch that shit.

Kai revs the engine of the car before peeling out toward the others parked in the infield of the track. His racing requires my focus. With his adrenaline-junkie ways, I've learned to sense the slight differences in light. The shift to real danger is minimal, but I can pick up on it as long as I'm waiting for it.

The drivers all gather, going over the same rules as every other race. The light hums through me, and I don't need a boost from the amulet to effortlessly drop to a shaded spot close to the track.

Before the race starts, I check on Avery. My perfect charge is at the apartment, snuggled up on the couch with a cup of tea and a book. Wild Saturday night. God, I adore that girl.

All the drivers head back for their vehicles, everyone clearing the track. There are a few seconds of calm while a breeze rustles the grass around me—warm for October in Colorado.

I close my eyes and breathe deep, enjoying the light pumping through my veins. The power. For a second, I almost forget what it's like to *not* feel this way.

The roar of engines takes over, the energy tingling from my fingertips. The cars all redline at the same time as their drivers tear off from the starting line. I don't watch because what happens out there doesn't matter, just the heat and light.

Footsteps swish in the grass, louder and louder until they force me to look. I barely have time to duck out of sight behind the wooden shed.

"See," a guy says, "I told you the view of the track is unbeatable from here."

His girl giggles. "You sure that's why you brought me over here?"

Then they start making out. Nope, sorry, kids. Uncle Chaz has more important things to do than listen to you dry-hump against the building. I step around the corner to suggest they leave, but as my eyes skim over to the bleachers, they lock on to Nyx, who's off to the side. Ned's arm is around her waist, urging her away from the crowd. She tries to stand her ground, and he all but drags her along with him.

Without thinking, I drop. The couple that had been a few feet away never even noticed me. I land on dirt, in the shadow of the bleachers. I'm not there long, though.

"Get off me," Nyx hisses, shoving at him.

"Hey now, don't be like that." The dude's not even being subtle anymore. His hand covers her mouth as I come out from the darkness.

"Hey, fuckbag."

Ned's head turns toward me, and my fist connects with his jaw, satisfying the urge I had earlier. The hold on Nyx immediately releases, him hitting the ground at her feet. She looks down at him in shock before she looks at me. Her shoulders are heaving, face attempting to mask the panic her eyes give away the moment they reach mine.

And I almost miss it.

The thrum of heat and power inside me falls out of rhythm—an extra heartbeat.

I look to the track. To Kai. He comes into the turn low, but the driver behind him turns too early and is about to catch his rear driver's side. I can't waste time getting back into the shadows, so I drop from where I am. Right in front of Nyx.

Car accidents are tricky. All about timing. Kai's already been nosed into a spin when I appear in the passenger seat beside him. No matter how he steers, the car will roll, so I click the button to unfasten his seatbelt, and as the first tire loses contact with the track, I grab on to him.

We drop to the opposite side of the track, away from the crowd and out of reach from the lights. The car flips for the first time, off the track to the infield. My fists in Kai's shirt help him find his balance. Once he gains his footing, the glow from my palms reaches his terror-stricken face. Part of me wants him to remember how this feels so he'll tone down his shit, but I need to cover. I latch on to his face, letting the light seep into him until he relaxes.

"You're one lucky son of a bitch, Kai Benson. You won't remember anything after that asshole caught your back end other than rolling. Not me, not leaving the car. Just getting hit and rolling."

I wait for him to nod and then glance up just as the car completes its final rotation and lands right side up. So, not all bad.

"All right," I tell him, moving my hold back to his shirt. "Sorry about this."

Then I drop us back into the car in the same position we left. I still have enough light to move at full angel speed and re-buckle his seatbelt in the time it takes the car to stop rocking. Now, for the part I apologized for. I grab the back of his head and bash his forehead into the steering wheel. Only hard enough to split open the skin without causing any damage—I would know with the danger gauge and all—but enough to look like he was in the wreck.

I vanish from the passenger side before any humans can see me.

When I get back to the bleachers, Nyx is cupping her mouth, staring at the track.

"Oh my God," she murmurs.

She starts to take a step like she's going to Kai, but I grab her wrist from behind and spin her around to me. She comes flush to my chest, and her eyes slowly rise. They reach mine, wide and filled with disbelief.

"You…" She shakes her head, and I think she might laugh. "You disappeared."

"I did," I say.

The light is mostly gone. Kai's not in danger, and I told him he doesn't remember anything, so he's not worked up over the accident. A little lingers from the adrenaline still clearing his system but not enough that I can alter her memories. Not on my own.

Now am I worthy, asshole?

Nyx stares up at me. Each of her ragged breaths rises against me. "And you can dematerialize because…"

"I'm a magician." My hands creep up to her neck. "Or an alien. Take your pick."

As my palms reach her cheeks, I chant the spell for the amulet under my breath. More heat pours out of my palms as Nyx relaxes into my chest. Her eyes soften. Her melty fucking eyes that nearly distracted me from the only reason I'm here. The only thing that matters. Eyes that could have cost me my eternity and Kai his life.

And there it is—we've reached life or death.

I can't wait for this to run its course. Nyx needs to leave and not come back.

"You won't remember seeing me here tonight," I tell her, keeping my voice low and soothing.

She nods and waits for whatever I say next. I hesitate, doubting if I should take away what happened between us in the bar too. But the amulet continues to work, so I guess my intentions are acceptable by whatever morals it operates by. Knowing Samy, that's enough for me.

"You've decided things aren't working with Kai, not even as friends."

"We have nothing in common," she says.

I force a half-smile. "You want to end things with him tomorrow. Even if he wants to work it out, you'll say goodbye and not contact him again." I pause until she nods again and then put the final nail in the Nyx coffin. "The first time we met was at Kai's apartment. We saw each other at the bar, the same night you saw Kai, but we never interacted."

"Did you want to?" she asks.

Fuck. I hate when the mind spits out questions instead of just adjusting, but sometimes, it needs more information to fill in gaps.

My thumbs sweep over her cheeks, and I shake my head. "No," I tell her. "You're not at all my type."

SEVEN

NYX

Kai refused to get checked over at the emergency room after the wreck. He claimed out of all the crashes he'd been in, he never walked away with more than a few bumps and bruises.

"I'm just lucky," he said.

Call me crazy, but I doubt luck has anything to do with it.

Tonight was so fucked from what I'd imagined. We were supposed to go back to his place, so I could make up for the extended *just talking* stage, but I asked for a rain check. I just wanted to go home.

Well, here.

Her worn eyes crease at the corners when she sees me in the doorway. It's the only part of her that smiles anymore. She hasn't spoken a word in months either. An effect of whatever disease is eating away at her or a choice—with her, I never know.

I cross the room to the bed and sit on the mattress. Her hand stays limp when I lift it, examining the lines and the veins beneath the skin.

"I really hope I don't look this terrible in my nineties." I scrunch up my face at her, and the creases deepen.

Her hand falls back to the bed, and I crawl over to sit against the wall on the other side of her. My legs create a bridge over her, my sneakers dirtying up the clean white sheets. They'll change them in the morning.

We sit in silence. She won't or can't talk, and I have nothing of value to tell her. Sometimes, we just need the familiar. A constant we can latch on to when the rest threatens to become deafening. And every day, I creep closer to losing that hum. I fall onto my side, bringing my legs over so I can lie down. I put my head on her shoulder, the tears soaking into the hideous white nightgown they keep dressing her in.

If I pull this off, the first thing I'll do is burn the damn thing. No, the second thing. The first thing I want to do is hear her voice again. I don't even care if Nyla yells at me for almost letting her go. I just don't want the last time my sister spoke to me to be the last time ever. Which means I need to figure out how to work around my latest obstacle—and fast.

"What's your name?" I'd asked. My hands were in his unruly blond hair, cool tiles on my back while his hard everything pinned me against the wall.

A low chuckle rumbled from his throat. *"Does it matter at this point?"*

It never did. I'd wanted him the moment I saw him at the bar, nursing his beer. Then his smoldering stare had landed on me, a dangerous brow arching. I'd known right then that I couldn't leave the bar without feeling his hands on me first.

I pushed down his jeans, his briefs, offering to moan his name if he told it to me. His rough fingers skidded up my thighs and under my skirt, but he still wouldn't even with his thick cock throbbing in my hand.

"You can cry out whatever you want, gorgeous," he said. *"Sex god or badger."*

He picked me up while I laughed, my legs tying around him. But I wanted him to tell me because I wanted to say it.

"I'm not calling you—" I couldn't finish because he pinched my clit, almost making me come right there. *"Oh fuck."*

I desperately rode his fingers until he finally rolled on the condom. Then he thrust into me in one smooth stroke, stretching and filling me. His lips found mine and then his tongue. He tasted of his beer and something more intoxicating. He pumped in and out of me, my heels pushing into him each time he retreated to bring him back. It made him fuck me harder, and I moaned into his mouth. He let out a harsh breath as his grip on me tightened.

"Chaz," he rasped.

My heart pounded when I heard him say it. Not because I didn't know it. I've known his name almost as long as my own. Chazaqiel. One of The Fallen. And I was already sorry for what I would have to do to him.

EIGHT

CHAZ

Once Kai gets back to the apartment after dropping Nyx off, I text him to let him know I'll be back tomorrow night. Convenient how fast a fake conference can wrap up when the reason it was created won't be an issue anymore.

Hit me up when you get in, he sends.

I will as soon as Nyx walks away and doesn't look back.

Not something I thought I'd say, but I actually miss my charges. Fuck me. I need to spend less time with Ros. Get my edge back.

For the first time since the fight, I sleep more than a few hours. Existence is already getting back to normal. When Avery leaves for her morning and afternoon shifts at the daycare, I follow along, knowing Kai will spend most of the day lounging around. The breeze from last night turned to a cold wind, so he'll stay in recovery mode an extra day. Then, tomorrow, he'll have me five hundred feet up on a rock face without any gear.

I check periodically to see if Nyx has shown up but no dice. All I suggested was she end things today. My bad for not specifying a time.

After Aves gets off work, I wait across the hall. Considering most of my time is spent hanging around and waiting, I shouldn't feel a need to keep checking the stone, but I'm pulling up Kai in ten-minute intervals. Then, around eleven, the door across the hall shuts. I summon Kai's image, breathing out a sigh when I see Nyx taking off her coat.

Fucking. Finally.

I set the stone on the kitchen counter, not interested in the specifics, and drag off the polo I've worn all day on my way to the bedroom. Once she's out of the picture, Kai will want to go to the nearest club to end his dry spell. I'm ready to end mine as well. He hasn't been getting any from Nyx, and I haven't gotten any *since* her.

Before I shower, I text Cass to let him know Project Nix Nyx is in the final stage.

When I called earlier, my brother wasted no time in barking out a, "Told you so," to Hannah, pretty proud of himself for predicting the necessary outcome from day one.

I swear I heard her roll her eyes through the speaker.

I toss my phone on the bed along with the amulet and snag clothes.

Twenty minutes later, I check the mirror one last time, dressed and ready to cheer up my charge. As I step out of the bathroom, music plays from across the hall, so I head straight for the kitchen to check the palm stone. Sure enough, Kai's alone and sprawled out in the living room, playing a video game.

My existence is mine again.

As I tuck the stone in my pocket, I smile and grab my keys off the counter. But my door isn't even shut yet when I come to an abrupt stop. Nyx is on the floor outside of Kai's apartment, her back against the wall and her knees to her chest with her hands covering her face.

Fuck.

Her head lifts when the door clicks behind me. She notices me and shakes her head. "Sorry," she says, pushing to her feet.

Once she's standing in front of me, I see the redness in her cheeks, her eyes.

"Were you crying?" I ask. I sound way more confused than I should because why would she be crying if she's the one who did the dumping?

She looks back at the door and whispers, "Yes," like she doesn't want Kai to know she's still here.

"He won't hear you with his game on. Even if it wasn't loud as shit, he zones out when he's playing."

Her shoulders rise with a slow breath. "Yes," she says louder. "I was crying. Kai broke up with me."

Now, my face matches my voice. "What? He dumped *you?*"

She nods, tears welling again. "Yep. I mean, I came over here to break up with him, but still."

"So, you're crying because he broke up with you first?"

The pink in her cheeks turns to a full blush, and she chooses the ugly carpet in the hallway instead of eye contact. "Partly." She blows out a breath before she looks up again. "I also left my coat inside and can't bring myself to knock and ask for it."

That part might be my fault with the whole *tell him goodbye and never contact him again* phrasing. I'm about to offer to get it for her, but she's not finished.

"And at this point, I can't knock, or he'll know I've been out here for fifteen minutes. Not to mention, I've already had a really shitty day. My car wouldn't start earlier, and I'm pretty sure I screwed things up for my sister…" A sad laugh escapes her, her head shaking again. "You're probably the last person I should be dumping all this on, considering your relationship with Kai. Sorry. I'll just buy a new coat tomorrow and wait for my Uber outside."

Nyx forces a smile, and with a small wave, she starts down the hall toward the elevator. For some fucking reason, I'm still standing here when she steps inside and turns around. Then we watch each other until the doors close.

I stare at Kai and Avery's apartment door, clenching my jaw while I reach for the knob. But before I touch it, I groan and rush down the hall to the stairwell.

Even though Avery has her finger ready on the pepper spray, I always make sure I'm there when she walks to or from the building at night. Nyx doesn't even have a coat, and I doubt her phone would scare away a fucking raccoon.

"Hey," I say, catching up with her just outside the entryway.

She glances over her shoulder, her eyebrows scrunching together when she sees me. "Hey."

I scan the front of the building, jogging the last stretch of sidewalk between us. "I can wait with you."

The wind whips around us, and Nyx's teeth are already chattering.

"Here," I say, peeling off my hoodie. Christ, I really am turning into Rosdan.

"No." She pushes it back at me. "Now, you'll be cold."

"I will. But I'm at least wearing a T-shirt." My head tips to the low neckline of her tank top.

She takes the sweatshirt, and fuck, it really is cold outside. Maybe I should have kept the amulet on and used it as a heater. By the time her head pops through the neck, I'm already over it.

"You order a car yet?"

She brings out her phone. "You stopped me, remember? Really, I'll be fine. Go inside. If anyone comes near me, I'll stab them with my apartment key."

She pulls a single key out of her pocket to show me, and I chuckle.

"That will do enough damage to piss them off." I dig my own keys out of my pocket and nod toward the parking lot. "Let's go."

She hesitates to follow me but then falls into step beside me. "Thank you."

I shrug. "I just want to make sure I get my sweatshirt back."

The drive only takes a few minutes. I let her give me directions, acting like I haven't followed her ex-boyfriend there multiple times. When I park in the lot behind her building, Nyx is looking at her hands while she plays with her apartment key. I rest my head on the seat, turned toward her. The console lights up her face, green instead of the blue cast from the screen the first night she showed up at the apartment. I study her one last time. The profile of her pouty mouth and the curve of her nose.

Her eyes flick up to mine, and the air feels thick from the heat blowing out of the vents. Even without her remembering how good we felt together, the tension's there.

I'm about to say *fuck it* and slam my lips into hers, but she beats me to it.

She whimpers the second her mouth is on mine, her hands skimming to the back of my head to pull me closer. I lean in over the console, bringing a hand to the side of her neck. But when my tongue dips in to stroke hers, she pulls back.

"Come inside," she says.

I force myself to stop looking at her mouth, and what the hell am I doing? I just erased her memories of us screwing, and now, I'm seconds away from recreating them with her in the passenger seat of my car.

"No," I say. "I can't." But I barely believe myself, so I add, "This was just supposed to be a ride. I don't want you to think it would ever be anything else."

Nyx slumps back in her seat like I slapped her. Then, after a beat, she recovers and sets her jaw. "Of course you don't. I broke up with your best friend less than an hour ago." She forces a smile and shakes her head, turning for the handle. "Plus, I'm not at all your type, right?"

She climbs out, and I sigh as the door slams behind her.

I should let the human sulk, thinking she's been rejected. Let her go about her life where she'll stumble into a rebound with the first person she comes across who owns both a set of eyes and a dick interested in pussy. But if I've learned anything about me and this chick, it's that *should* doesn't fucking matter, and I turn the key off in the ignition.

She keeps going, almost to her building when my door shuts.

I stalk up the sidewalk after her. "Nyx."

Her body freezes, her fists clenched at her sides. As she turns, I slow down, stalling out completely once she faces me. She looks like heartbreak, features crumpled with tears streaming down her cheeks. And I want to make her forget everything I just said.

I start to close the space between us, but on step one, the last words out of her mouth hit me. *You're not at all my type.* I told her that last night while I wiped her memories. She shouldn't have remembered.

A shadow moves behind her, and my muscles tense. A figure slowly steps out. He comes to a stop beside her, and she glances at him. Now, the light casts a yellow hue over her, over his slicked black hair and the suit to match. The demon from the fight. His pupils begin to glow a deep red before they drift over my shoulder, and then Nyx's line of sight follows.

Part of me already knows what they're looking at—or who. The scent of sulfur seeps through the air along with some tacky-ass cologne. I turn around to a smirk that ignites an existence worth of hatred.

The black-on-black-suit-wearing motherfucker tips his head to the side. "Chazaqiel."

Lower-level demons pour out of a portal next to him. I glance back at Nyx, under the arm of the other Upper.

She set me up.

Shaking my head, I chuckle, bringing my attention back to Abaddon. "Well, this should be—"

NINE

CHAZ

Chains. The Demon of Destruction, and he needs *chains* to hold on to an angel without any fucking powers? Abaddon is a disgrace to the name. My head throbs where I assume a Lower took a fucking cheap shot, but when I open my eyes, they connect with the slimy Upper from earlier, so maybe he's the one I'll have to fucking kill later.

I survey the rest of the dank concrete room. I'm on my knees in the center, my arms outstretched. A single caged light hangs above me, three Lowers hovering by a doorway off to the side. Shadows conceal one of the corners in front of me while the Upper perches in the other with Nyx nearby, her head down and hands hidden in the sleeves of my hoodie. If I were in any sort of a bargaining position, I'd demand she give that shit back, but we'll save it for another time.

The chains clink when I rotate my wrists, testing the give. Not much, but here's to Avery seeing a mouse in the next thirty seconds. A rough spot on one of the links digs in when I yank a little harder, but I keep tugging to fill the room with the irritating clanks.

"Probably not necessary since I don't have my powers," I shout over the noise, waiting for the ringmaster to reveal himself in some showboat, master-villain bullshit entrance. "Unless you plan on taking our *will they, won't they* to a whole new level, Abaddon. In which case, you should know my safe word is actually a phrase." I stop my assault on everyone's ears and roll my head toward the cluster of Lowers. "It's *Donny can blow me*. But given the situation, maybe I should switch it to *Justin Bieber*."

A set of red ovals lights up in the dark corner. "Just when I think I can't get any more joy out of killing you, you open your mouth." The rest of Abaddon appears, the demon slinking out with a smug smile that causes the scar just below his right cheek to dent.

I straighten up, pushing out my chest and raising my head, matching his expression with a smirk of my own. "Afraid I'll huff and puff and blow your flame out?"

He flicks his palm open, the blue flame springing to life as he marches toward me. His hand flattens against my chest. The fire eats at my skin, and a growl escapes me, but I don't back down. I push into the burn, jaw clenched tight and muscles fighting to pull away. Every second I challenge him pisses him off until he shoves me backward. Not having my powers leaves me at a disadvantage, and my ass lands on my heels.

When he moves to the side, my eyes connect with Nyx. Her hand covers her mouth but falls away when I wink at her.

"Don't worry, beautiful. I'll be loose in no time. Then the real fun begins, and I can hunt you down to return this little favor."

Her shoulders pull back in a sharp breath, her chin tipping up. But I catch the hint of doubt behind the façade. Donny's still walking away, being dramatic as shit, so I stare her down.

"What are you?" I ask, taunting her. "A demon groupie?"

She starts to take a step when the suit beside her places a hand on her shoulder. She shakes it off, shooting him a warning glare, and I whistle to bring her attention back to me.

"Please tell me you fucked Donny because I'm *dying* to know who's better."

"You sure about that?" She arches a brow and smiles.

All fucking bravado. But she confirms she remembers our time in the ladies' room. I wonder how she kept my light from working on her. A spell? Enchanted object?

"If you're finished whining about being outsmarted by a human…" Donny finishes his runway walk and holds his hand out to the suit beside her. "Hex."

I throw my head back, laughing. "You've got to be fucking joking. An Upper named Hex? You guys aren't even trying anymore, huh?"

The suit's cool demeanor slips. The darkness grows from his hands, vining up his arms, but Donny steps in front of him, hand still extended. After killing me a thousand ways in his mind, Hex reaches behind him. It's not until Donny turns around that I see what they handed off between them.

My fucking body ices over—muscles, blood, soul.

Light glints off the steel, Donny's talons wrapped around the handle.

The Dimming Blade.

"Surprise," Donny says, flicking his wrist and slicing through the air with the only thing outside of God that could end me. And I don't have my powers to defend myself. No Cass or Rosdan for backup. Nothing and no one.

"You good?" he asks, bending his knees to dip down closer to my level. "You look a little *dim.*"

"Save the puns, asshat." I swallow, refusing to show him vulnerability, no matter how fucked I am right now. I lift my chin to gesture to the weapon. "I'll bet my eternity you can't even work that little knife. You think you can just poke me and hocus-pocus happens?"

"Oh, Chazaqiel, you are always underestimating me." He twists the point on his fingertip—thin, dark shadows leaking from where he punctures his flesh. "I'm going to watch the light drain out of you, and then I'll wipe you from existence once and for all. Because an eternity of nothingness isn't enough. I want you to *be* nothing."

I might not be able to access my light, but it's still a part of me. Locked down, but there. Without the light, I'd be mortal with an angel soul. Killable yet unable to die. It's a strong blip in the matrix of existence, resulting in one of two outcomes. Either I fill the void of light with darkness and become a demon—an upper-level, of course—or when my mortal life ends, I cease to exist.

Abaddon squats in front of me, still scrutinizing the tip of the blade poking into his finger. "Of course, the blade must be activated first." His eyes meet mine, their red glow somehow more sinister than usual, and I growl as he leans in to whisper in my ear, "But that only requires a sacrifice."

The words hit me like a bomb blast, and it happens so fast that my gaze can't even beat the dagger to her. Abaddon's hand stays suspended in the air, a direct arrow to Nyx, who is clutching the handle in her hands, a look of shock in her face as she stares down at her chest. He teleports to her in less time than it takes me to blink. My breathing turns rough and jagged as I watch him pull the blade out before Hex lowers her lifeless body to the cold concrete.

But any mourning I might have wanted to do over the chick who landed me here in the first place is over when Abaddon vanishes. The blade's already slipped between my ribs by the time he reappears in front of me. The steel is hot, slicing through flesh and muscle until the hilt presses into me, and he twists. I stare him down, baring my teeth as the pain rips through me. All the light stored deep inside and just out of my reach ignites. An overwhelming sense of perfection. I feel everything I was—powerful and divine. Everything I'm supposed to be again. Then it seeps out of me, abandoning me and leaving nothing. A void that smothers my cells. I might not have been able to feel it before, but having the light truly gone is worse than anything I could have imagined.

I growl, thrashing against the chains, a wild animal deprived of oxygen. "I'll kill you!"

I don't feel the blade anymore, barely notice the clink of it hitting the floor beside me, and then icy fingers grip my throat, lifting until I'm once again on my knees, torso stretched straight.

"No," Donny says, his face in mine. "I'll kill you."

Then he squeezes, bearing down until I'm truly a wild animal without air.

About to go extinct.

TEN

NYX

Here's the thing about dying: it gets real old, real quick. And I've done it enough to know a thing or two.

For starters, there's more than one type of death. The first is physical. The body goes into shock, if you're lucky. The organs shut down, the lungs stop, and then the heart shudders through a final beat.

Next comes the death of the mind, which includes a full-life replay. Every moment, good or bad or mundane. Thank God this life only lasted a little over a year because I really don't have time for this shit right now.

It starts at the crosswalk, where a drunk driver clipped me and left me to bleed out in the middle of the night. Fast-forward to Hex, the demonic ex, showing up to offer the one thing I couldn't refuse. Then the vision lingers at the bar, the Watcher Angel watching me, his full lips on my skin while he fucked me against a wall, and then there was the rasp in his voice when he told me I didn't want to see him again. I can almost feel the heat of his hands on my face. The same way they felt in his charge's kitchen after I showed up with plan B and again after the car wreck when he tried to erase what had happened between us.

I wish he could have. Maybe then I wouldn't have noticed the change in how he looked at me, realizing I'd set him up. It cuts just as much to see the second time around, all the curiosity and heat in his eyes draining away and leaving me haunted. But it still fails to compare to the pain of my own realization. Abaddon's betrayal plunging into my chest and spilling out over my hands.

Then I relive the physical death itself, an intake of air as the steel broke through my sternum, the cool handle against my palms, hot blood coating them as he ripped out the blade. Finally, Hex lowers me to the ground with his lips at my ear. *"See you soon, love."*

The words echo until I open my eyes. I'm over my body, not quite here or there. A blue haze covers everything, sounds warble, energies shift. It only takes a glance at the pool of blood surrounding my physical form for the rage to slam into me. Hex might have known what would happen if I died, but Abaddon sure as hell had no idea when he killed me.

But he's about to find out.

The anchor to my physical body weakens by the second, not giving me long in my spiritual form, so I have to work fast. Seeing where my last plan got me, I let the primal need for payback drive me. Abaddon stole my life, so I'll take away what he wants more than anything—his revenge.

I seek out Chaz, still on his knees, and I focus on the life pumping through his veins, slowing the longer he struggles against the demon's hold on his throat. I have little to compare to with him being the first angel I've encountered, but the energy inside him feels different than any other I've sensed. I latch on to it with everything I have anyway and search for the same inside of Abaddon. The demon's essence is cold, harsh, and sharp-edged, like Hex's. When I pull it from him, it's blacker than black, a void and a complete contrast of the brightness inside the angel.

The forces repel, fighting to stay apart, but I drive them toward each other. Even though I'm stronger in this form, it takes all my focus to bring them together, and when they finally meet, they detonate. Two volatile chemicals exploding on contact. Pure energy, unlike anything I've sensed from life sources, unleashes around me, shock waves pulsing from ground zero until I can't hold on any longer.

I concentrate on the body beneath me. My lids fall closed, the rest of me falling right behind as my soul returns to where it belongs. I will myself to feel, to breathe, to live, my mind returning to life. Then the first of my muscles twitch, a hard beat of my heart, and my real eyes flutter.

ELEVEN

CHAZ

Abaddon's commentary about the pleasure of watching me fade from existence comes in and out. The words are heavy in my ears, and his hand is tight on my throat. Except then his voice cuts off, and I think that's it. I'm done, gone, a memory. But then coughing and sputtering. He stumbles backward, my vision going from black to red as the pressure on my neck releases.

I suck in a breath, choking on the rush of air to my starved lungs. Then another and another. Oxygen hits my brain, the ringing in my ears diminishing, and I realize the slack in the chains. I jerk until I can bring my arms in, struggling to my feet. We stare at each other—him grasping his own throat while I run my fingers along mine. After a second, he lunges for me but stops dead at a voice behind him.

"I wouldn't do that if I were you."

My eyes dart over his shoulder to Nyx, very fucking alive in my blood-soaked sweatshirt. Her brow arches when she pauses on me.

What the actual fuck?

Hex sidesteps, putting distance between them, before Abaddon spins around.

"What did you do?" he shouts, storming toward her. He's flaming—literally with fire blazing in his hand.

To be honest, so am I but in the nonliteral sense. It's one thing to be killed by your nemesis after one of the longest-running feuds in history, but it's another to be saved by the chick who'd helped him almost kill you in the first place.

Nyx stands her ground when he reaches her, letting the demon snarl and huff in her face like a raging bull. With her being the center of attention, none of the lackeys notice me dip down for the Dimming Blade. Any movement tugs at the edges of my wound, but I clench my jaw and push up the back of my shirt enough to slip the dagger through the belt loops of my jeans. Nyx glances over, too late to see anything, and her focus jerks back to Abaddon when he clutches her jaw in his non-burning hand.

"Tell me, princess."

"As is one, then so will be the other," she says, voice unwavering. "Think of it as your new tagline." Her eyes flash to me. "I bound you—your life forces. If he dies, you die."

The entire room stills at her words. His hand slowly falls away from her face. He whips his head around to me, but I'm looking past him, locked on to her and fighting the urge to charge forward and kill her again. Because even when compared with turning to dust or whatever the hell was about to happen to me, being connected to Donny the Destroyer might be the worse fate.

When I finally tear myself from her, he's waiting for me. A smirk appears as he turns all the way and comes toward me. I reach behind me for the handle before remembering he can't do anything to me. Not now anyway. No matter how much he wants me gone.

By the time he stops in front of me, I'm unwrapping the chains from my wrists. I toss them at his feet, the links clanking on the concrete floor.

"Since it looks like we're done here, someone want to drop me back at my car or…" I flash him a grin, faking the shit out of being back in control of the situation. If I can get the blade to Ros, we'll figure out a way to reverse the light. Stick it the fuck back inside me and destroy the weapon once and for all.

Except Donny gives a tsk, shaking his head. "I'm afraid we're not quite finished, Chazaqiel. But thanks to our little necromancer back there, I will need to keep you on ice while I sort this mess out." He slaps a hand on my shoulder, and my nostrils flare. I'm ready to kill us both if it means he'll stop touching me. "You understand, I'm sure."

Before I can spit anything back at him, he thrusts me backward. I expect to hit the concrete, but I keep falling. The dank room vanishes from in front of me, and only blackness remains.

A demon portal.

Of course.

My unplanned trip only lasts a second. The ground gives under my back when I land, my eyes clamping shut at the sudden change from doom and gloom to blinding light. Heat beats down on me as I crack them open a slit to scan around. Then I'm on my feet, hands clutching my wound as I rotate.

"Damn it, Donny," I shout.

Sand and sky and bright-as-fuck sun stretch in every direction, and apparently, he's not the literal type because I sure as hell don't see any ice.

TWELVE

NYX

The second Chaz vanishes through the portal, I'm slammed back against the wall. I bounce like a rubber ball, hitting the concrete before Abaddon grips the neck of my sweatshirt, dragging me up until I hover off the ground. I grasp his wrist, force-swallowing the panic lodged in my throat.

"Fix this," he hisses.

When he lets go, I fall all the way down. My palms flatten on the hard floor, but Hex shakes his head, warning me to stay down. I set my jaw, only now remembering how furious I am with him for bringing me into this mess in the first place. His word means less now than it did last century.

"I can't." I stare at the blood drying on my skin. "Or I won't until you give me the Essence of Creation you promised."

Abaddon lowers in front of me, grabbing my jaw and jerking my face up to him. "There is no more pure essence. Hasn't been for thousands of years."

I shake my head, fighting against his hold. "But you said there was a way to—"

"Create more?" he says dismissively. "Yeah, I lied. It's a myth. No better than the Fountain of Youth or…" He snaps his fingers at Hex. "What's the name of the cup?"

"The Holy Grail."

"Right. All nonsense."

I would slump to the floor if not for being held up by him. If there's no more pure Essence of Creation, then my last shot at saving Nyla is gone. I can't stop her from fading away. From permanent death.

Abaddon studies me while I fight to hide the devastating loss I'm already feeling. His breath is cool on my skin and his touch ice. "You aren't an alchemist like I was led to believe, or you wouldn't have resurrected. And a phoenix would hold darkness inside them, not to mention the lack of fire. So, what are you?"

My eyes dart to Hex as he tenses, looking up from his phone. He pockets it, moving toward the center of the room. "We should kill her for lying."

"What?" The word escapes as a disbelieving whisper. He knows what I am, what happens if I die again.

Abaddon digs his fingers into my face, forcing me to look at him. "Do you have to be dead to unbind us? Choose your answer wisely, princess. My patience is wearing thin."

I scramble for a lie, anything that will keep me alive, but before I can come up with anything, he tosses me aside like a doll.

"On second thought, I'll do my own investigation." He looms over me, wiping my blood off his hands with a white cloth. "Fair warning: if I find a solution that doesn't include you, I have every intention of watching you die until you stay dead. However long that takes."

Even though he could easily follow through on his threat, I won't take his shit lying down. I push up to my feet, ignoring a shuffle from Hex off to the side.

Abaddon smirks, his regard snaking over me. "Or maybe I'll find another use for you. Until then, try not to let Chazaqiel kill you and take away my fun."

He nods to Hex behind me, and I look back. Hex drags me backward, sparing me a quick glance before he pushes me toward the wall. I stumble forward, but instead of running into the concrete, everything goes black and cold, and a second later, I hit something else hard, different hands on me.

I squint against an assaulting brightness, leaving my vision white until it adjusts. And then I see the singed black T-shirt in front of me, my chest pressed to his, and when I look up, a set of infuriated blue eyes wait for me.

Out of one lion's den and straight into another's arms. Only this one might end up being the more dangerous of the two.

THIRTEEN

CHAZ

As if being stuck in the desert with a gaping wound and my existence tied to one of the most hated demons in history isn't bad enough, I'm now chest to chest with what landed me here in the first place. And while I've never killed a mortal before, I'm seeing no reason not to start with this one.

My fingers curl around Nyx's arm, her eyes wide when I reveal the blade from behind me.

"No." She struggles against my hold, not gaining any ground. "Please, Chaz. You don't understand. I had to——"

"Fuck me over?" I say, calm compared to her and the fight she's putting up to get away from me. "You had to lure me away from my charges, serve me up to Donny to be gutted, and then connect me to the one being in the cosmos I can't stand?"

She manages to pull me with her a few steps backward. "I was fucked over too."

"Well, in that case, I still don't give a shit."

I bring the weapon between us, pointing it at the hollow of her throat. As the steel meets her skin, she stops moving and clamps her eyelids closed. I hold the tip there, and each of her breaths becomes more ragged as I press inward until her skin dents beneath the flat side.

"You need me," she blurts out.

I withdraw slightly. "Oh, this should be good."

She peeks, checking the proximity of the blade, and then blinks all the way open. She licks her lips and swallows, still breathing hard. "We're in the middle of the desert as far as I can tell. Between the sand and heat, you're an infection waiting to happen, but I can heal you."

"You're the reason I'm here," I remind her. "The reason I won't feel Kai or Avery and heal from my light."

"I know." Nyx's voice cracks on the second syllable, her brows angling in. "And I'm sorry." She looks down at the knife creeping toward her neck and whimpers. "I'm so sorry."

I should kill her before she tries to do the same to me again, but the fear on her face, in her tone, and in her eyes when they come back to mine…

Fuck. Fuck. "Fuck!" I lower the blade and walk away from her, clutching the handle until my knuckles burn.

I've been without my light for minutes, and I'm already losing my shit. My stab wound aches with every breath, not that it compares to the way the rest of me hurts without the faintest flicker of light, but I know she's right. I'm mortal and susceptible to all the weaknesses that go along with it.

Stopping, I fish the palm stone out of my pocket. I'm not sure if I'm checking for them or me, but I pull up Avery's image. A tension eases when I see her with Kai at their apartment. Fucking safe. Given the shadows cast on the walls, the sun will set there in a few hours. That means, I've been gone about twenty.

"How do I know you won't just kill me to get rid of Donny?" I ask.

I put the stone away, not turning around even though Nyx doesn't answer right away.

"You'll just have to trust me," she finally says. The words sound weak. Probably because she realizes how insane they are, coming out of her mouth.

"Yeah, that's never happening." But I drag my shirt over my head. I tuck it in my back pocket and wait for her footsteps to cross the sand behind me.

She comes around, wary of the dagger as she stands in front of me. I clench my jaw when she lifts her blood-stained hands, but I let her place them on my chest, her palms cool.

"Please don't stab me when I close my eyes," she says.

"No promises." I follow up with a mocking smile, but really, I reserve the right to take her out at any point as far as I'm concerned.

She momentarily glares before her lids fall closed. She squares her stance and pushes into me. The feeling starts as a buzz where she touches. It spreads over my skin like static, turning to a hum when it sinks into my muscles and a thrum in my bones. My heart beats faster but not in a threatening way. More like she hit the fast-forward button. My eyes fall from her face to her hands and then to the gap between them. A fresh scar spans the space between my ribs where the blade went in, and the burns on my chest are all but gone.

"*What the fuck?*" I whisper.

Her eyes open, dropping to the scar and then connecting with mine.

"How did you do that?"

"I aged you," she says. "About a month." She must sense a repeat of *what the fuck* coming on because she quickly adds, "It won't affect you in any way, I promise. I only transferred enough of my life into you so that your body could speed through the process."

"You…" I shake my head, which is having a difficult time wrapping around what I just witnessed.

She starts to pull away, and I cover her hands with mine to keep her there.

"What the hell are you, Nyx?"

The handle of the blade presses between us, panic swimming in her eyes. But with nowhere to go, she takes a deep breath, looking up at me on the exhale.

"I'm a Descended."

FOURTEEN

NYX

My lungs burn, wanting to gasp at the hot air surrounding us, but I force my breaths to stay steady. I've only admitted what I am to Hex and only because he somehow figured it out. But this isn't some Upper killing his way to the top. Chaz is an original Watcher. One of The Fallen. A bedtime story Papa told us when we were little.

He searches my face, his nostrils flaring while his brow creases. "A what?"

I open my mouth and close it, confused by his response. "A Descended," I repeat, thinking he missed it the first time because my voice had trembled.

He blinks a few times.

Then. He. Shrugs.

"Are you fucking kidding me?" I jerk my hands out from under his, possibly more furious than when Abaddon freaking impaled me. "They say The Fallen are full of themselves, but this is beyond anything I could have imagined."

I start to march away, only making it a few steps before he grasps my wrist and tugs me back around. He steps into me, twisting my arm behind my back and pulling until I'm flush against his chest.

"How about you cool it with the insults and tell me what the hell you're talking about."

I try to wiggle out of his hold, huffing out a breath when I don't get anywhere. "The Watchers," I hiss. "The ones turned human as punishment for creating the Nephilim and left behind to repopulate the world."

His face darkens then, breath hot on my face. "What about them?"

"I'm from one of their bloodlines—Kokabiel, leader of the twelve Descended Watchers."

The mask slips, a flash of surprise in his deep blues before they narrow into an irritated glare. "Those assholes called themselves The Descended?"

He releases me without warning, leaving me off-balance in more than one way. I stumble backward a step and rub my wrist while he puts the knife away.

I expect questions, interest, something, but he walks away from me, shaking his head and muttering, "Is anyone fucking original anymore?"

"Where are you going?" I call after him.

When he keeps going, I glance around, not sure what to do. My choices seem to be wait in the desert alone until I die or until Abaddon blinks in to kill me again, or I can chase after an angel who still might very well kill me himself. The odds of me surviving the night suck all around, but at least with Chaz, I stand a slight chance of seeing Nyla one last time. The thought wedges in my throat, and I peel off the bloody sweatshirt. I drop it on the ground and follow him, sniffing away the threat of tears.

I can't spare the hydration right now.

The sun beats down on us, relentless while it treks through the sky. At first, the temperature feels bearable, but the longer we walk, the hotter it feels. Chaz hasn't said a word or even looked at me since I caught up with him. Even then, it was only long enough to roll his eyes.

So it surprises me when, out of nowhere, he says, "We call them The Others. Not that we talk about them often—or at all since the last one died off thousands of years ago. Until now, I wasn't aware we needed to worry about their human descendants."

"The stories say you abandoned them when they asked for help surviving, leaving them to suffer."

He snorts. "*The Descended*, or whatever, were full of shit. We avoided them because what they wanted was for us to risk further punishment by helping them get their powers back. They were obsessed with it." He looks over, giving me a once-over. "Looks like they figured something out just fine without us." A couple steps later, he asks, "What happened to the last one?"

"What?"

"Earlier, you said there were twelve Descended, but there should have been thirteen."

It takes him a few seconds to realize I've stopped, and he turns around. I stand there while he holds up a hand to shade his vision from the sun.

"Twenty original Watchers," he says. "Thirteen created the Nephilim, and seven passed along knowledge."

"The stories passed down to us said there were twelve Descended and eight Fallen."

His hand falls to his side, and he shrugs. "Further proof those assholes were full of shit."

Suddenly, I'm starting to think they might have been.

Chaz leaves me behind, still heading in the opposite direction of the sun. His back glistens from sweat, the black angel wings tattooed across the span of his shoulder blades gleaming. I haven't seen them before, and I almost smile. Both of us hiding in plain sight.

I rub the back of my neck, my stomach turning. Before I can think much about the tattoo that should be there, I hurry to catch up with him.

We walk a while longer before I quit trying to keep up with him. Each of his long strides spans two of mine, and my muscles are tired, my mouth dry. Chaz stops a hundred feet ahead of me. He doesn't turn around, but he waits. Progress. Or so I think until I reach him and see why he really stopped.

Up ahead between two bushes sits a red-and-white cooler.

"You think—"

"Donny needs me alive," Chaz says. "It's in his best interest to hydrate the mortal." His voice drops on the last word, and he makes his way to the cooler.

He tosses me a bottle of water, and I immediately twist it open. He pulls out another couple of bottles and closes the lid, so he can sit down.

"Cheers," he deadpans.

I sip my water, watching him lean his elbows on his thighs and drink. He looks paler than yesterday, even after walking an hour in the sun. Nothing else has changed. His features are still sharp, his body sculpted, but that small detail makes him look more … human.

"It was for my sister." I pause for any reaction from him, but he doesn't even look up. Just tips back the bottle, his throat working to swallow, and then hangs his head between his shoulders, staring at the barren ground between his feet. "She's dying—really dying."

I want to say more, but he stands up and stalks toward me. He stops inches away from me, and I can still smell his body wash mixed with his sweat. Every other time he's been this close, he's wanted me even if he wouldn't admit it. But now, his glare is cold enough to give me a chill in the desert. My breaths are shallow, his on my face.

"And now, so am I," he says.

Then he walks away, setting two bottles on the lid of the cooler as he passes.

One a water, the other sunscreen.

By the time the sun starts to set behind us, we've been walking for hours. The temperature lowers drastically without the sun overhead, and I rub my bare arms. Blood-soaked or not, I regret leaving the sweatshirt behind.

"Here." Chaz tugs the shirt out of his back pocket and holds it out for me.

Jesus. Déjà vu much?

But instead of arguing like last night, I pull it over my head. I leave my arms inside and wear the thing like a poncho. "Thank you."

He nods.

"You don't think Abaddon would go after Kai and Avery, do you?"

He spares me a sideways glance but ignores my question, and I sigh.

"Considering they're your charges, I thought you'd be a little more concerned. I mean, if he kills them and then you somehow get your light back—" I cut off, startled when he jerks toward me.

"I *will* get my light back. And with the Demon of Destruction lurking around, possibly with a weapon to end me, you don't think I have a contingency plan?"

He opens his hand, revealing a flat crystal in his palm. Kai's image appears in the center. He and Avery are both on their couch, carryout cartons spread across the coffee table in front of them.

I run my fingers over the smooth surface, biting back the guilt for having possibly put them on Abaddon's radar. "They're safe there?"

"Untouchable. And soon, a switch will flip in Kai's brain." He snaps his fingers beside my ear. "He'll whip out his phone, find *Rosie the Babysitter* in his contacts, and call my brother Rosdan." He pulls the stone away and shoves it in his pocket. "I set it all up after Donny resurfaced. If Kai ever goes more than twenty-four hours without hearing from me, he sends up the alarm. I texted him last night, so it will be any minute now. Ros knows what to do, and once he tells Cass…" He pauses with a hint of a smirk. "Let's just say, a pissed off Cass is the only being you need on your side."

"Armaros and Kasdaye?" I ask, using the names I've known as long as his.

He nods, and I can't help but smile. Papa told us stories about The Fallen every night until we were about eight. He meant them as a warning of how selfish and dangerous they were, using their charges to justify killing anyone who crossed them. Nyla and I refused to believe him, though, calling them *our* angels and making up our own stories. We'd divide them up—we thought there were eight, so it was fair. Armaros and Kasdaye were ones we would argue over and trade back and forth. But we each had one who was always ours without question. Nyla claimed Samyaza. My angel was Chazaqiel.

Of course, I thought he glowed, could control lightning, and would fall insanely in love with me the moment our eyes met.

"What the…" Chaz fixes on something in the distance. "Is that fire?"

When I turn, I see the faintest flicker. Small and barely visible against the serene purple backdrop of the fading sunset. The first sign of life we've seen since the cooler.

We follow the flame, the last of night falling while we walk. Once we're closer, Chaz reaches back to move me behind him. I want to think he cares if I live or die, but the gesture seems to be more of a habit. The green smudge behind the fire begins to take shape. A tent. His hold falls away from my hip, so he can check it out. I stop beside a change of clothes, folded neatly on one of the logs spread around the campsite.

"Empty," he says, flipping the flap back down. He picks up the paper from on top of the clothes and reads, shaking his head before he holds it out. "For you."

"Me?" I take the note while he disappears into the tent.

Stay warm. And alive.
—H

I roll my eyes and let the paper flutter into the fire. It will take Hex more than a pair of yoga pants and a clean hoodie to buy my forgiveness.

Chaz comes out with a cooler. As he sits on the other log and starts pulling out food, my mouth waters. Nope, still not enough.

As soon as Chaz unloads a handful of towelette packets, I grab for them. "Oh, thank God."

I leave him one and bring the rest with me into the tent to clean up and change. The blood smears as I scrub down my forearms and between my fingers. Chaz's shirt, along with my tank and bra, hit the floor before I sacrifice the rest of the packages to clean up my front and back. I'm down to my last two when I walk out of the tent, my new zip-up hoodie held over my chest.

Chaz bites into an apple, scanning me as I stand in front of him with my hand held out.

"Please?" I say, spinning around. "I can't reach the middle."

He blows out an annoyed breath that I consider a yes, and I rip open a wipe, handing it over my shoulder. It pulls from my fingers. He runs his hand across my shoulder blades, brushing my hair out of the way as he goes. I play with the drawstring while he works up the center of my back, trying to ignore his skin on mine.

"You have more?" he asks, standing up.

I tear open the last packet and pass it back. He moves my hair again, his presence looming over me. His hand slides down my back. It leaves a trail that chills in the cool night air. I fight off a shiver, adjusting the hoodie to better cover my arms. He dips beneath the waistband of my yoga pants, and I shiver again.

Once he finishes, he tosses the towelettes into the fire. I start to step away, but he grips my side. My breath catches, his long fingers splaying over my ribs. He moves closer until his body heat spreads across my back like a blanket, and he sweeps my hair away from the nape of my neck.

"Your tattoo." His voice is low, breath on my skin. It reminds me of the fight, the crowd and noise surrounding us yet completely separate. "The four lines," he says. "I couldn't figure out how I knew them before, but they're The Watchers' fall from grace."

A wave of relief washes over me as I nod. "It's still there?"

I've wanted to ask all day, but I couldn't face the possibility of it being gone.

He answers first by tracing his thumb down one of the curvy lines and then the loop of the Ouroborus—life and death. "It's faded more."

"It loses color with every resurrection, like a mystical power gauge."

"You have a limit on how many times you can come back?"

"The soul can only leave the body so many times before losing its hold permanently. Once the tattoo's gone, I'll be on my final life." I turn with the sweatshirt still loosely held to my chest. "Until then, my soul reenters my body, which reverts to its most ideal state."

His expression stays impassive. "How many times have you died?"

"Five. Twice of old age, once from consumption, a hit-and-run last year, and then…" I trail off, the evidence of the last time still burning a few feet away.

"And your sister?"

"Five." I look out over the desert, the sand white under the moon. "She came back five times before her tattoo disappeared."

"Let me guess. Sweet Donny promised you a way to save her."

"The Essence of Creation. The original Descended gained their abilities by fusing their blood with it. Back then, it was everywhere. It's gone now, but I thought if I could just find enough to reset her…" I shake my head, looking up at him. "It doesn't matter. Abaddon lied about there being a way to make more."

Chaz stares at me hard, his jaw working beneath the surface. "I could have told you he couldn't. Saved us all a lot of drama." He sits back down and nudges the cooler until it bumps my legs.

I turn around to put the sweatshirt on and zip it up before I grab a sandwich.

When we finish eating, Chaz pulls on the tee Hex left him. He stops outside the tent and holds up the flap. "In."

Despite the shortness of his command, I duck under his arm. "Sir."

Instead of sleeping bags, the demon, who's clearly never camped, left us three pillows and half a dozen blankets of various sizes. I start spreading out two to lie on. For some reason, it surprises me when Chaz steps in a few minutes later. He lowers down in the center of my blankets and stretches out on his side.

The space fills with him, and I have no choice but to drop down right beside him. I roll to face him, a safe foot of tent between us. "Should we create a blanket wall, or—"

I gasp when Chaz drags me toward him. He traps my arms behind my back, holding my wrists in his hand and pulling me closer. I'm plastered against his hard chest, his mouth inches from mine. And then I feel the fabric wrap around my wrists. My bra isn't in the corner anymore, and I realize too late what he's doing.

"No." I wiggle to free my hands, but he rolls us over so that half of his body covers mine. It leaves me nowhere to go while he finishes binding my hands together. I tug a few more times before I rest my forehead on his chest. An admission of defeat.

"In case you get any ideas in the night." He tightens the knot and rolls to his back. "As is one hand, then so will be the other."

Asshole.

FIFTEEN

CHAZ

I twirl the dagger in my hand, staring up at the green material of the tent. Nyx finally quit huffing and settled down, but I can't fucking sleep. All I can think about is that, for the first time in my existence, I'm aging. I said it earlier, but it didn't sink in until now.

I'm one day closer to dying. Not to going home or finishing my sentence. Dying.

The blanket moves when Nyx readjusts.

"How old are you?" I ask, twisting the tip of the metal against my palm.

"Tie me in front, and I'll tell you." When I ignore her request, she sighs. "When we met, I was twenty-three. Now, I'm twenty-two—at least, that seems to be my body's age whenever it resets."

"Cool. And all my shit says I'm twenty-four." I roll my head on the pillow to see her. "How *old* are you?"

She's still facing me, arms secured behind her. "One hundred and fifty-eight."

I do the math. Most likely, I would have been dropping around the East Coast then. Maybe a rogue charge still in Paris. With the last name Lamore, she was probably there, too, but I don't bother asking. We're doing the staring thing again, like every other time we're around each other. Except now, it's different. Now, I see her. And I move my head back to stare at the top of the tent, done fucking looking.

Sometime in the night, Nyx wiggles her way over. I wake up with her cuddled into me. Even with the blankets, it's fucking cold, and I'm not running hot for once, so I let her stay.

Traitorous or not, she's warm.

I readjust onto my side, draping my arm over her. A little while later, she's wormed even closer somehow. Her shoes are off, her feet wedged between my legs, her even breaths on my chest, and head tucked under my chin. I blame it on being half-asleep that I slide my other arm under her until I'm full-on snuggling with the enemy. Fuck me. I still can't keep my hands to myself with her.

We haven't moved by the time the first light of morning shines through the porous material of the tent. I detangle myself, moving Nyx's head off my arm, wisps of black hair across her forehead. She looks peaceful with her cheek pressed against the pillow. Angelic. Innocent. Deceitful, even in her sleep.

Once I've inched away, I put my shoes on and grab the blade from under my pillow. I'm halfway through the flap when I stop, still hunched over. A carryout coffee cup sits on one of the logs, another change of clothes the next over. Jeans, a gray tank top, new bra, and panties. None of it in my size.

Then I catch the tiniest whiff of burnt soul.

He faces away from me, on the other side of the ashes left from the fire last night.

Before I move again, I return the dagger to my belt loops and pull my shirt over it. "Come to apologize?" I straighten as Hex turns around.

Square jaw, straight-edged nose, and another goddamn suit. I never expected Donny to work with someone so … pretty.

"We weren't given an opportunity to properly introduce ourselves." He extends his hand, only to withdraw it a second later when I cross my arms. "Not a morning person?"

"Not a *you* person," I shoot back, keeping him in sight while I move to the coffee.

"That's for Nyx."

"Is it?"

He nods, so I make sure to maintain eye contact while I take a long drink. As I finish the lukewarm latte, the tent rustles behind me.

Hex's attention moves to the sound, and he grins. "There's my goddess."

Nyx steps beside me, her eyes slowly rising to mine. "Please untie me."

I pull apart the knotted straps until her bra falls to the ground. She rubs her wrist, rolling her shoulders a few times as she crosses the campsite. Hex smiles as she rounds the ashes. Then she walks straight up to him and slaps him across the face.

So, they've fucked.

He winces, his lips in a tight line. "I suppose I deserved that."

"You deserve so much more," she says. "I didn't think I could hate you any more than after you killed Nyla in Paris, but you've pulled it off."

"Love," he starts, only for her to slap the shit out of him again.

This time, the demon responds like a demon. He growls, catching her wrist before she pulls away, and he towers over her, lowering his furious face to hers.

"Watch it, Descended. That tattoo was looking a little worn the last time I saw it. I'd hate to be the one to make it disappear."

When she jerks away, he releases her and adjusts the cuffs of his jacket.

"Since you seem uninterested in playing nice"—he waves his palm off to the side of them—"we'll just get straight to resetting the game."

Nyx glances over her shoulder at me, concern etched on her face. I see the portal open, but before either of us can do anything, Hex grabs her shoulders and shoves her toward the rippling air. I take an instinctive step before she stumbles through, and then it's just the Upper and me.

I figure I'm up next for the portal ride, so I coolly dip down for the clothes on the log. "Chicks, huh?" But really, I'm scanning the area in the light. A cliff in the distance and a possible water tower on the horizon.

Hex teleports to my side, cocking his head while he studies me. "Keep your hands to yourself, Watcher. We wouldn't want for her to get attached to a mortal with a ticking clock."

I shake my head and back away from him. "Trust me, Hexagon…"

The cooler still has a few waters inside, and I swipe it on my way to the portal, not sure where it leads. Even so, I'd rather go through on my own than to be manhandled by a guy dressed like he might *actually* sell life insurance. I pause in front of the portal and look over my shoulder. "It's not my hands you should worry about."

His nostrils flare, and a flame appears in his palm right before I step through.

Uppers. So fucking touchy.

I pop out on the other side, bracing for … who the hell knows what? But it's more of the same. Sand, dried-up bushes, sun, and Nyx with a flash of relief at the sight of me. And at her feet is my hoodie she left behind yesterday, ripped to shreds from an animal.

Fuck. He really did reset us.

I start walking toward the sun, not quite in the same direction as yesterday. With more daylight, maybe I can get to some sort of civilization. A town, a highway, or hell, a dude in a dune buggy. I'm not picky.

As I pass, I shove the clothes at Nyx. "Gift from your boyfriend."

"Not my boyfriend," she bites back.

"Right," I call over my shoulder. "I'm sure you two are just feeling it out."

She lets out a frustrated groan from behind me.

By the time she reappears at my side, she's changed. She screws with the cooler, pulling the sunblock out and putting in her clothes from last night. After she finishes treating me like a packhorse carrying her fucking purse, we walk through the desert. And walk. And walk.

The sun looms overhead and stretches to the other side. We've both reapplied sunscreen a few times and drained the last of the water. Nyx keeps up for the most part. Every now and then, the sound of her feet dragging behind me slows and fades. Proving myself a real stand-up dude, I check back after a minute or so to see if she's unconscious on the ground. I don't know why I bother; she'll pop the fuck back up.

The Others—or Descended. They might not have gotten their angelic powers, but they did pretty well for themselves, apparently. The Fallen tracked them over the years, but they must have gone underground to make it look like they'd died off when they should have. We kept our distance, so if they pulled anything, we wouldn't get lumped in and screwed over.

Joke's on me with that one.

Nyx is right on my heels when I see it. I drop the cooler, coming to an abrupt stop, and then so does she when she slams right into my back.

"Ow, what the—" she cuts off, and I imagine she notices what my gaze is glued to ahead of us.

A fucking cooler.

Sure enough, when we get over there, we repeat yesterday. Four bottles of water and sunscreen.

"Shit." I kick the cooler over, the bottles rolling out onto the sand, and Nyx flinches.

Before I take my Donny rage out on her, I put some distance between us, flexing my hands as I go. A habit—but unlike the other times, there's no glow from my palms or fingertips. With the lack of heat, they feel empty. Cold.

"You think there's a tent waiting for us too?" Nyx's voice is quiet behind me, like she's afraid to rattle my cage any more.

I put my hands on the back of my head and turn around to look at her. "Probably."

And hours later, probably turns into definitely.

The same tent. Same blankets. A note for Nyx.

She throws it straight into the fire without reading it and sorts through the new cooler left for us.

I wander away from the campsite to see if any lights stand out in the night. If we were close to anything, we could keep going. If I weren't *mortal*, we would keep going regardless, but I'd rather not meet my demise because I stepped in a hole and fell face-first on a rattlesnake or some shit.

Nothing but sky and stars. Cass would be hard over this view.

I pull out my palm stone, Avery side up, and adjust the image to see the rest of the living room around her. Just as planned, Ros showed up last night. We'd come up with a code word, so the twins would take off their necklaces, and his light would work on them. He's not there now, but Cass and Hannah are—scrolls spread out over their feet and a torqued off look in Cass's eyes.

If this were a charge, he could use their blood to locate them. No vials of my blood lying around though. So, they'll have to figure out where the hell I am in a different way.

Come find me, brother.

After we eat, Nyx disappears into the tent with her change of clothes. I hang by the fire a little longer. The chill in the air bothers me more tonight. By the time I crawl in, she's lying under the blankets. I sit down and lean forward to fish her bra out from under her jeans in the corner.

"Seriously?" she says. "In case you haven't noticed, I'm on your side here."

"Cool. But I'd rather you be on *your* side, hands behind your back so I can tie your ass up and go to sleep." I circle my finger in the air, and she huffs, but then she rolls away from me, her hands sliding behind her.

Her pouting lasts a few hours before her need for body heat wins out. She moves closer and sighs. Then a little closer. Another sigh, followed by another inch. Since we both know where this will end up, I pull her the rest of the way to me. With her back against my chest, her hands push into my lower abs. Any lower, and we'd be in an entirely different situation.

At some point, she flips over and nuzzles into my chest, like last night. That's how we wake up too. Her encircled in my arms. My leg hooked over hers. And the demon who told me not to touch her staring down at us.

"The fuck?" I shout, sitting up.

Nyx jerks awake, panicked until she sees Hex leering at us from the tent opening. The flap falls down as he walks away, and she buries her face in the pillow. She yells something about him, but the obscenities are lost in the feathers.

Hex has a bored look on his face when we crawl out. He hands her the coffee today, not chancing any interception. Then he waves his little palm to open the portal. This time, we both walk through of our own accord, taking Nyx's change of clothes and the cooler with us.

And we're back at the damn sweatshirt.

I start in the direction we went the first day, thinking about the water tower.

Nyx almost has to run to keep up with my fast stride. "Why are we bothering to walk if he's just going to find us again?"

"The better question is, how is he finding us? A demon's not going to hang around all day, watching us traipse around the desert."

She looks up at me. "He's tracking us somehow."

I nod, trying to figure out how, but a few seconds later, her steps fall behind.

"Shit," she says when I turn around. She's taking the cuff out of her cartilage, and then she holds it out for me. "Could he be using this?"

I pick the earring out of her palm. "He gave this to you?"

She bites her lip, averting her gaze. Once I see the crystal embedded in the gold, I know why.

Sonofabitch.

"This is why my light wasn't working on you," I say through clenched teeth.

Nyx nods, but it wasn't a question. Slap a spell on it, and the earring works exactly like Samy's amulet, the gold diverting light into the crystal. My light never affected her because it never reached her brain. The bar, Kai's kitchen, the hallway, at the racetrack. She bullshitted her way through it all.

Impressive if I wasn't the one fucked in the end.

"Would Hex have—"

"The diversion spell would have overridden any other spell cast," I tell her. "So, unless he got his paws on it between you lying at the racetrack and lying in my car…"

"No," she says. "I haven't taken it out since I met you at the bar."

I nod and drop the earring back into her hand. "Well, he's not using it to track us then. And you blew your secret for nothing."

She has an apology in her eyes when I look up. Before she decides to voice it and I have to tell her to fuck off, I shrug off a chill working down my arm and unload the cooler. I'm already sick of carrying it.

"Demons have a trick where they can sense mortal heartbeats." I give her a water, the sunblock, and her clothes. "With no one else around, he's probably scanning the desert until he picks up ours."

"So, what do we do?" she asks as I walk away, abandoning the cooler. And her—but only one will stay where I left it.

"We get somewhere with more than the two of us." Because of her little boyfriend, but also I just need to be away from her. Every time I look at her, the absence of light throbs within me. No heat, light, or life, but a cold ache.

Nyx must sense she needs to give me space, or maybe she's just as desperate to get away from me. Either way, we have little to do with each other until afternoon—when we run across the cooler we both knew would be waiting for us.

I take my shirt off before snagging a water. She grabs one, too, but doesn't drink it right away. I tip my bottle back and watch her, holding the water in her arm and twisting at the sunscreen in her hands. By the time I spin the lid back on my bottle, she's walking over with a determined look to her.

Not in the mood, I start to walk again.

"Do we have an actual plan?" she asks. "Because I'm done wandering in the desert like what's his name."

Moses, but I don't supply the answer.

When it becomes clear I'm not coming back, she shouts, "When are you going to forgive me?"

She can't be fucking serious with that question. But when I look, she's standing there, waiting for an answer.

"I don't know," I say, facing her. "You plan on forgiving your boyfriend for killing your sister anytime soon? Because I'll fit you in a century after that."

She shakes her head, glaring. "*Ex*-boyfriend. And you won't fucking be here in a century."

I growl, my hands flexing on my first step toward her. "Because of you!"

Nyx's eyes widen, lips parting with a quick breath. "Chaz…"

"No." I stalk toward her, my chest heaving and the rest of me seething. "I've been *nice*, considering the part you played. You're the reason we're here. You and your fucking—"

"Chaz!" She stumbles backward, the bottles falling to the ground while she tries to get away from me. "Stop, stop, stop," she begs. "Please!"

The shrieked plea brings me to a stop, real fear in her eyes. I might be twice her size and pissed off, but her response seems dramatic. She's taking short breaths, staring at my hands. That's when I see the shadows escaping from my palms. Swirls of darkness are circling my wrists and going back into the skin, where more appear.

Oh, fuck me.

SIXTEEN

NYX

"What did you do?" Chaz whispers the words, but they sound thunderous in the silence around us. Then he repeats them, his eyes shifting to me. "What the *fuck* did you do to me?"

I swallow, watching the black fade until it's just his hands again. "Nothing. I bound your life force with Abaddon's—"

"What exactly does that mean?" His tone stays calm, but I have a feeling he's anything but below the surface. "Life force."

"It's hard to explain. A lot goes into life, but it's sort of like an essence tied to your soul."

"O-kay," he says slowly, a little more edge to his voice. "But a demon doesn't have a soul. The darkness smothers it out and takes its place. Darkness is what keeps a demon alive."

My breath stops, my entire body numbing. "Oh."

"So, that would mean…" His jaw tenses, the control slipping. The shadows return for a second until he closes his eyes. They dissipate, and he takes a few more breaths before looking at me again. "I have darkness inside of me."

"You shouldn't. Only one life force can exist at once. There shouldn't be room for anything else."

"Except I'm not whole," he says. "I lost my light, Nyx. A rather important part of the angel equation, which means there's a massive void." He stretches out his hands and lets the shadows flow from his fingertips. "Or there was. It looks like your little stunt gave the darkness an opening to move *the fuck in.*" He practically growls the last few words, and I fold my arms across my chest.

"How was I supposed to know any of that?" I ask. "In case you missed it, my ancestors were more worried about bitching than giving us useful information, like what powers a demon."

Chaz storms toward me, his temper flaring along with the darkness. "So you shouldn't have been screwing with what you didn't understand."

I backpedal, and I'm pretty sure I just reached his breaking point and am about to wake up in my spirit form.

But then his shoes skid as he stops in front of me. His eyebrows shoot up, and out of nowhere, he smirks down at me. "They didn't teach you what powers a demon? Or what powers a demon has?"

"Both? I knew nothing about them until I met Hex during my first life."

"Well, lucky for us," he says, holding out his hands, "I've known everything there is to know about them since my beginning."

I'm about to ask what the hell he's talking about when he waves his palm off to the side of us. At first, nothing happens, but then I notice the air. A slight ripple, like a mirage, except right beside me and not from the heat. My eyes snap up to Chaz, and he shrugs right before he sidesteps and disappears.

I suck in a breath, my head taking a second to wrap around what just happened. And then the air returns to normal, and my shock flips to irritation. He did *not* just create a demon portal and leave me here.

"Hey," he says from behind me.

I jump, grabbing my chest as I whip around to face him a few feet away. "Jesus. I thought you'd left me."

He picks up the cooler and my clothes. "Wouldn't do me any good to abandon my hostage."

"Hostage?" I say.

He nods and opens another portal. "Plus, there seems to be a small caveat with the portals."

"And what's that?"

"It seems that since I only have some darkness in me"—he vanishes through the portal, and in a blink, he reappears so far ahead that I have to squint to see him cupping his hands around his mouth—"they have a limit." He steps out in front of me again. "But we should be able to track down some extra heartbeats before your boyfriend checks in."

"Ex-boy—" I drop the last part of the word because he's already gone.

I blow out a breath and gather the waters and sunscreen from the ground, and then I follow my captor through.

Because what the hell else am I going to do?

Chaz notices the outline first, set low on the horizon.

I've been gripping his bicep for a while, trying to keep up as we portal-hop. He closes one, opens another, drags me through. Wash, rinse, repeat. But once we see the building, he pulls on his shirt and tosses the cooler behind a bush. He crouches down in front of me. I don't hesitate to climb on, and he hikes me up as my legs wrap around his midsection. For only being a few hours into demon powers, he's got this part down. One hand opens while the other closes. We blink our way across the desert until the shack takes shape.

The last portal brings us out behind the building. Wooden siding and shingles in the middle of nowhere, but none of that matters because music is beating through the shabby, spring-loaded screen door. I slide off him, and Chaz grabs my hand, bringing me with him. He leans around the corner, and the tension melts out of his shoulders. When he spins around and half-smiles, I peek to see what has him sliding down the wall.

Motorcycles. Parked in a long line that extends past where I can see. And behind them are cars and trucks and a four-wheeler.

"Thank God," I say.

"Nah, baby. God didn't carry your ass here." He climbs off the ground and hooks his head toward the corner. "Let's go."

I stay close behind him. Part of me still expects Hex to jump out, yell *boo*, and start us all over at the sweatshirt again. But we step onto the forward-slanting porch at the front without him appearing, and once we're walking under the overhang, it feels like we're in the clear.

"*Patty's Saloon*," Chaz reads the sign beside the green metal door before swinging it open and directing me inside with his chin. "Hostages first."

I roll my eyes, passing him. He follows right behind me, and I'm about to smart off when an entire bar's worth of people stop what they're doing to look at us. The music is still thumping from a jukebox in the corner, and the door bangs shut behind Chaz, but everything else seems frozen. Bikers wearing a whole lot of leather—like you'd expect bikers to wear—bandanas, sunglasses tucked in the necks of their shirts, and then everybody else. Tables full of ripped jeans, T-shirts, caps faded from the sun, and a whole lot of skirts and crop tops.

A hand creeps onto my waist, Chaz's protective hold reminding me to breathe, but after the initial shock of us walking in, the room reanimates. People turn back to their beers and conversations. A few stares linger as Chaz nudges me forward, his arm staying across my back.

"What can I get you?" The graying redhead behind the bar smacks her gum, her tone wary. "Water from the looks of it."

"Phone?" Chaz asks.

"Pay phone." She nods toward the back, somehow filling six shot glasses of whiskey while still keeping a careful eye on us. "Slip your hand in the slot where the phone book should be. You'll find yourself some quarters."

Chaz busts out a grin that I've been on the receiving end of a few times. Not lately, but before he hated me. He raps his knuckles on the bar top. "Thanks, Patty."

She winks, and he ushers me around tables until we reach the far corner. The decorations are limited to road signs, except for a single deer head with a pair of bright pink panties hanging from an antler.

"Classy," I say under my breath, but Chaz's lips twitch.

He leans against the wall and snatches up the phone while I run my hand to the back of the shelf, dragging a few quarters out. But before I feed them into the slot, Chaz taps the receiver against his forehead.

"Shit," he says. "Shit, shit." He hangs it back up and rubs his face. "I don't know anyone's phone number."

I close my eyes, realizing I don't either.

A low chuckle rumbles from behind us, and seconds later, a guy slings his arm over Chaz's shoulders. "Need an old man to show you how this thing works?" The top few buttons of his blue jumpsuit are popped open, his white undershirt wet from recently spilled beer. "You two look like you've been through it. What brings you here?"

Chaz blows out a breath. "I need a fucking drink."

He heads back to the bar, leaving me with—if I'm to believe the name stitched above his pocket—Jerry, who takes over Chaz's spot on the wall.

"Desert tour," I say. "They left us behind." Then before he can put too much thought into whether it's a viable excuse, "Do you know if anyone has a cell phone we could use? We need to look up the number for the tour company."

Jerry barks out a laugh that makes me jump. "No cell phone reception out here. No Wi-Fi either, before you ask. You'll need to get on the highway and go for about forty minutes."

Great. Chaz and I have both been around since before cell phones *and* landlines, yet here we are, screwed the second we lose access to modern conveniences.

"Thanks anyway."

I make it a few steps before he says, "My kids are heading that way in the morning. They can take you and your boyfriend if you still need a ride."

I force a smile over my shoulder, so he knows I heard his offer.

When I land on the barstool next to Chaz, he already has two empty shot glasses in front of him and is lifting a third. He glances over, throwing it back, and then slides me a fourth.

I take it, the whiskey biting on the way down. I make a face, my nose burning. "We probably shouldn't be drinking until we've had some water and eaten."

"You're probably right." He smiles as Patty refills the glasses and pushes two over. "But I don't think either of us gives a fuck right now."

I can't argue. It looks like we're stuck here—wherever *here* is— and I could use a few hours of not thinking.

He takes one shot after the other, then he watches me tip mine back.

The next time Patty walks by and sees our empty glasses, she leaves the bottle.

"She won't hit anything," Jerry says.

It's the same thing he said on my last turn and the one before. And like those other times, my next dart lands on the board for triple points.

"I'll be damned," he says.

Like the other times.

I've been kicking his ass at darts while Chaz nurses a beer at a table nearby. Night only fell an hour ago, but we've already been drunk and back again because we have nothing better to do. The crowd of heartbeats is concealing ours, and leaving means we'd chance Hex tracking us down, so we're stuck in the middle of nowhere in Arizona for the night.

Jerry offered to let us sleep in his cousin Rudy's camper. A bunch of the people here live a few miles away in what sounds like a Mojave version of Slab City but with electricity and running water. Rudy's out of state, visiting his girlfriend in Nevada. At a prison.

The group around Jerry is still roaring over my win when I glance over at the broody angel. He's spinning the crystal stone that shows him Kai and Avery on the tabletop, but he's focused on me. Our stare holds like the first time we were in a bar together.

His eyes soften, back to the way they were then, magnetic and drawing me in.

It only lasts a few seconds. Then he blinks. Looks away. And the moment's gone.

The pull remains though.

I sit down beside him, but his head stays down, tension refilling the space between us. As I fold my feet up on the chair, I watch his hand flexing underneath the table. Shadows appear in his palm and then disappear once it closes. I force my eyes up, pretending I didn't notice.

We ride with Jerry and his wife to the little collection of RVs and trailers. They're scattered around like a real neighborhood, most with lawn chairs or a picnic table outside. A few have Christmas lights strung around fabric awnings or fake grass on the ground outside the doors.

Rudy's Palace—as the sign out front states—is stuck in the seventies. Brown shag carpet stretches from end to end, orange cushions cover the bench seating on either side of a bright yellow laminate table, and the tiny Formica counter beside the sink has a daisy pattern. All that really matters is the real bed in the back and the bathroom with a shower stall and hot water.

Within twenty minutes, I've used a fourth of a bottle of generic vanilla-smelling body wash and just as much strawberry shampoo. I rip the tag off the underwear I found in the bedroom, still in the bag. Turns out, Rudy's girlfriend and I are close in size. The only other things I'd wear of hers, though, are the pair of sweatpants and plain black tank I dug out of the closet.

I'm still combing my fingers through my wet hair when I come out. Chaz is leaning against the counter. He's tall enough that if he pushed onto the balls of his feet, the top of his head would graze the ceiling, and even after he straightens, I brush against him as I pass.

He has gym shorts in his hand and a gray shirt. But what I fixate on is the blue tie with an unfortunate flower pattern.

Since I doubt he plans on wearing it, I roll my eyes. "We're in the middle of nowhere with a demon chasing our heartbeats. I'm not going anywhere."

"The tie isn't for now," he says, walking to the bathroom. "It's for when we go to bed."

Before I can respond, he drags the paneled accordion door closed. The shower turns on a second later.

Even though I've spent the last three days outside, I leave the inside door open and sit on the steps. I relax back against the metal screen door and sigh. Tomorrow, we'll be back in civilization. I can check on Nyla, move her somewhere Hex can't find her. Somewhere Abaddon can't find *me*.

"Trailers work best if you sleep inside of 'em."

I raise my head. The guy is standing next to the Rudy's Palace sign with a plastic bag in his hand. Long legs bring him the rest of the way. I take him in—the checkered shirt with a pocket, distressed jeans, gorgeous brown eyes with dark hair to match.

"Nyx, I take it?" He smiles when I nod and hands me the bag. "Jared." Then he quickly adds, "Jerry's son. My mom thought you two might need a few things."

"Oh my God," I say, checking inside. Unopened deodorants, toothbrushes, toothpaste, a comb. "Thank you. I mean, tell her thank you."

"I'll deliver the message. She keeps extras on hand for trips, but they never go anywhere."

I laugh, and he smiles again.

"My dad said you and your boyfriend need a ride into town in the morning?"

"We do, but he's not my boyfriend."

"Brother?" he asks fast. "Close cousin? Best friend who would kill anyone who touches you?"

"None of the above."

He blows out a breath and gives an exaggerated nod. "Good. The truck is very close quarters. I'd rather not have any issues when I'm pressed up against you. In the morning … you know, when I give you a ride."

I narrow my eyes at him. "Are you hitting on me, Jared, Jerry's son?"

He puts his hands behind his back and shrugs. "Not very often my dad brings a beautiful woman home with him."

"Your mo—"

"Fine," he cuts me off before I finish. "He's never brought home a gorgeous chick with a smile like yours, and if I haven't been clear, yes, I am hitting on you."

He's cute and coming a step closer. "Let's go somewhere."

"Where? The truck you want to give me a ride in?"

That earns me a surprised quirk of the brow. "We would need to take it if I'm going to buy you a drink. Long way to the bar though. Might get lost or—"

Metal bangs above me, and I jump off the steps, my heart pounding when I whip around. Chaz glowers at us from the other side of the screen, his jaw hardened and focus over my head on Jared. Then it lowers to me.

The way he used to look at me made me all heart-fluttery and weak, but I can't be weak when it comes to him. I need to be impenetrable. With the look he's giving me now, I have to be, or he'll eat me alive.

I stare him down through the steel mesh until he hooks his head for me to come inside and then walks away.

"Not your boyfriend?" Jared says.

I shoot him a smile before I climb the steps. "I'll see you and your truck in the morning."

He's still standing there with a disappointed look on his face when I shut both the doors. I take a deep breath, touching my forehead to the inside one. When I can't stand Chaz's stare on my back anymore, I turn around.

His hair's still wet, haphazardly pushed up, and the gym shorts and V-neck look a few sizes too big but still manage to hang off him in all the right ways. God, he's gorgeous. It's truly unfair how he can be such an ass and still make my pulse race without trying.

I grab a few things out of the bag before tossing it on the table on my way to the bathroom. When I come out a few minutes later, Chaz has a toothbrush stuck in his mouth. He's propped against the counter, so I have to sidestep to get to the table. He smells spicy, like whatever brand of deodorant Jerry's wife sent for him.

"Getting friendly with the locals?" He throws the toothbrush in the sink beside him and twists for a purple plastic cup behind him. A row of them are upside down, drying, but he must have filled one.

"Only the one," I say, returning everything to the bag.

One side of his mouth turns up in a smirk. "Maybe we should vacation together more often. You get a fuck buddy. I get my soul tainted."

I sigh as he sets the cup in the sink. He stretches out his fingers, bringing his hand back. I don't even think he's aware of it until he catches me looking.

"The darkness is cold," he says, turning his palm up. "I thought it was because I'd lost my light, but I'm cold because of what's currently inside of me, not what isn't anymore." His brow pulls in, real pain on his face. "I once said there was nothing worse than being mortal."

"You could be dead. I'm sure, as an angel, you think it's worse, but I've died enough times to know—"

His eyes flash to mine, stormy and intimidating, and I know I shouldn't have said anything.

"You don't know shit," he grinds out. "I was brought into existence with divine light. Every second without it has been like drowning. I've spent my entire punishment gasping for air, filling my lungs with water. And I keep sucking it down, waiting for the slightest bit of oxygen to surge through me because those moments are worth every second of suffering. But now, those moments are gone, and the water's cold and muddy." He pushes off the counter, taking a step toward me. "Let's not forget whose fault that is."

"You know what?" I snap. "Go ahead and blame me. For pretending to date Kai and trying to save my sister. The Dimming Blade, the darkness—all of it. If you want to hate me for it, then hate me, Chazaqiel. I don't care. But while you're hating me, remember the only reason you're even here to do it is because of me."

My voice trembles at the end, and unwilling to give him my tears, I start to walk away until he spins me by the waist, trapping me between his arms and his hard body. I have to lean back to put space between us, and I tip my chin up to meet his harsh glare.

"Trust me," he says, "I want to hate you." One of his hands moves, and I can't tell if he means to or not, but his cool fingers graze my back under my shirt, making me shiver.

"You want to, or you do?" I sound out of breath, and I realize how fast I'm breathing, my grip digging into his biceps.

He licks his lips, his eyes falling to my mouth at the same time, then they come back to mine different, darker. "Want," he rasps. "I want to hate you. So. Fucking. Much."

Two breaths—one mine, one his—and then his lips are on mine. I grab the back of his neck as he sets me on the sad excuse for a kitchen counter, knocking over the row of plastic cups. No part of him is asking permission, not his hands tugging my straps down my arms, not his tongue sinking into my mouth. And I know he won't be trying to take any second of it away from me this time.

I shove his shirt up and we break apart, so he can yank it over his head. He groans as his lips crash into mine again, like it took too long. My head falls back when he moves down my neck, running his tongue across my skin. He pushes down my top, kissing his way to my breasts. The low-hanging cupboard presses into my back while he sucks one nipple into his mouth, his cold palm on the other. I whimper at the mix of sensations, and he jerks me to the edge of the counter into him. When my legs wrap around his waist, I feel how hard he is and lift my hips, wanting more friction. He grinds his cock perfectly against my clit, his mouth still on me.

"Chaz…" My back arches into him, and he slips his arm behind me to hold me up.

"Say it." He raises his head enough to see me. "Tell me you want me. That you've always wanted me." He thrusts forward harder, working my sweatpants down with each one. "When you were with Kai, in my apartment, when my hands were on you at the hotel, five minutes ago while you flirted with the redneck."

"Yes." I circle my arms around his neck and bring myself up until we're face-to-face. "I've wanted you the entire time."

He growls, picking me up, and he carries me to the bedroom at the back of the camper. My feet touch the mattress, and he lifts my shirt. I raise my arms, taking over once he pushes it over my head. I toss it on the floor, and he's already kissing down my chest and over my stomach. I close my eyes when he bites my hip and slips my sweats further down. His thumbs drag my panties down, and then he pulls me to him and lowers us onto the mattress before he takes them both the rest of the way off.

While he rips open the drawer to the nightstand in search of Rudy and his prison girlfriend's condom stash, I push down his baggy gym shorts. In one quick move, he finishes the job. I drag him to me by the back of his neck until he's between my legs. He grips his shaft and rubs the head of his cock through my slit before teasing it over my clit. I shudder from the spark of pleasure.

"Admit you wanted me too," I say.

Chaz studies me, his movements slowing.

"All the times you acted like you didn't, tell me you did."

He tosses the condom package on the bed and dips his head to free himself of my hold. He licks and nips his way down my body. My fingers grasp his hair as he goes, and then he nudges his shoulder against my thigh, so I'll spread them wider for him. I suck in a breath the second his mouth covers me. He groans, dragging the flat of his tongue through my core and then flicking my clit with the tip.

"I've wanted to fuck you again since you bitched I'd only made you come once." His words hum through me, my pussy already dripping when he slips a finger inside me. "Every time I caught you staring at me." Another. "Or you touched me." He adds a third, stretching me around his thick digits.

My hips rock to find his tongue again. He clamps his free arm around my thigh and sucks on my clit, causing me to moan, then he bites it. I gasp, my body jerking, but he holds me tight against him, and I have nowhere to go.

"Oh, fuck."

I tug at his hair, and he grunts, dragging his teeth over the sensitive nerves before an almost sweet swipe of his tongue.

"I'm gonna need you to come on my face, Nyx," he rasps.

He pumps his fingers faster and sets an entirely different rhythm with his mouth. Quick thrusts and languid licks.

My entire body is on fire for him. Because of him. Then the cold hits me from the inside, his fingers curling to set me off. The icy sensation clashes with the heat pulsing through me in the most delicious way. My thighs tighten around his head, and he groans into me while I come. His lips latch onto my clit, and he sucks, not letting up until I cry out his name.

"Fuck." Chaz pulls his fingers out of me and grabs my legs, yanking me down the bed to him. He rips open the condom and rolls it on, his pupils blown out when he lowers between my thighs. "Now on my cock."

His hips surge forward, and I fight to keep my eyes from rolling back as he sinks inside my swollen pussy. He takes me in deep strokes, his forehead dropping to my shoulder.

"Shit, baby. You feel so fucking good."

His grip moves to my ass, and I feel up the muscles of his back, his shoulders, and chest. Greedy now that I can touch him. When I reach his neck, he lifts his head, eyes heavy-lidded. With one look, I'm drunk on them. His mouth crashes down on mine, and I moan, my body bending into his.

"Oh God," I say into the kiss.

"Sex god," he mumbles back.

I feel his lips turn up seconds before he pins my wrists over my head. He presses them down into the mattress while he thrusts harder, his tongue mimicking the movements. I lock my legs around him and tip my chin up when he shoves his face into my neck. His teeth nip at my skin, his hold on my wrists tightening. It isn't like the first time when we were on an even playing field. He's in complete control and not letting me think otherwise.

When Chaz's hand dips between us and rubs circles on my throbbing clit, another chill surges from his fingers. I suck in a harsh breath as my climax slams into me. My pussy constricts around his cock, his name becoming a part of every exhale until I can't tell if I'm breathing or chanting.

Chaz's control finally shatters.

"Fuck, Nyx. Fuck."

Keeping my hands pinned, he fucks me faster and then groans, driving deeper. His body tenses, his brow pulled in.

Somehow, he's even more beautiful.

As he relaxes, stubble drags over my chest, up my neck, and across my jaw. My body's still shaking beneath him when he kisses me slowly. His lips are soft and tongue gentle, and I sink into the bed. His arm leaves my side, his hand abandoning my thigh. The kiss deepens as he pulls out and shifts on top of me.

Fabric tightens around my wrists.

I break my mouth away from him, looking up to where he's knotting the ugly tie. Once he finishes, I pull my arms down between us and shove against his chest, but it only results in a smirk.

"Just because I fucked you doesn't mean I trust you."

I huff as he climbs out of bed, and he looks up and winks before walking out.

But at least he tied me in front this time.

Progress.

SEVENTEEN

CHAZ

Standing at the bathroom sink, I examine the scar from the blade for the first time from something other than a downward angle. The flesh is smooth and the edges clean. It's not even all that badass-looking. A genuine disappointment, considering the hell I went through in getting it.

I run a hand through my hair, opening the door. Instead of checking myself out, I should have been preparing for any aftermath there might be from screwing Nyx again. But fuck was it worth it.

When I walk in, she's rolled onto her side under a blanket. I lift it, confirming she's still naked before I lie down. Sexiest damn prisoner I've ever kept. She doesn't try to cover up, but her glare narrows until I let the comforter fall over us.

"What did you do to Donny?" she asks as I stretch out on my back.

Goddamn it. I'd rather talk about my feelings.

"You've never called him Donny before." I stack my hands behind my head. "And why would you assume it's the angel's fault and not the demon's?"

She adjusts her pillow. "I guess you're a bad influence," she says dryly. "Okay, what does *Abaddon* blame you for?"

"Upper-level demons have a code where they keep what they kill—money, possessions, darkness, titles. It all means power, and most spend their existence scrambling for more. Figuring out who needs to die to get them what they want. Like the Demon of Destruction."

"Is he not the original then?"

"Nah, Abad*don't* isn't the original anything. He had himself lined up to take the previous one out though. Except then a small war broke out between the angels and demons. God had to reboot creation by the time we were done. It's when Kasdaye gave him the scar on his face. I banished the darkness from a lot of demons during the fighting, the most well-known of them being the last Demon of Destruction."

Nyx sighs. "He wants to kill you because you killed the guy he was going to kill. Nothing more alpha bullshit than that."

I can't disagree, so I continue, "Donny ended up defeating the other Uppers who'd tried to claim the title, but he still had it in his head that his legacy had been tarnished because he didn't earn it the right way. The Almost-Legitimate-Except-for-a-Tiny-Loophole Demon of Destruction. The solution is to wipe me from existence to prove himself worthy."

"But you hate him too," she says.

I look up at the ceiling, over the conversation. "You were supposed to siren-song me away from Kai and Avery, so Donny could snag me without my powers, right?"

She fidgets, and I take it as a yes.

"So, why did we hook up at the bar? Kai was nearby, and demons wouldn't dare attack me there. You could have suggested your car or asked me to take you somewhere." More wiggling, so I turn my head. "Why did you have sex with me that night, Nyx?"

She shrugs. "When else was I going to get the chance to be with one of The Fallen?" Her melty eyes engage until they suddenly lower to the bed between us. "And I tried to get you to leave with me after, but you used your light on me. I wasn't supposed to care if I saw you again or want you to call me. I couldn't exactly…"

She says more, but I'm in the middle of a *fuck me* moment.

Call me.

A second later, I'm rolling out of bed. I grab my dirty-ass jeans off the floor, dragging them on instead of the shorts, and I throw Nyx's clothes at her. "Get up."

She sits up on the edge of the bed, confused, her hair a mess. She looks fucking hot, and I can't help myself. I dip down to kiss her and push her onto her back while I crawl on top of her, and I definitely have a problem because I'm thinking about being inside her again instead of untying her hands. I tug apart the knot and force myself off the bed, leaving her panting and even more confused.

I find my shirt at the front of the camper and pull it on along with my shoes. Then I open the cupboard under the sink and grab the Dimming Blade from where I wedged it between the pipes. By the time I tuck it behind me and stand up, Nyx is in the doorway.

"Are we going somewhere?" she asks.

"Yep."

"But Jared won't be here for hours."

"Fuck Jared. And not in his truck." I tack on the last part to be an asshole.

She doesn't get a chance to be pissy about it, though, only getting to open her mouth before I cross the trailer and scoop her up.

"What the hell?" she says, but her arms go around my neck.

I pull open the inside door and nudge the latch for the screen door, kneeing it the rest of the way open. At the bottom of the stairs, I swing Nyx onto my back and open a portal.

"Chaz, wait. What about Hex?" she whispers like he'll hear her, holding on while I readjust her.

"Hex has until we reach Patty's Saloon to catch us."

Then we're through the portal. It seems to go farther than the last one I created. Unnerving as shit but helpful nonetheless. In no time, we pop out beside the bar. I keep Nyx on my back, going behind the building. I pull open the screen door and see the padlock on the inner one.

"Hold the screen," I tell her.

She tightens her hold with one arm and plants a hand on the wood framing the door. I blow out a breath and close my fist around the lock.

"What are you—"

I shush her and concentrate on earlier when I walked out of the bathroom and heard her laughing. For the fucking dude in a checkered shirt. How his eyes were glued to her tits when I pulled down on the slats of the blinds. My jaw clenches, the urge to drop him in the middle of the desert resurfacing. Then, just like last time, ice shoots down my arm and into my palm. A flash of cold flame, and when I jerk down, the lock breaks. I unhook it and throw it on the ground.

Fuck Jared.

"Shit," Nyx says as I open the door. "You make flames now?"

I shrug, and once we're inside, she slides off my back. She holds on to my arm, following me through the dark kitchen and out into the main bar area. When we reach the pay phone, I swipe my hand underneath for quarters. A couple of coolers light the room, and I see Nyx squinting at me when I pick up the receiver and drop the quarters into the slot.

"I thought you couldn't remember anyone's phone number."

I smirk, dialing the one phone number I do know.

Mine.

Something inside me relaxes at the sound of the first ring, and by the second, someone answers.

"Hello?" she says. "Oh my God. Chaz, be you."

Hannah fucking Kelley.

I smile, slumping against the wall, and I can sense her pulse pounding. "I knew you wanted me, beautiful, but breaking into my apartment and stealing my phone?"

I've barely finished when the bar fills with divine light. Now, both Nyx and I are squinting until the brightness fades. And then there's Cass, standing in the center of the room, and I, for one, have never been more grateful for caller ID.

DARKENED SOUL

The first few hours after Nyx and I get back to my apartment are eventful, to say the least. I tie Nyx up—obviously. Then Cass ties *me* up because he can sense the darkness taking up residence. Ros shows up shortly after and rushes to untie me, only for them to all find out I've taken care of it myself with the help of my new little buddy, the flame. After that, there's a bunch of sitting around and staring at the floor while I tell them about my last few days. And Nyx.

"Whose lineage is she from?" Cass asks. "Which of The Others?"

Ros perks up, both of them waiting to see if she has ties to their Nephilim.

"Kokabiel," I say, locked on Cass.

The muscles of his jaw work overtime beneath the skin, but he gives nothing away.

"You said you have the Dimming Blade?" Rosdan moves us along like the exchange means nothing, and Cass shoots him an appreciative look.

We both know if Cass wants to tell Hannah that she shares a bloodline with Nyx, he will. Not our charge, not our choice.

When I whip out the dagger, they both lean back on the couch, instinctively putting as much space as possible between them and the thing that could end the ride.

After a minute of no one moving, Hannah comes and throws her arms around my middle. "I'm so sorry," she mumbles.

"Fuck, Kelley, not in front of the guys." But I wrap my arm around her shoulders anyway, letting out a long breath. Even with the ache from the missing light, the cold of the darkness, and the scar on my chest, it only now takes hold how screwed I am unless we undo what Donny's done. How one wrong move can wipe me from existence.

"Chaz…" Ros doesn't go any further with the pity, his sad eyes darting to Cass. "We just have to reverse the direction of the light from the blade, right? The light will banish the darkness, and then we can figure out the rest."

Cass is honed in on Nyx with a look that even causes Hannah to shift uneasily at my side. "She has to die to unbind you?"

Nyx shrinks into the chair, giving all the answer we need.

"All right," he says, "so we get you back the light, and then we kill her."

"What?" She sits up, shaking her head. "No, I—"

"That's how it works, right?" Rosdan, the only one of us who might have been her ally, raises a curious brow. "Why else would Abaddon have kept you alive?"

She turns to me in a panic. "Please. I probably only have one resurrection left. I can't die again."

"And he can?" Cass crosses the room. "You'll still come back. He'll cease to exist."

"He what?" she asks, but I look away as Cass pulls Hannah away from me.

He tucks her into his side. "You cool with lying low until we figure out the blade?"

I nod. "Not a huge fan of being connected to dickhead Donny, but that just means Armaros needs to get me up and glowing faster than he did the amulet."

Ros flips me off. "I could just stab you again and see what happens. Speaking of"—he stands up and digs the amulet out of his pocket—"put this on. It might help mask the darkness inside of you."

I catch the amulet and slip it over my head. "Why? You fighting the urge to strike me with a lightning bolt?"

"Yes," Cass says, flexing his hand. "My powers have been on since you started breathing the same air as Hannah."

"You're welcome then." I mean it as a joke, but it's not.

He's swimming in light because the darkness is a threat to his charge. Brothers or not, he'll end me before he chances anything happening to Hannah. And I wouldn't blame him for a second.

The amulet must remember me, and once I mutter the spell, it flashes. The cold sucks out of my extremities and knots in my chest behind the crystal, which is fading to a faint glow. I barely feel the darkness other than a soreness where it converges, but Cass nods, telling me he can't sense it anymore, so I suck it up. Uncomfortable or not, no one in this room wants to kill me now.

My eyes land on Nyx.

Right. *Almost* no one in this room wants to kill me.

With a tentative plan in place, I guilt my brothers into taking me across the hall. The past few days, they've been pulling double duty with my charges. When Hannah's school schedule allows, Cass drops them in from Boston, so Avery can go to classes or Kai can go out for a while. Rosdan takes one or both of the twins to Seattle or hangs at the apartment if he can. And the switch-offs will continue until I can protect them myself again. The in-between times neither of them can be here, Kai and Avery are on lockdown with a blocker bag they only disengage when they hear either of my brothers' voices.

Kai looks up from his video game when I walk in, Avery from her book.

"Hey," he says at the same time she smiles.

I land on the cushions between them like nothing has changed. In their minds, nothing has. They are blissfully unaware I haven't been around and that they can't leave on their own. They won't even try while under the suggestion to stay inside the apartment.

It feels strange to come back to my place, knowing I won't go across the hall later. Donny will be looking for us soon enough if he's not already. Depends on how clever Hex is at keeping our disappearance under wraps. Either way, one of them will be staking out the building with Lowers, waiting for me to pop up. I can't chance them stumbling onto my charges.

Cass has already dropped Hannah, but before he and Rosdan leave for the night, we duck into the kitchen. Just the three of us.

"What do you want to do about..." Rosdan tips his head toward Nyx in the living room.

"She stays here with me."

Cass raises an eyebrow. "You sure that's a good idea?"

"Would you rather she go with you?" I ask.

"Fuck no," he says fast. "Hannah would use the Dimming Blade on me if I brought another chick home. Just do us all a favor and don't find a way to make this worse."

"Love you too, Cassie."

After a heartwarming, "Whatever, asshole," he texts Hannah for a burst of light out. They've gotten timing her adrenaline down to a science.

With him occupied, it leaves me to deal with Rosdan's pity eyes.

"Come on," I tell him as I hold out my arms. "Bring it in."

He gives me a hug, slapping me on the back. Our dude moment gets an eye roll from Cass before he drops out of the kitchen.

"I'll be here tomorrow to start working with the blade," he says, bringing his phone to his ear.

"Thanks, buddy. I'll owe you one if you pull this off."

His charge must spook from the late-night call. He drops without saying anything, and I toss the crystal into the blocker bag, sealing us off from everything Heaven and Hell.

It's past middle of the night when I walk into the living room on my way to the bathroom. I smell like that shitty body wash in the camper, so a second shower it is.

I pass Nyx, still sunk into the chair. "Consider this home until we clean up your mess."

She opens her mouth, but I shake my head, cutting her off before she can argue.

Prisoners do not get negotiating rights. And since she made herself an integral part of my existence, she's not leaving my sight until one of us is dead.

EIGHTEEN

NYX

I rush to follow Chaz into the bathroom, where he's setting the amulet Rosdan gave him on the counter.

"I have to get to Nyla. Hex knows where she is, and if he—what are you doing?"

His shirt hits the tiled floor, and he's unbuttoning his jeans. "I'm going to scrub off the camper"—he pushes them down and straightens up, stepping out of the legs—"and then sleep. Unless you want to..." He gestures toward the shower.

My eyes travel down his body, lingering on his bare cock. But instead of taking him up on his offer, I hold my wrists up, knot out. "At least untie me."

He turns on the water. "No can do. You're a runaway risk."

Then, he steps into the shower, and a second later, the curtain separates us.

I sag against the counter, exhausted on every level. Nyla would have loved tonight—three Fallen in one room together. She would have willingly been restrained for it to happen too. If I could, I'd trade places with her in a heartbeat even if it meant I was down to my final life.

I stare at a loose thread on the black tie Chaz found to use when we got back. "Can I ask you something?"

He doesn't answer at first, but then a bottle snaps open. "You're going to anyway."

"Kasdaye and Armaros—"

"Cass and Rosdan," he corrects. "Modern names for modern angels, baby."

"They're your brothers, right?" I only pause a second before I rush through the rest in case he tries to cut me off. "Look at everything they've done for you these past few days. To protect you. Nyla and I have always done that for each other, and she's helpless right now. If it were Cass or Rosdan stuck in a bed and unable to defend themselves, you'd do whatever you could. So, it's not fair to ask me to just sit here when Hex could lead Abaddon straight to her. He'll use her to try to get to me, and then—"

Chaz pops his head around the shower curtain, his wet hair dripping down his face as he nods at his jeans on the floor. "Get my phone."

I drop to my knees and pull it out of the pocket. He's wiping his hand on a towel hanging by the tub when I hold it up for him. He shakes his head, tapping one-handed, and then he tosses it onto my lap before disappearing behind the curtain again.

My eyes fall to the screen and the message he just sent to *Whipped One.*

> *Blocker bag to protect the other Descended from Disastrous Donny?*

The phone buzzes with a response: *Address?*

A relieved sob escapes as I set the phone on the floor and enter the address for the farmhouse. Armaros—Rosdan's nickname is Cursed One, which leads me to believe I'm texting Cass.

> *Nothing like chanting in the middle of the night*, he replies. *We're going now.*

I sit back on my heels and wipe the tears. I almost laugh because Nyla would probably die just from knowing he was there. Her little old lady heart wouldn't be able to take it.

"Thank you, Chazaqiel." It comes out soft. I'm not even sure he hears it over the shower until I put his phone away and stand up.

"Yeah," he says. "Now, can you shut the damn door and let me wash my junk in peace?"

I smile and pull the door on my way out, turning the handle when it doesn't latch and tugging again so it stays closed.

I'm on the couch when he comes out a little while later, dragging a towel over his head. He barely glances at me before going straight to his room. I sigh and slip my shoes off. As I reach for the blanket at one end, he steps around the corner in low-slung sweatpants with a Q-tip shoved in his ear.

He doesn't say anything. Just raises his eyebrows and gives me a *what the fuck are you doing* look. Then, he clicks off the light and disappears. I decide that's his way of telling me he doesn't trust me out here on my own. Which is fine because I want to sleep in a real bed.

Neither of us says anything after I follow him. We get under the covers and lie in the dark, facing away from each other. It's hard to believe we were naked in the camper just a few hours ago. Now, we're here, where the sheets and the pillows and the comforter smell like him. Everything except me, which is still a mix of artificial strawberries and cheap vanilla.

"You were talking about killing me earlier."

The mattress shifts under his weight. I think he rolls over, but I don't look.

"How else did you think this would play out, Nyx?" he asks. "You thought Abaddon would abandon the grudge he's held for an eon? That I would be cool with my existence, relying on no one killing him? Neither of those is happening."

I squeeze my eyes shut, wanting to hate him for what he's saying. For all but telling me what he'll do to me once he regains his light. Or what someone will do for him.

In the desert, Chaz's life was at risk, and I was safe. But the second we left, the coin flipped, and the safer he becomes, the closer I am to death. The scales haven't been in balance once since we met, and somehow, I'm only realizing it now.

One of us has been dead all along. We just haven't figured out which one it is yet.

When I wake up, my hands are free, and Chaz isn't beside me anymore. I stretch, looking around the room in the morning light. All black furniture with nothing personal in sight. Not that I can imagine him framing pictures of Kai and Avery or the other angels. But it does make him look slightly like a serial killer.

Feeling the effects of two and a half days in the desert, followed by a half-day of drinking, I want water, shower, and food. In that order.

I climb out of bed in search of all three but pause at the sound of voices in the living room. The amulet's gone from the nightstand, so I'm guessing it's Cass or Rosdan.

I consider listening, but in case they're planning my murder, I'd rather break up the conversation. The door creaks the rest of the way open, and Chaz looks up as I step around the corner. He's on the couch with the Dimming Blade while Rosdan stands several feet away, fingers steepled under his chin. Rosdan's eyes flit to mine and then down to my hands.

"She won't suck the life out of you or something?" he asks.

Chaz only shrugs a shoulder, his focus returning to the weapon. "Water's in the kitchen. Towels in the cabinet."

"Thank you."

But neither is paying attention to me anymore.

"Human sacrifice." Rosdan dips his head for a better look. "Should we see if straight blood works first?"

"Nephilim," Chaz says as I open the fridge. "I'll grab a vial."

As I drink my water, I notice a black velvet bag on the counter. The drawstrings are loose and the top open. A crystal lies beside it and a few more inside.

"It's a blocker bag." Rosdan's propped in the doorway. "When active, it prevents anything light or dark from entering other than whoever cast the spell."

"This is what's protecting my sister?"

He cautiously approaches, like all five-four of me will attack the towering and muscular angel at any given moment. "Cass set one in the house last night."

I nod and force a smile. "Good."

Chaz rounds the corner, rubbing at his chest. "Ready?"

Rosdan passes him, and I leave my glass on the counter, following them.

"When can I go to my apartment?" I ask.

"You can't," Chaz answers, sitting down.

Rosdan looks between us, his face saying he wants to be anywhere but here right now. "I'll check on Avery and Kai." He quickly strides across the room and into the hall.

"I need clothes," I say. "And my phone."

Chaz reaches in his shirt and takes off the amulet. "A swarm of Lowers will be waiting for you the second you step foot into your place. And Hex is one hundred percent the kind of ex who would be tracking your phone."

"What if Nyla's doctors need to contact me?"

"Give them my number."

"What am I supposed to wear? I have a shirt, sweatpants, and one pair of underwear. Do you expect me to do laundry every day and hang out in a towel until it finishes?"

He smirks and spreads his arms across the couch cushions behind him. "Suddenly shy of strutting around my apartment in a towel?"

I let out an exasperated groan and stomp toward the bathroom, but he cheats with a portal and appears between me and the door, bracing his arm on the frame.

"Fine," he says. "You can get some clothes from your apartment."

"Fine." I duck under his arm, and he switches direction, pressing his other forearm to the wall.

"But you still aren't stepping into the building."

Rosdan lands us directly in the center of my bedroom.

Chaz cocks his head to the side. "Lucky shot, Ros?"

Rosdan steps away from us, scrunching up his face. "I might have been here before." I raise an eyebrow, and he says, "Kai mentioned your name when I went deep-diving for anything useful in finding Chaz. When his car ended up being in the parking lot, I thought it was worth checking inside."

Chaz moves to the dresser and picks up one of my bras. "So, you raided her panty drawer?"

I rip it away from him, and he winks.

"Recast your amulet spell," Rosdan tells him. "Your darkness is showing."

He flips Rosdan off, but his lips move.

"You have a bag?" Rosdan asks. "We need to hurry before Mark and Scarlett, uh…" Dimples appear with his half-smile. "Before they—"

"Ros's charge is banging his wife on his lunch break," Chaz says. "So, we need to be in and out in the time it takes him to be, well, in and out."

"In the closet." I shoulder past Chaz and show Rosdan where it is on the shelf.

He brings it down for me and opens it on the bed while I gather a few shirts. I toss them in and return to the dresser for the rest. Jeans, underwear, another few bras. When I turn, Chaz is beside the bed with shampoo and body wash. I nod, surprised he's helping.

He stuffs them in along with my armful of clothes and shakes the bag to make more room. "Anything else?"

I scan around, looking for my clean laundry. "Let me grab something to sleep in—"

With my first step toward the door, a hand clasps on to my upper arm. Chaz drags me backward until I hit his chest, and his other arm snakes around my waist. I look up at him behind me, but he's watching something outside my room.

The rest happens fast.

He whips to Rosdan by the bed, and his brother throws my bag at us. At the same time Chaz catches it, Rosdan hurls a lightning bolt from his palm. It strikes the chest of a man in the doorway. He flies into the drywall but vanishes before he hits the ground.

Demons.

They pile in through the door then, and Rosdan dives for us. The bright light from earlier surrounds us, Chaz's hold on me tightening as the world turns white and hot around us. I only get through a single breath before we're in Chaz's living room again.

He lets go of me and my bag, shaking his head as he runs into the kitchen. "Sorry, dude, but—"

"No," Rosdan says. "Blocker bag in case they followed." He no more than finishes when he disappears.

By the time I get to the kitchen, Chaz is cinching shut the black velvet pouch. He tosses it in a cupboard and slams it closed. Sighing, he turns around and plants his hands on the countertop, hanging his head between his shoulders.

"You good?" he asks.

He looks up, and I nod.

"Good." He takes off the amulet and lays it on the counter. "Everyone's fucking good, and you have clothes."

"Right," I say, deciding not to tell him I only have *half* my clothes.

In about twelve hours, he'll find out on his own.

NINETEEN

CHAZ

Cass continues to glower at me from the opposite end of the couch while I dick around with the blade. Since he and Hannah are on Kai and Avery duty tonight, he thought he'd come here to help—or babysit, as he put it. He's not ecstatic that we left here to go to the only other place guaranteed to have Lowers watching, and that it resulted in us being on the receiving end of a demon firing squad.

"Recast the amulet spell," he says, "so I'm not tempted to finish what the goddamn Lowers started."

But he's hiding the emotions well.

I mumble the spell and fight not to wince as the darkness balls in my chest to get away from the light.

"You think a few drops will do it?" I ask, unscrewing the top from a vial of Nephilim blood.

He shrugs, and I decide *fuck it* and pour it all out onto the steel.

Cass leans forward, and we watch the blood smooth over the broad side. I flip it, and the other side is entirely covered too. Sparks of light seem to flicker beneath, trapped inside the metal.

"Shit." I set the blade on the table. "Is that my light?"

He reaches out, curling his fingers back in a moment of hesitation before he snatches the handle. "Now, how the fuck do we get it out of there?"

We exchange looks, and because we've known each other since our beginning, I know we're both thinking about Rosdan's offer to stab me.

I tip my head in suggestion, and Cass shakes his in a hard no.

"I am not dealing with Hannah if she finds out I stabbed you when you can't heal." He rotates his wrist to pass me the knife. "You're on your own with this little experiment, brother. In fact, I don't even want to be here when it happens."

I put the blade down as he stands up. "Not sure I'm up for it tonight anyway."

He looks at the closed bathroom door. Nyx has been in the shower for-fucking-ever, and I'm starting to wonder if she's staged an elaborate escape plan. Dug a hole through the wall or something.

"Are you telling Hannah they're related?" I ask.

He shrugs, still staring at the door. "If I wait, she won't have to live with the guilt of choosing to save you over her only living relative."

I see the torn look on his face and have a Rosdan moment, swooping in for a hug.

He stays absolutely still and lets out a slow, impatient-as-fuck breath. "You really want me to wipe you from existence, huh?"

I chuckle, slapping him on the back a few times before I pull away. "Come on. We all know the Kasdaye lineup of love." I hold my hand like a shelf. "Hannah." I move it down a notch. "Chaz." Then another with each item. "Your motorcycle, cigarettes, and then Rosdan."

He blankly stares at me and then walks out without a word. The door across the hall shuts a few seconds later, and I imagine Cass is already bitching to Hannah that he wants me immortal again, so he can punch me in the face.

I go back to the blade, still flickering and taunting me with what's just out of reach. Sighing, I flip it around and press the tip between my ribs. Right over my scar. I blow out a few quick breaths, and then just before I plunge it into myself, the energy dancing through the metal fizzles out. A second later, the blood starts to drip onto me and the carpet.

Of course, this is the exact position Nyx finds me in when she finally swings open the bathroom door—bloody dagger poking into my side.

"Chaz!" she squeaks more than says. "What did you do?" She rushes over and moves the blade out of the way, lifting up my shirt. Her hand is already splayed over my abs when her eyes snap up to mine. "You're not hurt."

I shake my head but get distracted as my gaze rakes over her. She has on a familiar-looking T-shirt—mine—that hangs to her mid-thigh, and everything from there down is bare.

Her hand falls away, and she stops holding up my shirt. "I forgot a few things at my apartment."

She flushes and starts for the bedroom, and I have no issues with watching her go.

After I reengage the blocker bag, I clean up my mess in the living room. Maybe I'll give Rosdan a little time with the blade. See if he finds a method that doesn't risk massive blood loss and a trip to the ER.

I lock it in the box hidden behind books on a shelf in the living room. In case Nyx gets any ideas.

The amulet is still active. Just like Rosdan predicted, each time I cast, the longer the spell works before the crystal powers down. It's also getting stronger. Badass because, soon, I'll be able to use it in place of my light. But the space between the light and dark is hurting more each time.

I'm rubbing my chest as I walk into the bedroom. Nyx is cross-legged on the bed. She has the tie, dragging the silk through her closed palm. Trying not to smile, I bring the chain over my head and lay the amulet on the nightstand. Then I beckon her over, and she walks on her knees to the edge of the mattress.

"Why don't you tell them?" she asks, holding her wrists together.

"Care to add any specifics?" I fold an end over the material bridging her hands.

"Why don't you tell your brothers what the amulet is doing to you?"

I consider bullshitting her with a, *No idea what you're talking about*, but with the look she's giving me, she won't let me dismiss it.

"Angels are created with light to protect from the darkness. I'm not going to force them to deal with something they're programmed to fight because it makes me uncomfortable."

I finish the knot with a gentle tug to tell her I'm done. She sits back on her heels, and before she digs deeper into where she doesn't belong, I strip off my shirt and walk away, making sure not to massage the spot on my chest until after I get out of the room.

Nyx has only been here since yesterday, but her scent already covers my bathroom and is all over my sheets. Every single time I turn around, I'm breathing her. Eating, showering, sleeping, and most definitely when I wake up in the middle of the night with her ass nestled against my cock. The shirt she's wearing has ridden up, leaving her warm skin torturing mine.

Christ, if I were ever going to lose my mind, it would be because of her.

I run my hand over the curve of her hip, and she relaxes into me, the sexiest hum escaping her. And there's no chance I'm going to stop touching her now. I keep skimming down the front of her bare thigh, and her body shifts further into me. Her head lulls back against me as my palm glides back around, and when I nudge her panties down, she sucks in a breath.

"Chaz," she starts as a warning but never finishes.

I'm right there with her, reminding myself of all the ways this goes wrong. I just can't stop with her. Fuck, I'm not even sure I want to anymore. Everything's so screwed, so why not enjoy the ride?

My lips graze over her shoulder. "Tell me no."

But she doesn't. She rubs her ass against me. I pull her against my erection, grinding right back. She whimpers, immediately letting me slip my hand between her thighs.

"Always so ready," I say, dragging her arousal up to her clit.

Her focus goes from her ass on my cock to my fingers stroking her clit. Hips chasing more anytime I lighten the pressure.

"Eager to come for me, baby?"

"God, yes," she breathes.

Nyx brings her arms up and hooks them around the back of my head. I drop down and lick up the side of her neck, redirecting my fingers. I start with one pushing into her, only for a breathy, "More."

Not needing asked twice, I fill her tight pussy with three. Her inhale's shaky at the sudden stretch, but she clenches around them, hips chasing again.

She presses her head back, lips parted with erotic pants and moans spilling out.

"Come so I can fuck you." I nip at her ear and then her shoulder through my T-shirt, pumping into her faster with every desperate whimper.

"Yes," she cries out. "Yes, *fuck*."

She rides my fingers through her release, and then I roll to grab a condom, pushing my boxer briefs off on the way.

When I turn over again, Nyx lifts her arms over the back of my head again, forcing my face into her neck before I even roll on the condom. She arches into me, and I pull her leg back enough to slide into her from behind.

The way her hot cunt envelops my cock feels so good that I drag all the way out just to push into her again. I thrust slowly while she pushes back, her fingers tangling in the back of my hair.

"Chaz." The breathy way my name spills out of her mouth makes me groan. I drive into her faster, hooking her leg over my hip so I can go deeper.

My fingers return to her clit, causing her to moan. I pinch her peaked nipple through the fabric with my other hand, arm holding her tight against me.

When Nyx tugs at the back of my head, I bite down where her shoulder meets her neck until she whimpers, but then she's tugging at me again, asking for more.

"What are you fucking doing to me?" I ask, then I drag my teeth over the shell of her ear. "So goddamn irresistible."

She moans, already close, and so am I. I unhook her arms from around my head, pulling out of her long enough to push her onto her back. Our lips collide as I ram into her. She loops her arms over my neck, her knees pressing into my hips. The chill starts in my spine, working its way out until her skin cools where I'm gripping the back of her neck.

"Yes," she says. "Put your hands on me."

Not about to argue with the chick I'm burying my dick in, I run my other palm up her leg. Her breaths become desperate, and when she comes, her pussy strangles my cock. I barely get through another three rough thrusts before I'm growling out my own release.

My forehead rests on her cheek for a few seconds. I'm still panting, semi-coherent after I pull out. I take care of the condom and drag on sweatpants before I flop down beside her again. "You've got to be pretty fucked up to get off on the darkness."

"Well"—Nyx drags my arm across my chest to her—"I guess we're pretty fucked up then."

She moves my hand under her shirt and flattens my palm over her stomach. Shifting to my side, I let the shadows out against her skin and watch her. The more I expel, the cooler our skin becomes, and the more she squirms under my hand, her thighs pressing together. She's right. We're both fucked up because my cock jerks at how she responds to it alone.

But our darkness-play ends when my phone vibrates on the nightstand at the exact moment the pounding on my apartment door begins.

Nyx sits up. "Who's that?"

"You really don't want to know."

I untie her and grab the amulet off the nightstand and a shirt on my way out of the bedroom. Both are on a minute later when I walk into the kitchen to get the blocker bag out of the cupboard, the amulet giving off a faint glow concealed by the fabric.

"Chazaqiel," Lydia says outside the door. "I can hear you walking around in there."

Before I pull out a crystal and disengage the spell, I take a deep breath. Here's to the amulet hiding my dark side.

The crystal plinks onto the counter.

"Come in," I call, my tone lighter than a goddamn balloon.

Lydia drops into my living room, and I walk past her as dismissively as ever. She doesn't immediately strike me dead with a bolt of light. A good sign.

"And to what do I owe the pleasure?" I ask. "Here to beg me to help you relive the best night of your existence?"

"Ew. No." She straightens her shoulders, her cheeks pink. "I told you I'd be checking in more frequently. I need to make sure you three aren't trying to—"

"Serve out our punishments in peace? Job well done, gorgeous. But I think Armaros might be a little too comfortable up in Seattle at that swanky house his charge owns. You might want to send a few locusts and nip that shit in the bud."

"You are quite possibly the most annoying being ever created."

I splay a hand over my heart. "Touched."

Something moves behind her, and Nyx peeks out from the hallway. Fucking hostages. Never staying where you leave them. Lydia follows my line of sight and then turns back slowly.

"Who the fuck is that?" she whisper-yells at me.

I shrug. "You expect me to remember her name?"

I nonchalantly walk over to Nyx and hook my arm around her, pulling her into the living room. She looks just-fucked and like she's second-guessing her decision to snoop. Completely understandable, given the death glare beamed at her.

"Great." Lydia shifts her look to me. "Hurry up and report on your charges, so I can clean up your mess."

"Kai and Avery Benson," I say. "They're asleep, but I can grab them if you want to meet them too."

"No, I think we've had enough mortals listening to our conversation for one night." She takes a step toward Nyx, holding out her hands like she's approaching a skittish forest animal. "What's your name?"

Nyx glances up at me as I step away from them, waiting until I'm out of Lydia's line of sight to shake my head. She looks back to Lydia, who is lifting a hand to her cheek. Nyx's eyes widen, but the second the light touches her skin, she falls into character. Pliable, innocent, defenseless. Everything she's not.

"What's your name?" Lydia asks again, her voice almost sickly sweet.

"Corey." Nyx sounds dazed, hypnotized.

I stand there, witnessing two venomous snakes trying to convince each other they're as dangerous as baby bunnies.

"Corey"—Lydia tips her head to the side, condescending as shit—"you won't remember seeing me or anything you might have heard, okay?"

Nyx nods slowly.

"After I leave, you're going to go home and never come back. You can do better than someone who can't remember your name after leaving bite marks."

My eyes dip to where Nyx's shirt has slipped down, her skin red. Then I quickly mutter the amulet's spell under my breath again for good measure and step forward. "Such a cockblock. Anything else you want to interfere with while you're here? Maybe hit up the rest of the women in Colorado?"

Lydia's hands fall to her sides, and she turns around to face me. "Mortals are beneath even you, Chazaqiel. I'll be back, so don't get comfortable."

The second she drops, Nyx reaches for the gold cuff. She almost rips the earring out, her ear pink where it touched. "Why did it burn so much? Usually, the gold just heats up."

Fucking Lydia. She used too much.

Once I reengage the spell bag, I take off the amulet and go back to rub my thumb over the hot spot. "Good thing you had something to divert the light."

"Why?" she asks, dagger vision aimed where Lydia was standing.

"Instead of your ear burning, she could have melted your brain." A problem we learned the hard way when we first arrived. The line between using enough light to shape the human mind and straight-up lighting it on fire could, without a doubt, be wider.

The shadows have lowered the temperature of her skin, and I leave Nyx with a panicked look on her face, flipping off the light as I go to the bedroom. Then I pick up the tie for whenever she recovers and follows me in.

TWENTY

NYX

After almost having my brain melted by a gorgeous—and totally in love with Chaz—angel, the days start to run together. In the mornings, Rosdan stops by to work with the blade before he has to nanny his charges. Sometimes, he stays in the living room. The rest of the time, he goes across the hall. In the evening, Cass is around.

I try to stay out of their way. Partly because I still feel like a little girl playing make-believe when in a room with more than Chaz. Mostly though, it's less awkward for everyone when I lie low. Even though he took me to my apartment and saved me from demons, Rosdan is still cautious around me. Most of the time, he looks like I might attack him at any moment, and then there's Cass giving off major vibes that *he* might attack *me*. So, not only am I stuck in Chaz's apartment, but I also spend a lot of the time strictly in the bedroom.

A week after escaping the desert, I wake up to the groan I have most mornings. Chaz gets out of bed and isn't even gone a minute before he shuts the door and crashes onto the mattress beside me, landing on his stomach.

"Rosdan." His voice is raspy and tired, and he drags his pillow under his arms to lie on. He's softer when he's only half-awake. Not just his features, but him in general.

I nudge him before he falls back asleep. "Hands?"

He barely cracks open his eyes as he unfastens the knot and tosses the tie to the end of the bed.

I get up and sort through my bag. I'm almost to the bottom and grab the last top. My knuckles touch metal. Thinking I must have forgotten to unpack something the last time I used the bag, I pull it out.

Everything stops for a second.

I cover my mouth to hide a gasp when I see the picture that should be hanging in the hallway of my apartment. A black-and-white of Nyla and me from the fifties a few years after her last resurrection. The last time we were in our twenties together. Chaz must have taken it when he went for my body wash and shampoo.

When I look back, his head is buried under his pillow. I go to his side and kneel on the floor, shaking his shoulder. He grunts and tips the pillow up, so I can see him.

"You brought this from my apartment?"

Heavy-lidded eyes search my face before they move to the frame in my hand. "It was probably Ros."

Then he lifts his head, turning it the other way and putting the pillow down. But I know it was him. Rosdan never left my room.

By the time I've showered and dressed, Chaz is still sleeping, so I reluctantly go to the living room. Rosdan glances up from where he's sitting on the floor with the Dimming Blade. He's wearing work gloves, refusing to touch the metal. I give an awkward wave to let him know I mean no harm, and he gives a halfhearted smile before lowering his head again.

I think he's the most different from what Nyla and I imagined. His hair is darker, and his eyes are only a few shades from black. Not as close to the color as Cass's, and his dimples aren't as pronounced either.

He adjusts as I move toward the couch, so his back isn't to me. I'd like to believe it's to be polite, but I know better. I understand why, but it still bothers me, considering I've spent all my lives thinking he and his brothers would adore me from the get-go.

I curl up on the cushion and watch him sift through some of the scrolls he brought with him. From what I've overheard while walking to the kitchen or hovering at the bedroom doorway, they've figured out how to activate the blade without a human sacrifice. As a previous sacrifice, I am grateful. The problem seems to be getting the light *out* of the blade. And as the person who dies when they do, I am again grateful.

"Chaz told me about the desert," Rosdan says after a few minutes. "That you gave him life to heal his stab wound."

He keeps reading, and I'm not sure if I'm supposed to respond since he didn't ask a question. But then he glances up, and I nod.

"How does it work? I can't find records of The Descended or any mention of a race that can influence another being's soul or whatever."

I hesitate to answer him. Papa drilled into our heads that, if anyone found out what we could do, they would use it to their advantage. Hex proved him right. First, by killing Nyla when she told me to dump his demon ass, and then again with Abaddon. But if I can help Rosdan find a spell or anything else that can unbind Chaz and Abaddon, they won't need to kill me.

"Life force." I sit up and pull my knees to my chest. "Think of it as energy. It can be manipulated and transferred. In my case, it can be generated from the essence in my blood."

"Can you take it then? Someone's life?" His interest drifts to my hands, and I tuck them under my legs.

"No. Or maybe in my spiritual form."

"That's when the soul leaves the body?" he asks, and I tip my head in question. "I'm an angel, Nyx. I know some shit."

I give him a small smile. "I'm stronger then, but I've never tried."

Usually, I'm more interested in getting back into my body before anything happens—last time excluded. Then again, until Abaddon, no one had murdered me in cold blood. Other than the guy who ran me over with his car, but he was long gone by the time I flashed through eight years of memories.

Rosdan considers me for another moment, and then his focus returns to the knife. "So, what could you do to me right now?"

I ignore his phrasing, an unconscious reminder that he views me as a threat. "I can sense your life force if I focus hard enough—feel the essence of it. Most of what I can do involves my own life though. If you were mortal, I could transfer part of mine into you and then manipulate it like I did to heal Chaz, but I'm not sure how it would work on an immortal."

"And it wouldn't work with your sister?" When I don't answer right away, he adds, "Sorry. I'm sure if you could—"

"It would just prolong her suffering."

He wants to ask more. I can tell by the way he opens his mouth to say something, but he turns it into an, "Ah."

"The second generation tried it," I tell him, fully betraying my ancestors. But really, I've always kind of thought they sucked. "After the original Descended started dying off, they realized we could only resurrect so many times. They found ways to determine that limit and then forced their offspring to transfer life into them. Except the spell infused with our blood resets us *after* death, so they stayed old and decrepit. When their extended lives ended, their souls lost hold like they were supposed to, and they couldn't return to their bodies."

"I'm sorry," he says again, to which I shrug.

I watch his glove run along the sharp edge like he's searching for a hidden message. "Our lore says there's a possible workaround. Supposedly, by injecting more Essence of Creation, like in the original spell, we can reset while still alive. There hasn't been any pure essence since right after creation though. And as I've recently learned, there's no way to create more dust."

Rosdan's hand has stopped moving over the blade. When I look up, he's staring at me. His eyebrows draw in, but the line between them smooths out just as fast, and he looks away. "I wish I could help. But like I said, my scrolls mention nothing about life force and infusion spells or anything to help…"

"Nyla."

"Nyla," he repeats, and I smile, hearing him say her name.

I know she has always been a Samyaza fan, but I think she might be Team Armaros if she met him.

DARKENED SOUL

I think about Nyla the rest of the day, staring at our picture that I set up on the dresser. She's safe, which is what truly matters, but I'm starting to worry she won't be here when I finally can go see her again.

After my shower that night, I'm combing through my hair when Chaz creaks open the bathroom door. We haven't been in the same room for more than a few minutes all day. My eyes meet his in the mirror, and he crosses his arms, leaning in the doorway. He stays there until I finish.

"What?" I ask, finally turning around.

"You enjoy your little heart-to-heart with Rosdan this morning?"

"You enjoy eavesdropping on it?"

"My damn apartment," he says. "Plus, you left the door open, and the two of you were loud as fuck."

I'm about to push past him when he unfolds his arms and holds up a clear orb. "You'll have to learn a spell or two to work it on your own."

He sets it in my hand, and my heart almost stops as I look down at an image of Nyla. It's like what he uses to see Kai and Avery. His fingers wrap over mine, and more of her room at the farm comes into view. The ugly white nightgown, one of her nurses adjusting her IV. After Chaz mumbles something under his breath, I hear the record they have playing by her bedside. Something from the jazz age shortly after we came to the States.

I'm shaking my head when I look up to see him watching me. The picture and now a way to see her anytime. It feels like a glimpse of *my* Chazaqiel. The one a little girl dreamed up in her head. And I want to believe it's him, not a twisted version of the warden offering the death row inmate their last meal.

"Why are you giving me this?" My pulse picks up the longer he studies my face, and then his eyes lower.

"I don't know, Nyx," he says. "But now, you have it."
"Yeah," I say as he backs away.
And I still have no idea what it means.

TWENTY-ONE

CHAZ

Two weeks. I've been stuck in my apartment for two weeks straight. Fourteen days with the chick who, three weeks ago, I was doing everything to avoid. It's gone about as well as expected. I've fucked her most nights, given her shit, spent an afternoon chanting over a fucking crystal ball for her, watched her—fuck, have I watched her.

Like tonight. I have the palm stone out to watchdog Kai and Avery across the hall. The twins are on their own until Cassannah gets here later, and I prefer to have eyes on them until then. But while I switch channels from one charge to another, there's substantial Nyx interference to tone out.

She's draped over my couch with her crystal ball. My attention follows as she rolls it back and forth on her stomach. Along the edge of her shirt and above the inch of skin between the hem and her jeans.

I force myself to quit looking, solely focusing on the stone. I have mild success until jazz fills the room, coming from the couch. They only play one record in her sister's room, and after the first few times through, I started to regret showing her the spell to listen through the orb.

"Cut the sound," I say.

But she ignores me.

I'm about to tell her again when she jerks upright.

"Nyla," she whispers.

The crystal ball starts emitting another sound then. Hard and labored breathing. And then gasps for air.

"She can't breathe." Nyx looks up at me, her face morphing from alarmed to downright terrified in a split second. "Chaz," she says, her voice breaking. "She can't—"

A loud beeping comes from her hands, and her eyes shoot back to the orb. I move to her as she stands, and I take the crystal. I manipulate the image, pulling back. Two nurses rush into the room, and Nyx is gripping my shirtsleeve.

She bolts for the door.

"Damn it, Nyx."

All I do is think about going after her, and I'm across the room. She slams into my chest, shocked by the unexpected collision.

"Did you just…"

"Teleport," I finish.

But I can't worry about that with Nyx trying for the door again. I catch her in my arms, pulling her farther into the apartment.

"No!" She struggles against me with every step. "Chaz, please! I need to go. I have to be there in case she—"

All the fight from her stops, both of us knowing what she was about to say. *In case she dies.*

I let her go in the center of the living room and move back to give her space. Nyx follows the orb in my hand, and after I quiet the beeping, she swallows hard and blinks up at me. We stay locked on each other, her chest rising in short, shallow breaths. No more attempts to run. No pleas or threats. Just sad fucking eyes on mine until she says, "She's all I have."

Her voice trembles at the end, but it doesn't matter. I knew I was going to find a way to get her there the moment it broke on my name.

When we portal in on the porch of the farmhouse, Nyx dashes inside.

"Where's the bag?" she asks over her shoulder.

"Try the top shelf in the kitchen cupboards."

She passes the windows, and I track her to the last one. The thin white curtains are transparent enough that I see her climb on the counter. She stands on her knees, rifling through one cupboard and another. I'm about to doubt Cass's predictability when I see her pull out the black pouch.

By the time she pulls a crystal to disengage the spell, I'm back at the doorway. I cross the threshold without any problems and shut the door behind me. Not that it will protect us from anything other than the wind chimes blowing outside.

I'm well aware that the last fucking thing I should have done was trek ten miles away from the safety of my apartment without backup, but I wasn't exactly drowning in options. Rosdan's been skittish about Nyx's sister since their little chat, and I still owe Cass for bringing what I needed for the crystal ball.

I pull out the fresh blocker bag I assembled from my magic stash before we left. Instead of chanting for three hours to create a permanent block, I dump the contents onto the floor in front of me. If I can use enough light from the amulet, I should be able to create a temporary one.

Nyx rushes in as I take the amulet out of my pocket.

"Five minutes," I tell her.

She stops long enough to give me her melty eyes before she runs up the stairway off to the side.

A nurse called my phone a few minutes ago and said Nyla's breathing was under control, but we were already portal-jumping at that point.

Clutching the amulet in my hand, I hold it over the scattered ingredients and chant its spell. The light glows brighter than usual. Much brighter. Heat coats my palm and creeps up my forearm. It sends the darkness fleeing. I ignore the ache shooting down my other shoulder and pooling in my fingertips and mumble the words I've chanted so many damn times. Soon, the crystals on the floor move into a cluster, forming a short-term barrier to prevent anything with angel or demon powers from entering.

"Excuse me?"

I spin to a woman walking down the stairs. Stethoscope, scrubs, and quite the mean mug set on me and my mystical mess.

Luckily, the amulet seems to be in a giving mood tonight, and I slip it over my head. The cold knot forms in my chest, but the light balances out, and I call it into my palms. I meet her at the bottom of the stairs and quickly bring my hands to her cheeks.

"Don't step on my stuff, okay?" I say as she glazes over. "After we leave, you won't remember it was even there." She nods, and I give her a quick smile. "That's my girl. Now, tell me what happened with your patient tonight."

"From what we can tell, she was short of breath and worked herself into a panic attack." She stays monotone, delivering the answer without feeling. "Her breathing has stabilized, and we're giving her oxygen and monitoring pain levels."

My gaze flashes up the stairs before returning to her. "How much time do you think she has left?"

"Not long."

I feel the power wavering. "You won't remember talking to me, but once we leave, you'll call her contact at the slightest change."

After I let her go, I make sure she blinks out of the daze and then deactivate the amulet on my way upstairs.

The second floor is small. Only three rooms—one a bathroom, one closed off, and the other where I find Nyx. She's on the bed with her back against the wall and her legs over top what I imagine is Nyx plus seventy-some years. From the doorway, I don't get much more than long white hair and pale, wrinkly hands, and I can't say I've paid much attention through the orb.

The old wooden floor creaks under my feet, and Nyx is beaming before she even looks up at me. She scrambles off the bed, not worried at all about crushing the poor woman. Her eyes are bright, and I've never seen her look more alive. Everything about her is warm and light.

"How is she?" I ask.

She shrugs. "She's weaker than the last time I saw her. I told her about Abaddon and where I've been without triggering another panic attack, though, so that's a plus." She glances over her shoulder, chewing her lip when her face comes back around. "Will you meet her?"

"Will I meet your sister while I'm holding you hostage?"

Before I have a chance to say no, Nyx is hauling me toward the bed. Once we're close, she spins and holds her arms up to cover me—because she can hide the six-two dude three feet away. But she commits. With her hands on my face, she checks behind her. "Promise you won't quit breathing?"

Jesus. I pull her wrists away, and she whips around. The playful glare she serves reminds me of the first time we met. So much fire beneath her surface, stoked and ready to burn.

She pulls me another few steps and keeps her fingers curled around my arm after we stop. "Nyla, this is Chaz."

I look down at the frail, old woman in the bed. She has oxygen in her nose and tired eyes. Nyx's eyes but duller in color. I've followed hundreds of charges from birth through death. So many that I could accurately sketch what Kai and Avery will look like in fifty years. The reverse happens with Nyla. I can smooth her skin, add color and shine into her hair, bring out her cheekbones. I adjust her features in my mind, rewinding her to match the picture I took from Nyx's hallway, and it's like seeing them both at every age.

Having no gauge as to what the fuck I'm supposed to do when meeting my captive's sister, I lift my chin in a nod. One side of Nyla's mouth perks in response, and Nyx tightens her grip on me. She squeaks and looks up at me, her face even more illuminated than when I walked in.

The guilt finally hits. It's not the twinge from in the desert when she told me why she'd helped Abaddon. Not the wave last week when Rosdan asked if I knew *what* she needed to try and save her sister. The guilt washing over me right now, as I see her this fucking happy over a half-smile, it settles in my bones.

TWENTY-TWO

CHAZ

After Nyx returns the crystal to the bag and cleans up the protection spell in the entryway, she meets me outside. She's already dimmed a little by the time I open the portal. Since mine max out, we leave the front lawn of the farmhouse and step out on the highway, maybe a mile away.

The second my shoes touch asphalt, something instantly feels wrong. The air is tight and too still. My hands hook around Nyx's legs while I check in each direction down the abandoned highway. Then the breeze picks up, carrying the faintest scent of burnt soul.

"What's wrong?" she asks.

I shrug so she slides off my back, and I bring her to my side while closing the portal. As I fish out my phone, the first shadow moves in the ditch. Then another and another.

"Chaz." Nyx tugs on my arm, but I don't need to look. She's seeing the same thing on the other side of the road.

"Are they grungy? Like you want to shower just from looking at them?"

"Yes," she says. "Four of them."

Lowers. And seven of them total. Not a usual demon number. Then I hear, "Hello, love."

I turn toward the voice, and standing on the centerline with his hands behind his back is who has quickly become my second least favorite Upper.

"I've been looking for you." Hex is locked on to Nyx and not paying attention to me in the least.

"Stall," I whisper, tapping away on my phone.

Nyx side-eyes me, doubtful, but then she sends him a venomous smile. "Are you here to grovel out an apology?"

Hex laughs. "I tried the apology route. You repaid me by disappearing and leaving me to face the boss all on my own."

Finished ratting myself out to Cass, I pocket my phone. I texted Hannah to save time. Poor girl will see the thirteen exclamation points at the end of my message and flip her shit.

Nyx runs her hand up my arm. "It's not my fault I found someone who plays the game better than you."

His eyes flick to me, tension creeping across his face. By stall, I didn't mean get me maimed with a fireball from her jealous ex. But I'm an asshole, so I hook an arm around her waist and wink at him. The flame flares to life in his hand. I consider showing him mine since he's showing me his and all. Only the fire extinguishes a second later when he looks beyond us.

Fuck.

"Is Abaddon behind me?" I ask.

She glances, and her entire body tensing is my answer.

"Of fucking course he is." I rotate enough to see the demon's red beams.

Hex opens a portal. "We're square then, Abaddon. Consider my debt paid in full." He offers Nyx a tight smile and steps through.

"Chazaqiel," Abaddon says. "What a pleasant surprise. And with my little mystery princess."

"Gang's almost all here," I deadpan. I blow out a breath and hand Nyx my phone. "Send another round of exclamation points to—" A burst of divine light interrupts me, and I take the phone back. "Never mind."

Cass appears in a blaze between us and where Hex was standing before he bailed. After a *fuck you* look to me, he lifts his glowing palms and juts his chin in Abaddon's direction. "You finally had your chance to end him, and you blew it? Damn, Donald." His eyes cut to us, and I move Nyx between us, creeping toward him while he distracts. "I don't know how you'll recover from something like this."

We stop when the demon's shoulders heave in a growl, his flame reflecting in his eyes.

Uppers. *So* damn touchy.

"Aww, look." I pout my lip out. "You hurt his feelings."

Donny zeroes in on me, giving Cass an opening. "It's not over yet. I *will* end you, Chazaqiel. I'm coming for you next, Kasdaye."

And we slide backward.

"Any damn day," he says.

"But, Cass"—I glance enough to note my brother's a few cool steps closer—"how will he come after you without the Dimming Blade?"

Abaddon's face goes slack, and then he snarls at me. "*You* have the dagger?"

"Did you not know that?" I ask.

"How could you not know that?" my brother asks, taunting him as Nyx and I inch.

I tug her belt loop before taking over again. "I'm pretty sure *everyone* knew that."

We must get cocky then—it happens with us—and move at the same time. Donny darts his eyes between us, realizing we've more than halved our distance to each other right in front of him. He doesn't take it well, his palm flashing.

I can't tell which happens first—Cass's drop or the Upper's teleport. But I know where they're going. I barely swing Nyx out of the way before light and dark clash where she was standing. Donny immediately retreats to a safe range, and then the rats pile in. Lowers hit Cass from every side, and when Nyx screams, I jerk her away from the one with his hands on her.

"Don't hurt him," Donny commands, dodging an arc of light Cass managed to fire at him.

"Yeah." Cass drops to within a few feet of us. "What he said."

A fireball flies close enough that it forces him to drop farther away.

"He's going to have to cull the herd," I tell Nyx.

My brother's focus goes from getting to us to taking out as many demons with one bolt as possible. It kills me to sit out of the action. I flex my hands, playing out all the moves I could be making, but instead of a rush of heat, my palms ignite with cold, shadows appearing in place of light.

"The amulet," Cass shouts. "I can't tell what's them and what's you."

I mutter the spell, and the amulet bursts to life, not stopping at its usual intensity. The white glow grows until it encircles us. The Lowers flinch about as severely as I do, but they have the option of getting away from the light. Right now, we need the protection even if it's tearing me to pieces on the inside.

"That works too," Cass says before impaling a demon.

But while the Lowers scatter, Abaddon is stalking toward us. He reaches the perimeter and grunts as the light hits his skin, only slowing as he continues to push through.

"We can't stay here," Nyx says. "Can't you angel us somewhere?"

"If by angel us you mean drop, then no. It requires wings, which require my light."

Abaddon stops, and it looks like he might give up. Until the shadows twist and swirl around him in a demonic tornado. He takes another step, using it like a fucking shield.

Shit. I really hate not being able to land a house on him right now.

Our clothes flap in the wind from Donny's vortex.

"Cass," I shout over the growing roar. "We need to go."

"You think?" He dodges a fireball, reappearing closer to us but not close enough.

"Portal." Nyx moves farther behind me, wincing at the dirt being kicked up. "You can portal to him, right? Or do the teleport thing?"

"I can't access the darkness when I'm using the amulet." But I can *feel* it, ready for release. Like at the house earlier while I spell-cast.

I check Cass, who's still battling it out, and I rip the amulet over my head. As I hold it away from my body, the darkness storms to the opposite side.

Nyx is ducking behind me, and I crouch. "Get on."

She jumps up, and I straighten, stretching out my arm so the amulet stays as far from the darkness as possible, as I concentrate on upping the power.

"So," I say over my shoulder, "this is either going to work or go really fucking wrong."

Her arms tighten around me, and I blow out a long breath. Then, I shut off the light from the amulet.

The sudden loss of resistance throws Donny off-balance. He loses control of his shadows and stumbles forward, his eyes bulging when I open a portal and wave with the amulet hand as I step through.

We come out just short of Cass, who drops in the opposite direction to avoid a fireball.

"Chaz." Nyx jerks on my left shoulder, and I turn in time to see the Lower aiming at us.

I activate the spell and blast him with a flash of divinity, grimacing until I return to shadows. And like she's riding a damn horse, Nyx tugs me around, so I can catch another with a wave of energy. I teleport then, popping up beside a Lower on the sidelines. It feels fan-fucking-tastic, watching him blow backward when I light him up.

We knock out a few more before Nyx shrieks. I jerk sideways as a demon tries to drag her off me by the leg. With him so close, I press the amulet straight to his forehead. The darkness races out of him to escape the shock of divinity, and he collapses beside us.

This time, I teleport in right behind Cass. He whips around about to nail me with his light, but his hand falls when he sees us.

His shoulders slump in a deep exhale. "Jesus, man." He spins to pitch one last bolt at Abaddon, a smirk on his face as the demon goes soaring. "Bad dog, Abby." And then he grabs on to us and drops.

As soon as my feet land in the hallway outside my apartment, I throw open the door and cross the threshold with Nyx still on my back. Once we're protected by the blocker bag, Cass drops again. He'll bounce around to guarantee no demons are following him, and then he'll want to see Hannah. He always does after an attack. I would text her to tell her we're safe, but he needs her light.

I shut the door, feeling Nyx slide off. "You good?" I ask.

She doesn't answer, so I check over my shoulder. She's standing a few feet behind me, her focus far away.

"Hey," I say, spinning around.

She's taking shallow breaths through her mouth.

"Nyx." I dip down to bring my face level with hers and brush the backs of my knuckles over her colorless cheeks. "Look at me, gorgeous."

She focuses in on me, her chest rising faster. "I can't … I can't—"

Her eyes drift off again, and I pick her up and carry her through the apartment. Apparently, panic attacks run right alongside resurrection and life manipulation in the Lamore family.

She's clinging to me when we reach the bathroom, so I slip off her shoe and sock, then I switch arms with her and nudge off the other side's. I set her bare feet in the bathtub, breaking her hold to take off her shirt and jeans. Her leg's already a deep red from the demon's grip, ready to bruise.

It only takes a few seconds for me to strip to my boxers. I step in with her, turning on the shower. Her breaths are still fast and shallow, but the cold water hits her and she sucks in a deep one.

"There you go." I hold her to me, rubbing up and down her back. Cold as fuck.

After she breathes deep a few more times, she throws her arms around my middle. Her face buries in my chest, her body shivering against mine. I adjust the water, making it warmer, and smooth a hand over her hair before I wrap her tighter. Sobs shudder through her, and she wilts into me more with each one. And I let her, the stream beating down on us while I hold her up.

I've witnessed this woman die and come back to life without a single tear. She's traipsed through the desert, been locked away with the promise of another death, and in the past hour, she thought she'd lost her sister and was dragged around by a demon. I'm not moving a goddamn muscle other than to turn the temp higher, so she can cry.

After her sobs turn to whimpers, she shakes her head, her forehead sliding against my skin. "I'm so sorry," she mumbles into my chest. "You knew it wasn't safe, and I made you—"

"Hey." I curve my fingers under her chin and bring her out of her hiding spot. "I hate to break it to you, but you didn't force me to do shit."

She's still looking down, and I tip up her face until her eyes come to mine. They shine with fresh tears, her lashes wet, water streaming over her. She's fucking beautiful and heart-wrenching, twisting at something deep inside me. I drop my mouth onto hers, only letting her go to turn the shower hotter.

I've always imagined how the light feels on the mortal brain. Soothing heat that lulls while reality bends and curves, and then what you know isn't what you know anymore.

Nyx isn't like the light. She's fire, singeing the nerves. I don't get to forget the before. She just makes me brutally aware that it won't be that way again after her.

The spray runs cool before I cut off the water. I didn't bother pulling the curtain, so I reach for towels on the rack and fold her up in one. She pulls it tight around her, pushing her nose into the fabric while I wring out her dripping hair.

With us both semi-dry, she follows me to the bedroom. Even though her eyes are clearer now, she still has a daze to her. She swaps out her wet underwear for dry ones, and I find her a shirt to wear. I change into sweatpants, knowing I'll need to deal with Cass later. Only later becomes now.

Nyx is crawling into bed when the knocking starts, and I pull on my shirt.

"It's Cass," I say, crossing the room.

As I click on the lamp, my eyes land on the tie. My hand is still hovering over it from turning on the light, and Nyx pushes onto her knees. She moves to my side of the mattress, holding her hands out. Like she expects nothing that happened tonight to change anything. I can hold her, soothe her, tell her any number of things, but our ending stays the same. Our beginning, our middle. None of it is pretty.

I quickly tie the material around her wrists. "I'd better let him in before he beats my door down."

"Tell Cass I'm sorry?" she asks, and I nod, finishing with my usual final tug.

On my way out, I turn off the overhead light and close the door behind me. I force myself to the kitchen to disengage my security system and then trudge into the living room, not looking forward to the next few minutes. I brace for the ache and activate the amulet, but I end up grinding my teeth anyway.

"You can only come in if you don't yell at me," I say.

Cass appears an instant later. "Then kicking your mortal ass it is."

But instead of following through, he blows out a breath and goes to the kitchen. He comes back after raiding my whiskey and hands me a glass. "Here's to the look on that fucker's face when he realized we have the blade."

He clinks his glass to mine, and I huff out a laugh.

"No matter the millennium, handing him his ass never gets old." I finish my drink in one swallow and head straight to the kitchen for more. "Kelley recover from my text?"

He snorts and leans on the counter as I refill our drinks. "She's going to lay into you one day, and I can't fucking wait."

I smile, thinking of Hannah going all pissed-off-kitten on me. "Me either."

We fall quiet, sipping round two, and while I pour the third, he studies me the way Kasdaye does when he sees straight through the bullshit.

"You plan to give me smoldering looks all night, baby boy, or are you going to ask me to dance?"

"Okay," he says, picking up his glass. "Are you getting attached to The Descended?"

"Nyx." I set the bottle down and brace myself on my flattened palms. "Is that really your question?"

"No. I really want to know if you're nailing her and if, because of it, you'll pull some *spare her life and let me go* shit. 'Cause this only ends one way, brother—with you getting your light back and being unbound from Abaddon. I don't care what has to go down for it to happen. Then we're going to banish the darkness from this asshole once and for fucking all."

"None of it matters without my light. The only way I stay in existence until then is being directly plugged into Donny."

"We'll figure it out. We haven't even stabbed you yet." His lips turn up into a smirk, and he throws back his drink.

"Right," I say dryly. "Plan Z."

I rub a hand over my face and bypass my glass for the bottle. Which works out since, by the time I finish a long pull, Cass has emptied mine too. The second one hits the counter harder than the first.

"And don't think dodging the Nyx question isn't an answer." Then he grabs the crystal from beside the bag. "Please stay put for the rest of the night. I'd really like to get my girlfriend worked up for a reason other than to save you."

He waits for my nod but not long enough for me to comment before he tosses the stone into the bag. It forces him to drop out of my apartment, and I put the bag away, mentally listing all the things I could have said.

The lamp's off when I go back to the bedroom. I lay the amulet with my phone on the nightstand, the crystal still active. Its soft glow touches Nyx's face and shows her tied hands tucked under her pillow. I wonder if she tested the give. If she noticed I'd left the knot looser than usual. Not enough that she could get it undone, just a little less secure. Less than last night when I hadn't tightened it all the way and the night before that.

Cass's words swim in my head while I watch her. All the reasons to shut down whatever this is with her. Our messy ending where both she and her sister die, one of them not coming back and the other hating me.

I drag my shirt over my head, throwing it on the floor as I climb in with her. She sighs the second my lips find hers, and then her hands slide up my neck, her fingers pushing through my hair. I roll her onto her back, needing to feel her against me. It's the only time my mind shuts off all the shit—locked in my fucking box with her.

Us. Here. I want her. Just her.

I'm a pyromaniac who's been left alone with an open flame. It was only a matter of time before I lit myself on fire. Fuck, am I ready to burn.

TWENTY-THREE

CHAZ

The next morning, I ask my brothers to come over at the ass crack of dawn before Nyx wakes up. Cass and Rosdan are already exchanging glances on the couch, Hannah between them. Since we rarely surprise one another, I doubt what I brought them here for will come out of left field for either of them. So, I jump straight into it without offering pastries and coffee.

"I want to tell her," I say.

Cass exhales and slouches into the cushions, and Rosdan tugs at the back of his hair. Then the silence kicks in—and it's loud as fuck. But I need all three of them to be on board, so I wait through it. I stare at my hands, slowly passing the glowing amulet between them. It keeps the shadows mobile, more tolerable while they shift from one side to another.

"She'll want to use it on her sister," Rosdan finally says.

I nod. "Yeah."

"You can't let her," Cass adds.

Another nod. "Yeah."

I might not know what the fuck is happening with Nyx, but I know all of this. But she also deserves the truth. That Abaddon lied about lying. Pure Essence of Creation *can* be made, and not only that … I've had access to it all along.

"Wait, what are you telling her?" Hannah looks first at me, then at Cass before ending on Rosdan. "What will she want to use?" Her questioning comes back to me, and Cass's jaw tightens.

"The essence Nyx wants for her sister." He massages his temple with one hand and her shoulder with the other. "It's the dust that was left over from creation."

Rosdan sits back and sighs. "A few scribbles on a paper and a Nephilim, and we can make more."

"*The* dust?" Hannah asks. "*My* dust?"

I almost laugh at *my dust*, like the very essence of all things created belongs to her because she's one of the eight beings currently in existence who could create it without God's assistance. She didn't even know what it was a few months ago. About the dust or the Book of the Speech from God that was used for every reboot of creation, let alone that she could read the language it was written in.

Her eyes drift around the room while she pieces the rest together. "So, if her theory about the dust works, then she could keep her sister alive?"

"It doesn't matter," Cass says.

"She can't even try," Rosdan continues. "If she only has one resurrection left, we'll need it to unbind Chaz from Donny after we get his light back."

He looks to me, waiting for my reaction. But fuck if I have one. So much of my existence has focused on protecting man—and I've spent the *entirety* of my mortal life watching over Nyx.

Now, I'll need to let one die and crush her if I want to save myself.

NYX

Before I even attempt to open my eyes, they feel dry. I rub one and then peek at the single hand, my other still on the mattress. Not something that should normally confuse someone, but in my current situation, I expect my hands to come as a pair this early.

Chaz looks amused when I blink the rest of the way awake. "Here I thought you'd appreciate not being tied up in the morning.

Guess I'll make a note—hostage *wants* to be bound. Not a beneficial method of torture."

I laugh, and he smiles. It fades fast, but his expression stays soft. Something about him feels different after last night. Warmer despite the coolness of his skin. He studies me for a long time and then sweeps my hair away from my face.

We haven't done this before, just lie here together. I creep my hand across the space between us. His gaze flicks down when I reach the scar on his side, but he brings his eyes to mine again without stopping me. I run over his abs and up his chest and neck. The stubble on his jaw scrapes my fingertips. He turns into my touch, closing his eyes as he kisses my palm. His lips brush my skin again and again. Only then, his brow draws in. He slides his hand over mine, pressing it to his mouth harder before he pulls it away.

"Fuuuck, Nyx," he says. He opens his eyes, and they've changed in the past few seconds. His thumb rubs over the inside of my wrist, and he's watching the movement instead of me. "I have to tell you something."

"What?" I ask.

He lifts his head, and I haven't seen this Chaz yet. A hard swallow bobs his throat, concern etched in his face. His perfect fucking face, sending me into a panic.

"Did Nyla's nurse call? Is she…"

"No." He shakes his head, emphasizing.

I let out a relieved breath, my entire body relaxing until he moves my hand back to my side of the gap.

Then he lets go and rolls to his back. "Abaddon wasn't lying about the Essence of Creation. More can be made."

My skin chills and not from his touch this time. I shift, so I can see his face, bracing myself on my forearm. "But why would he say it couldn't?"

"Because *he* can't make any." Then he adds, "Who knows? He might not even know it can be made, so he thought he was lying to you."

"So…" I lick my lips, hesitating. I should be diving on him and squealing in joy, but a warning sounds inside my chest. "How do you know this?"

Chaz moves onto his side again and pushes up on his elbow. He hangs his head and drags his finger over the back of my hand, resting on the mattress. "Because I can."

The heartbeat rises into my ears, my pulse throbbing everywhere at once. "You've known the entire time? When I told you in the desert that it's why I…" I swallow, remembering the harshness of his stare after I mentioned it. He said he could have saved us the drama.

I scramble to the foot of the bed and to my feet, holding a hand to my forehead as I take a few steps. Then I face the bed. I face him and his guilt-ridden features, and reality sinks into my belly. I told Rosdan how the essence supposedly worked—about injecting Nyla with the dust after I transfer my life into her.

The life they need. Why I'm even here with him in the first place.

"Can I have the dust?" I ask, and I drop my arm to the side.

"Nyx," he starts, rotating to get out of bed, but I shake my head.

The tears burn in my throat, my lip trembling as he walks toward me. "Answer me, Chazaqiel. Can I have the dust?"

He stops in front of me, only holding my gaze for a second before he looks to the floor. "No. We won't give you the dust." He reaches for me, grazing my hip. "You can't use it on her—"

"No." I shove his hand off me and back away from him. "No. You don't get to tell me you have the one thing that can save her and then forbid me from using it. It's *my* life. My death."

"If your tattoo disappears—"

"It's not your choice," I shout. "She won't come back, Chazaqiel. She'll die and be gone. I can't just let her go without trying. I can't. I don't…"

The tears are falling in earnest now, and I don't even bother wiping them as they drip off my face. My insides are crumbling, leaving holes as they cave in on themselves, and I don't fall to the floor; I disintegrate. I slump against the dresser, legs folded in front of me. I rest my head on the wood and close my eyes, trying to grasp on to anything to stop spinning.

Everything I've done to try to keep Nyla from permanent death is now a part of the reason I can't. I finally met my angel, and he'll take the life meant for my sister. Save one; lose another.

After a few minutes, an ache in my eyes replaces the tears. The last of them are drying on my cheeks as a shadow falls over me. I look up at Chaz. It feels like I should fight him more. But before I can, he lowers to his knees.

"I'm sorry, Nyx." His fists clench like he's stopping himself from trying to touch me. "I'm so fucking sorry."

He never loses eye contact, tilting his face up when I push off the floor to my feet. I start to walk past him, but he stops me by wrapping his hands around my waist. They stretch almost all the way around me.

He stares up, and I stroke his cheek.

"I'm sorry too," I tell him.

Then I leave him there, on his knees, his eyes begging for forgiveness.

TWENTY-FOUR

NYX

At some point, I forgot the reality of my situation. I'm not a guest or a part of anything. I'm a tool kept on the shelf until needed—one-time use. I appreciate that Chaz took the time to remind me.

I haven't talked to him for three days. I haven't talked at all. Not to Rosdan or Cass. Even Hannah, when she gives me a sweet smile from the other end of the couch, gets ignored. They work on the blade in the living room or conference in the kitchen. I stay wherever they are not.

The most interaction I share with anyone is at night while Chaz knots the tie around my wrists.

The first night, he said, "I need you to believe me when I say I'm sorry. If we knew you had more than one resurrection left, I'd give you all the fucking dust you wanted."

I waited for him to tug the last loop through and rolled away, giving him my back until morning when he unbound me.

Night two: "I understand why you're upset, but you need to forgive me."

By last night, he was feeling otherwise. "You set me up to lose my light, bound me to a demon, and in the process, let the darkness inside me. It was all you, Nyx. I didn't ask for any of this." He jerked the knot as he finished but kept ahold of it, so I couldn't move as he leaned in close. "I want you to fucking remember that."

Then he marched out of the room, and I slept alone for the first time in weeks.

This morning, I woke up, already untied. I haven't seen him at all, other than the few seconds it took me to pass to and from the kitchen. But when I come out from my shower in the evening, the bedroom door is shut. A relief. I need a break from the same four walls.

I grab a glass of water from the kitchen and flip on the TV. Halfway through some trashy reality show, I hear yelling and cursing coming from the bedroom. A minute later, the door swings open. Chaz hovers in the doorway as I sit up, ready to switch rooms once he comes out. He stares at me, his features hard lines and zero give. If I wasn't so mad, I'd find it intimidating. I do when he starts stalking toward me, and I sink into the couch. He stops a few feet away, his fists clenched.

"Here," he says, but it's more a growl. He throws something on the cushion beside me and slams a set of keys on the coffee table before storming away. "Now, get the fuck out."

While he bangs drawers and the cabinet in the bathroom, I carefully pick up the clear vial next to my leg. The bottom half is filled with a nearly translucent white dust. A shocked breath leaves me. It's the Essence of Creation. I look up at the hallway where Chaz disappeared and then at the keys. *His car keys.*

It takes a second for my brain to catch up, but once it does, I snatch the key ring off the table. I dash for the door, only thinking about Nyla until I hear footsteps behind me. I glance over my shoulder just as Chaz collapses into the recliner, facing away from me. My fingers rub over the glass tube in my hand, the other hand squeezing the keys.

Shit.

I breathe deep and turn around. Each step feels like a betrayal to Nyla, but I can't leave until I know why he's doing this. Why he gave me the dust when it might mean he'll stay bound to Abaddon.

As I get closer, I see a pile of white cloth on the table. No. Bandages. Then his thigh comes into view, red streaks on his jeans, his bloody shirt on the floor.

"Oh my God," I say, rushing around the chair.

Chaz glances up, irritated. "What part of *get the fuck out* was unclear?"

He winces, trading a saturated gauze pad for a new one and pressing it to his side. Right over his scar from Abaddon. Where, a few weeks ago, he was holding the tip of the Dimming Blade when I panicked that he'd stabbed himself.

And now, he has.

The vial and keys fall to the floor, and I push the already-soaked pads off his leg.

"Seriously, do you need an escort out of the building?"

"Do you need one to the ER?" I bite back.

I crawl up to straddle his legs and shove his hand away, so I can apply pressure to the wound. I expect more of a fight, but I don't get one. He grunts and readjusts my knee before he rests his head back, his chest rising and falling with sharp intakes.

"What the hell were you thinking?" My voice is weak from not speaking—or from speaking to him. "You agreed to wait until Rosdan ran out of ideas before you—"

"There wasn't time." He watches my hands. "I needed to know."

I lean back for a clean square, and he grabs my thigh to keep me balanced. He keeps his grip there after I straighten up. Like maybe he's missed touching me. I hate admitting that I've missed it too.

"What was the big hurry all of a sudden?"

"You," he says, and I look up at him. His fingers flex, squeezing my leg tighter. "I thought if I could get my light back … I don't know. Maybe we could lure Donny to the farm, and you could give your life to Nyla and unbind us at the same time. Two birds, one resurrection. Then you could keep her, and I could…" He tips his head toward the side. "Obviously, it didn't work."

A few shadows spill out as I switch the pads. "But you gave me the dust anyway?"

Chaz nods, running his other hand up the outside of my other thigh.

"Why?" It comes out a whisper, probably because I'm terrified of the answer. "Why would you do that?"

He was going to let me try to save her. Without knowing if I would be able to help him after. Without proof that the dust would work or if he was sealing his fate over a myth.

"She's all you have," he says. "I won't be the one to take her away from you."

I feel a catch in my chest—my breath or my heart or both—and the realization spreads over me like a smooth wave. It pulls me under before I even have a chance to fight or thrash around. I was right to be scared of his answer. Of the truth it would bring to the surface.

Save one; lose the other. But it was never meant to be a choice.

It was always going to be him.

Chaz is rubbing his thumbs in circles on my thighs.

"Can Rosdan or Cass take me to the farm tonight?" I drop the gauze and place my hands on his chest, so I can heal him. "I don't want to worry about demon attacks."

His thumbs stop moving. "Nyx, they won't—"

"Please." I push down until I feel his heartbeat beneath my palms and glance up into his blue stare. "I want to be able to say goodbye to my sister in peace."

After Rosdan drops us to the farmhouse, I leave him and Chaz on the porch and head for the kitchen. One of the night nurses pops around the corner from down the hall. They set up shop in the den when they're not in Nyla's room. She gives me a soft smile before disappearing again.

I find the black velvet pouch right where I left it last time— behind a dusty stack of china. The house came furnished, so who knows how long it's been out of commission. As I jump down, I un-cinch the top and pluck out one of the crystals. I bring both with me in case either nurse wanders in, and I return to the entryway.

"Rosdan said he'll drop back whenever," Chaz says, shutting the door. "I'll take care of the nurses after I set up the protection barrier."

I nod while he empties another blocker bag onto the floor. "How long will it take?"

"It will be up and working in a minute. I'll chant for a few more, so we can stay however long you want."

He fishes the amulet out of his pocket, wrapping his fist around the crystal. I can already see his muscles tensing, and it hasn't even activated yet.

I set my pouch and crystal on the small table along the wall. "Only chant as long as you need to."

He watches me, a grateful look in his eyes. I'm the only one not begging him to use it all the time to cover up the darkness.

At the top of the stairs, I pause for a calming inhale and then a blow-out-the-bullshit exhale. Nyla's already waiting when I walk in, and the first thing I notice is her nightgown. Blue and not at all hideous. I hid the white one the last time I was here. Someone needed to.

"Did the creepy twin thing tell you I was coming, or were we just that loud?" I ask, toeing off my shoes at the bedside.

She doesn't answer, of course, and I climb over to the wall side of the bed. I stretch out, tipping my head against hers on the pillow. Her arms are thinner than a few days ago, her face more gaunt. According to the doctors' original timeline, her body will only last another month. I've only made it to eighty-eight before I hit the fast-forward button.

"How are you feeling?" I ask.

Tired eyes move to their corners in a look that says, *Like shit, Nyxie.*

In my mind, she still sounds young, her laugh bright, hair dark, and she has a never-ending supply of shimmer to her.

"Do you remember when we were eight, and Papa was still trying to tell us stories, warning about The Fallen?" I pause as if she might answer. "Then you sat up in bed one night and told him he was a liar. They were strong and fearless, and you were going to find one and prove him wrong. He said you'd never live long enough and then stormed out, refusing to tell us bedtime stories ever again."

I pick a piece of fuzz off the pillow between us. "*I'm* the one who found him, so you're welcome."

Her eyes smile, and mine tear up.

"I can't save you, Ny. You've been telling me that for a long time, but I finally get it." I wipe my cheek on the shoulder of her nightgown. "I don't know a world without you in it. I don't know what it looks like or feels like..."

There's a brush of something on my shoulder, and when I look down, her hand's coming up to smooth over my hair.

I smile and let out a sob disguised as a laugh. "Such a show-off lately."

Her chest moves a little, a soft hum with it. She brings her hand up again and runs it down. I close my eyes, amazed at how much a simple touch can hold. All the words and smiles I've missed the past few months are right here.

"I'm sorry I can't keep you longer," I say.

And I'm sure she's sorry she can't stay.

I lie with her the entire night, falling in and out of sleep. The floorboards creak more than once. I watch Chaz's shadow eclipse the light from the hall. Not once does he come in and ask if we can leave. Just darkens the doorway for a few minutes and then retreats.

Eventually, I stay asleep, waking up after dawn has already started streaming through the windows. Nyla's resting comfortably despite the slight rattle with each inhale. A sound I've heard before.

I sit up to scoot down the mattress to her feet when I notice Chaz across the room. He's passed out in the most uncomfortable-looking rocking chair. The knit blanket he has draped over him only covers his chest and arms.

Trying to keep from waking *two* people, I carefully move to the end of the bed and untuck the sheet and comforter. I draw the covers back and sigh at the purplish splotches from her toes to her ankles. The doctors' timeline was off. She only has a week—or she would have only had a week. But we made a deal a long time ago to let each other go before the *end*-end.

One of her big toes taps, and I look up to her waiting. So much for being stealthy.

"Sorry," I whisper, flipping the covers down.

The springs squeak as I crawl over her to the edge of the bed. I slip on my shoes to avoid the draft on the floor and check the angel in the corner. Once I see his deep and steady breaths, I cross the room to her side. Nyla rotates her hand, palm up, as I reach her. I slip mine into it and squeeze. Hard. Then I stare at the sheets beside her.

A tug brings my attention up, and I swallow back the threat of tears, seeing the worry in her eyes.

I force a small smile. "I'll be fine. Eventually."

Her eyes move behind me and then back to mine, and her grip tightens. I want to ask her if she's scared, but she'd say no regardless of the truth. She stares up at me for a minute before her eyebrows dip. I know what she wants. She wants me to say goodbye.

"Not until you do."

She squeezes my hand again, and I shake my head.

"The deal is, we say goodbye. I don't trust you to uphold your end if I go first."

And now, my sister is glaring at me on her deathbed, but when I loosen my hold, hers bears down. We stand off until her lids close.

"Goodbye." Her voice is hoarse, the word a whisper, but it's everything I fucking need.

I clamp my eyes shut, burying a sob. "Goodbye, Nyla."

My jaw clenches, and I only focus on breathing. Her pulse speeds under the tip of my thumb where it touches her wrist as she manipulates the life inside her to its end. The pace quickly slows, the space between beats growing longer and longer ... and then nothing. My eyes stay shut while I search for any hint of what's always been there, but I can't sense the life force inside her anymore.

I can't feel my sister.

I whimper, and the rocking chair groans behind me. Nyla's hand falls back to her side when Chaz pulls me to him. His arms envelop me, and I fist the back of his shirt. My nose is buried in him when I take my first breath without her.

TWENTY-FIVE

NYX

With the exception of my last one, Nyla and I always moved after a resurrection to avoid people noticing one of us had aged in reverse overnight. We'd be each other's aunt or grandmother, depending on who looked the part. I haven't dealt with a permanent death in over a century. Fortunately, being taught to live under the radar with minimal acquaintances cuts out a lot of the work. A few phone calls, a little paperwork. Still plenty more than when Papa died though.

By the time I get in the shower that night, I've gone from raw nerve ending to desensitized. My heart is beating, my lungs breathing, my soul in my body. I'm not the one who died, but I've never felt less alive. Numb and in slow motion. I get it now—why Kai jumps off cliffs and chases the adrenaline rush. Not feeling alive while you still are is terrifying even if it allows you to avoid the pain.

When I get to the bedroom, Chaz is on the edge of the bed. His hooded eyes dance over me in the towel, and the spark reaches my skin. My fucking cliff. He plants his hands on the mattress behind him as I crawl right onto his lap, my hair dripping on his bare chest. His is still damp from his own shower. I put my arms around his neck, and he leans back, tipping his face up.

"Touch me."

"You've had a long fucking day," he says.

"I have. And right now, I want you to touch me."

He shifts his weight to one arm, and he pushes his hand into my hair. "You forgot to say, *Simon says.*"

He's studying my mouth, so I bring it closer. Our noses graze, but his lips stay a few charged air particles away, his breath teasing my skin. I press a palm to his chest, wanting his heart beating against it. Then I push further below the surface, down to the life flowing through him.

We both move at the same time then—him sitting up and me sliding forward.

"Touch me," I say again, feeling him hardening beneath me. "Please."

My breaths are more needy, and he pushes under the towel, up my thigh. He slips his hand the rest of the way around, gripping my ass to hold me to him while his hips flex, grinding his erection into me. I skim my hands up his neck, into his hair, and when I rock my hips, his fingers dig into my flesh.

"We don't have to do this tonight, Nyx." But he keeps drawing me to him, rubbing my clit over his covered cock. His lips stay just out of reach. After four days of missing them on me— and hating myself for it—the near touch of them pulses through me.

"Kiss me."

His chest heaves against mine, his face conflicted until his gaze drops to my mouth.

"Fuck it," he says.

He slams his lips onto mine, growling, and in the next breath, his tongue plunges into my mouth. My body responds the way it always has to him, slowly coming back to life.

I gasp as he tears the towel off, flinging it across the room. He breaks the kiss and dives down, grazing his teeth over one of my nipples before pulling it into his mouth. When I arch into him, he leans forward, lowering me onto his arm behind me, and then he sucks the other nipple in. I lock my arms around his neck and let him bite and lick the sensation back into me.

"God," Chaz rasps, "I missed this body."

He drags his tongue down, pushing me back until he can trail it all the way to my stomach. I move my hips against him, and he groans, dipping into my belly button before he pulls me upright.

I kiss him again and then slide backward off his lap, onto the floor, so I'm kneeling in front of him. He runs his fingers down the side of my face as I reach for his waistband. My eyes stay on his, and I tug down the front of his sweatpants and boxer briefs far enough to expose his cock. I stroke him a few times, and then I tease the crown with my tongue.

Chaz's fingers tangle in my hair. "Nyx—*fuck*."

I suck on the head of his dick before dropping down his shaft. It elicits a groan from him. He starts pumping into my mouth, shallow at first and then deeper. When he hits the back of my throat, he grunts and grasps my jaw, lifting me off him. He tugs me up, and I land right back in his lap. His lips capture mine, slow but hungry.

Our mouths stay fused while he turns us around. Chaz crawls onto the bed with me wrapped around him and nudges his sweatpants and briefs off all at once. He lowers me to the mattress and pulls away to finish kicking them off, and then he's grabbing a condom and between my legs. He hovers over me, mouth out of reach while the wide head of his cock nudges my entrance. I'm aching, needy with my skin on fire. "Chaz."

"Yeah, baby?" he says, his hand cooling against the back of my thigh. "You want something?"

"You, Chazaqiel." I bring myself up to kiss him. "I want you."

His lips turn more demanding, teeth tugging at my bottom lip, and then he suddenly scoops me off the bed.

"I don't want a condom," I mumble against his mouth. "I want to feel you."

Chaz kisses me harder, nodding. "Then you'll feel me."

He pulls me into his lap as he sits back on his heels, so I'm straddling him again. His hands roam over me before they settle on my hips and urge me up. I gasp as I sink down on his bare cock, and he pushes his forehead into my collarbone.

"Fuck," he hisses. "You have no right to feel so perfect."

I slide up and lower back down with Chaz gently thrusting up into me. One of his hands runs the length of my back, a chill crawling my spine. I feel the shadows on my skin. Every touch and breath from him. He's resurrected me from wherever I was. The emotionless limbo that was fogging my brain.

My lips latch on to his. This time, they press harder, asking if he missed more than my body. If he wants all the pieces of me like I want all the pieces of him. When he cradles my face in his hands and pulls back, I see it in his eyes before I hear it.

"I want us to be done now," he says.

Our bodies keep moving, almost as if they were working separately from the rest of us. His arm wraps around my waist, and his other's hand grips the nape of my neck.

"What are we done doing?"

He kisses me, deep and heated, and then his blue eyes drag me so far under that I know they're not letting me out again. "Pretending you haven't been mine since the first time you said my name."

I really have been. He just has no idea it was long before the bar.

My lips race back to his. I thread my fingers through his hair, riding him harder. My thighs tighten around him, and I'm sure he can feel my heart hammering through my chest, crushed to his.

Chaz sweeps over my clit, his skin warm, but then he does it again, and it feels like ice. I gasp into his mouth, and he smiles against mine. He keeps switching back and forth and pumps into me while he inches me over the edge. The fall hits me hard, and I cry out, so overwhelmed that I barely notice him hiking me up until he tosses me onto the mattress.

My head hits the pillow, and he's right there, between my thighs. A needy sound rumbles in his throat as he thrusts back in. My body continues to shudder around him, and he drives into me faster, rutting deeper. I hook my legs around his waist and take everything from him. The light, the dark, anything *him*. Finally, his muscles grow rigid, and he groans, coming deep inside me.

Breathing hard into my neck, he stays inside me while we come down. He starts to skim his lips over my sensitive skin. I close my eyes, back to a raw nerve ending. His mouth brushes me, and his tenderness hurts. But I fall into it as he carefully kisses my cheeks and nose and eyelids. Even the tears that escape get chased by him, and when we go to sleep, I'm in his arms.

And the tie is on the nightstand—where it stays.

TWENTY-SIX

NYX

Nyla is cremated. She always thought it was poetic for our kind to return to dust. It's not only where we came from, but it's also a part of our blood.

When I moved her to Colorado, I chose the farmhouse because of the view. The upstairs window faces the back of the property. It has a large yard that leads to a lake with a dock. At first, she'd sit in her wheelchair, staring at the water.

"Just stand still and look, Nyx." She still talked the first month and would catch my hand before I left after visiting her.

I would face the window until she let me go, but I wasn't looking. I was too busy trying to keep her alive. To keep her with me a little while longer.

A few days after her death, I'm in her room. I'm standing at the window. I'm looking.

And it fucking hurts.

The floor creaks as someone crosses the threshold into the room. He steps behind me, and I close my eyes, wanting to feel him—the life in his veins.

Chaz grips my waist through my plain black dress. "Cass and Hannah are by the shelterbelt to the east. Rosdan's near the barn with the amulet."

Demon watch. I search the tree line until I see them. Hannah's leaning back into Cass, his arms wrapped around her like he'll never let her go. Then I find Rosdan pushing off the barn. His attention is set toward the front of the house.

"And you?" I ask.

Chaz doesn't step back when I turn around, his hands sliding over me until I face him. He's in a long-sleeved white dress shirt, wearing the black tie that, as of the other night, appears to have been retired. He moves closer, his arms encircling me.

He rests his forehead on mine. "I'm right here."

His cool thumb skims over my cheek, and I try to lock all of this into memories in case it's the last time. Because right now, everything feels like it might be a last time.

Muffled slams from car doors out front force me back a step. His hand falls away, and I wipe my cheeks. "They're here," I say. "We should go."

I look over my shoulder out the window one more time. The table sits on the dock, white linen cloth on top and the urn surrounded by loose stemmed roses.

I fucking hurt.

When we get downstairs, Chaz hands me the wool jacket Hannah grabbed from my apartment earlier. I put it on as we go out the sliding doors that open to the lake. I'm still hooking the buttons when Chaz comes to an abrupt stop on the back porch.

"Are those all…" He trails off, scanning the yard.

They come from both sides of the house. If Chaz knew what to look for, he'd see the division between the bloodlines. Clusters that keep distance from the others. Furtive glances.

"It's the only time you'll see the remaining Descended in one place," I say.

"All of them?"

I nod, stepping down onto the grass. "Twenty-seven of us now."

The others have created a scattered formation near the dock, and I stop in the middle. My lineage has stayed rather neutral within the remaining nine. We—or *I* have no one with ill will toward me or hard feelings over bullshit that happened centuries ago.

I nod to an older man by himself, scanning the faces. "Amadeus is the last from Gadreel's lineage. He's the eldest, outlasting three children."

"Gad was a prick," Chaz says, curling his arm around my waist.

He tucks me against his side, holding me there like it's where I belong, and I smile into the collar of my coat.

Amadeus visually counts The Descended, hesitating on us for an instant before he moves on. But that's the thing with a group this paranoid—everyone notices. The calculated glances begin, and Chaz brings me closer.

"Step right up to see the infamous Watcher, folks," he deadpans.

Maybe I won't leave here quite as neutral.

Amadeus steps in front of Nyla's urn, kicking us off with a not-so-brief listing of every person in my lineage, ending with the original. I would have skipped this entire part and just scattered her ashes in the lake, but they would have shown up eventually even if I hadn't invited them. Tradition. And such a waste of airfare.

After the excruciatingly boring list of monotone names, the end of the ritual lasts all of five minutes. Each lineage approaches the urn, and every member leaves something meaningful to them behind. A piece of their life for the one who lost theirs.

The stares transition to gawking when I tug Chaz with me to the dock. I find an old, crumpled receipt in my coat pocket and set it under the edge of the urn. Chaz lifts a brow, side-eyeing me, and I shrug.

"I gave her part of all my lives," I say quietly. "Plus, I have, like, five things at your apartment and forgot to ask Hannah to bring something from mine. Why? You bring something better?"

He smirks and loosens the knot on his tie. "No, but I have an excuse." He drags the loop over his head before dropping it over the urn. "I've only had a mortal life for twenty-three days, and it's all revolved around you."

His hand glides over mine, and he winks, walking away to give me a second. I wait until he's far enough away that he won't see what I pull out of my other pocket.

"You can have this for the sake of ceremony," I tell Nyla, "but I'll need it back."

I tip the urn and put the picture all the way under to keep it from blowing away. During my stint in solitary—when I wasn't talking to him—I found it tucked away in the box he keeps in his closet. Given the quality and style choices, I'd place them in the early nineties. Cass is midway through an eye roll while Rosdan mean-mugs and Chaz flips off the camera. The guy beside him has dirty-blond hair and a different shade of blue eyes, and he has an arm slung over Chaz's shoulders.

Samy, according to the name on the back.

"I told you they'd both be blond," I say before I catch up with Chaz.

Now, we each have our angel.

The group disperses rather quickly after everyone's left their offering, which I will get to figure out what to do with later. A few of the lineages linger. Amadeus and two others who have formed alliances over the years. They warily approach like Chaz might strike them down at any moment. They must have deep-dived into his life force to sense the darkness or the unique energy tied to his angel soul.

"Nyx," Amadeus says, reaching for my hand, "you have our sincerest condolences."

The three men and four women with him stop staring at Chaz long enough to mumble similar sympathies.

Amadeus motions to them. "You're familiar with the children of Rameel and Arkas."

Chaz tenses beside me, and his eyes dart to Rosdan as he makes his way from the barn. "I'll be right back." He walks off toward Rosdan, glancing over his shoulder once in Cass's direction.

"Yes, of course," I say, forcing a smile. "Papa always had such nice things to—"

"The Fallen." Amadeus lowers his voice while most of the others track Chaz and Rosdan's every movement across the yard. "I didn't realize any of them still remained, let alone three."

"They look so normal." One of the women grasps on to the shirtsleeve of the man next to her, not looking at me. "Are they dangerous?"

What she's really asking is if the fairy tales of the monstrous Fallen Watchers are true. If they murder with abandon and rip mortal men to shreds. I could ease her fears, but I've had a really shit month, so when she glances over for my answer, I shrug.

"Thank you for coming," I say, walking away.

Chaz turns around then, his lips curling up at me before he narrows a glare at the others. Rosdan's beside him, arms crossed, and once Cass and Hannah drop in, they appear anything but normal. Three towering and muscular angels alongside a Nephilim. To everyone behind me, they look absolutely terrifying.

With everyone gone, the last thing to do is shut up the house until I decide whether or not to sell it. We go inside, so I can double-check that all the lights are off and see if anything else needs to be done. It feels final, walking through the downstairs for the last time. The others wait by the door until Chaz and I meet them there.

"Oh," I say, pausing by the banister. "The curtains in the upstairs bedroom need to be closed."

Chaz tugs my hand for me to stay. "I'll grab them."

Relieved to not have to see the lake again through the window, I half-smile and mouth, *Thank you.*

On his way past, he drags his fingers across my stomach. The first outward sign of affection he's shown me in front of his brothers. He's kept me close all day, but from the looks they give each other, demon duty distracted them from noticing.

Chaz climbs the stairs as Cass's jaw clenches. He walks out the door without a word, and Hannah flashes me an apologetic face and follows him, leaving just Rosdan. He pulls at the back of his hair, staring at the wooden floor.

"I should unplug the TV," I say, but really, I'd unplug the couch if it meant not standing there.

Stepping down into the den, I smell a familiar cologne hanging in the air.

Hex.

I suck in a breath to scream but barely get out a squeak before a hand clamps over my mouth. He pulls me against his chest with his arm around my middle.

"Shh, love," he whispers in my ear.

But I thrash against him and kick out my feet, catching the lamp on the table and sending it crashing to the floor. In a blink, Cass appears by the couch. Sparks fly from his hands, but when Hex lets go of my mouth and slaps his flaming palm to a sigil painted on the wall beside us, Cass vanishes.

I spin as Hex releases me and glance around until I see Rosdan outside the doorway. He looks distorted, the sound muffled as he bangs on an invisible barrier that's keeping him out.

"What the hell?" I shove Hex in the chest. "Today? Really? I haven't even spread Nyla's ashes yet, and you're—"

"Saving you," he shouts. His shoulders slump, and he rakes his hands through his hair until it sticks up every which way. "I'm sorry about Nyla, I am, but you're not safe with the Watcher."

"And I would be with you? You'll hand me over to Abaddon, so he can kill me again."

Both Cass and Rosdan are at the blocked doorway now. Cass looks ready to murder someone, and for once, it's not me.

"I won't." Hex comes forward, and I withdraw. A hurt look crosses his face. "I've been working on something big, Nyxie. I needed Abaddon distracted for a while."

"So, you sacrificed me."

"I knew you'd come back," he says, frustrated.

"Well then, all forgiven." I take a step, and he grabs my arm.

He checks the doorway. "You need to come with me. I'm the only one who can protect you right now."

"Pretty sure we have that handled, asshat."

I follow the low voice to the fireplace. Chaz straightens up from where he was leaning against the brick. He shifts his attention from Hex to me. The look he gives weighs down my chest, and I shake my arm away from Hex.

"How the fuck are you even in here?" Hex asks, genuinely interested. "Even if you had your light, I have this place blocked from all things divine."

Chaz crosses the room, stopping beside me. "Good thing I came equipped with the darkness then." Shadows spill from his palms and vine up his arms, sweeping over mine closest to him as they go.

Hex cocks a dark brow. "The game just got interesting." His eyes dart between us before they settle on Chaz again. "Fine, consider this your warning. The other Uppers know, and word is spreading like wildfire—kill the Watcher to kill Abaddon. They'll be coming for you."

Chaz shakes his head and smirks. "I wonder how they found out."

A smug smile spreads across Hex's face. "Not a damn clue." His gaze slides to me. "Stay alive, love." He quickly looks at the floor and then up again before he disappears.

"Fucking Uppers," Cass says from the doorway.

The barrier is down, and Chaz passes without acknowledging me other than a quick, "Let's go."

Not sure what I've done to deserve the cold shoulder, I scoop down for the scrap of paper at my feet as I follow. I crumple it in my fist until after Cass drops us at the apartment, and Chaz heads to the kitchen. I shrug off my coat and sigh once I unfold the note. Hex's number.

Since I programmed it into my phone the last time he gave it to me—in case he got ahold of mine and called—I throw it away in the bathroom trash can. I've just stepped into the hall when I screech, startled by Chaz's sudden appearance in front of me.

I barely have a chance to process him before he crowds me back against the bedroom door, his face severe. Once my back flattens to the wood, he boxes me in with his hands on either side of me.

"Would you have gone with him?"

"What?" I ask.

"If I hadn't teleported in," he says, his voice softening, "would you be with him right now instead of with me?"

His eyes reiterate the question, his brow furrowed, and I shake my head.

"No. Not unless he—"

Chaz's mouth presses hard to mine, all his doubt from a second ago gone. I hook my arms around his neck as he picks me up and turns the doorknob, using my back to push it open.

"Good," he says against my lips. "Saves me from tying you up again to keep you."

He smiles, and I laugh for the first time since Nyla died. Then I kiss him again, knowing it's true.

Even if he were to tell me to leave, I couldn't. I won't. I've been in love with Chazaqiel since long before I met him. I'll be in love with him long after he gets back his light. In this life, and into the next.

TWENTY-SEVEN

CHAZ

The week after the funeral sets a new pace around the apartment. Cass rarely stops by when he takes his turn with my charges. If he does, he brings Hannah and is less than his usual chatty self. We haven't talked about Nyx or the blade, and I know why. My brother told me where he stands on this matter. He views Nyx as a liability, and that certainly won't change now that I fell for the one woman who could easily sign my death sentence.

Rosdan has shown up every morning like clockwork, taking advantage of his charges' mother working from home in an effort to "get to know her children." Get to know in a sense that she can still call up Ros at any moment, so he'll swoop in and save her from them. He tinkers with the weapon here or ducks across the hall and then tries to swing by in the evenings when all his charges are tucked safely away in the McMansion.

Meanwhile, my living room has enough dusty-ass books stacked around that it looks like a monastery library. Since I have limited options on what to do, I spend most of the day sifting through them, trying to find anything remotely helpful. Any mention of a dagger crafted of divine steel or weapon imprisoning the light of God.

Of course, my reading would go a lot faster if I were surrounded by nuns and not Nyx.

"Stop fucking watching me," I tell her without looking up from my page.

"But I like looking at you." She shifts on the couch above me, and her bare foot nudges my shoulder.

I dodge my head out of the way when her toes climb my neck. Fucking seducing me with her damn feet. Slamming the book closed, I whirl around and climb on top of her. She laughs as I cover her body with mine and nip at her jaw.

"You fucking better." I graze my lips over hers and tug at her bottom one with my teeth until she whimpers. Then I kiss her once more and slide off her all the way to the opposite end of the couch before I lose all will to research.

I switch to a different book with a crumbling tan cover, and she leans over to pick up my other one from the floor. She lies back again and flips it open, placing the bottom of it on her chest.

"Fluent in Latin?" I ask, biting back a smile.

She pretends to ignore me, turning the page. "Fluent in jackass?"

I chuckle and lower my eyes to my own work.

Within a few excruciating pages, she disappears into the bedroom. She mentions yoga or some shit, but I wave her off, already buried in mind-numbing passages.

After a while, she reemerges in some crisscross-strapped bra and leggings that hug every curve. Hannah did me no favors when she and Cass gathered clothes from Nyx's apartment.

"You've got to be fucking kidding."

"What?" she asks, throwing her hair up into a messy knot on the top of her head.

I groan and restack the books, tossing the scrolls on top. "You're a fucking distraction."

Not even tempting myself by going near her, I head to the bedroom with a plan to lock myself in until I get through this shit. Before I even shut the door, someone blows it out of the water by knocking.

"I ordered food," Nyx calls.

Fuck. She's prancing around like a goddamn wet dream, and now, she's bringing food into the equation. I sigh, setting the pile on the dresser, and go back to the living room.

As I round the corner from the hallway, my first thought is that I'm going to murder the delivery guy if he looks at her tits. But that's quickly overshadowed before I even see where his eyes land—because the delivery dude is wearing a shitty uniform with dress loafers and a designer watch.

It happens fast.

Nyx holds out the cash, and her hand extends over the threshold.

"No," I shout, but it's too late.

The demon's eyes flash red, and I teleport just as he latches on to her wrist. I reappear where Nyx was standing, missing them by a fraction of a second.

I no more than *think* about the amulet, and it activates in my pocket. Chasing down the Upper who just abducted my chick must rank pretty high on Samy's list of worthy causes. My darkness scatters, but the light hones in on the demon's. I switch to shadows and flash into the hallway right as they materialize.

"Chaz," Nyx whimpers.

The demon arm across her throat shifts, and the arrogant asshole it belongs to grins behind her. "Chazaqiel," Braxis says. "Long time."

"Not long enough."

"Feel like coming the easy way?" he asks. "Or do I need to give you more motivation?" His grip on her tightens, but he won't waste his only leverage so soon.

"You know I like to play hard to get." I notice the ripple at the end of the hall by the elevator and blink to his other side, placing myself between him and his exit strategy. "Looks like you still have a bad habit of leaving your portals open."

His eyes cut behind me, and I wrap the chain of the amulet around my hand, crystal in my fist while I wait for him to move. But then another portal opens behind him. And another fucking Upper steps out and nails Braxis in the back with a fireball. Zagan—even douchier.

Braxis lurches forward, his arm slipping from around Nyx.

I teleport to her. She grabs on to me just in time for the amulet to light up, and I blast Zagan with divinity as soon as he pops up next to us.

Then Lowers start slinking out of his portal, and I glance back to the same by the elevator. They brought the sewer rats.

Fuck, fuck, fuck.

In a matter of seconds, the corridor fills with demons, flames start flying between Braxis and Zagan, and I teleport to the apartment door. I shove Nyx through it and spin to face the hell breaking loose on the second floor.

She yanks on my arm from behind. "What are you doing?" she shrieks.

With Kai and Avery so close, I can't just chill behind a barrier and let it all play out. The Uppers seem more concerned with duking it out over who gets to kill me and claim Abaddon's title than *actually* killing me, so I only have to worry about the dozen Lowers stalking in my direction.

"Sorry, gorgeous," I say over my shoulder. "We have a rat infestation I need to handle."

I jerk the door closed before she can argue, tightening my grip on the amulet. With the douche twins bouncing around on one side, I swing right. I pick the Lower closest to the elevator, appearing beside him. He lights up nice and pretty, and I hurl him through the portal he came out of. Since he doesn't poke his head right back out, I move up the hall. Each flash of light drives the other Lowers away, and they almost make it easy.

I clear the first side and am marching toward my next target when the door beside me yanks open.

Rosdan looks at me, shadows swirling around and up my torso, and then he leans his head out to check down the hallway. "Holy shit," he says.

He launches a bolt of light at the nearest set of demons, and they fly all the way to the other end, landing between Braxis and Zagan.

Rosdan catches the amulet when I toss it—in case he loses his light left over from whichever charge helped get him here. He drops, I teleport, and we surprise the shit out of a Lower. I snatch hold of an arm and look away, bracing for the rush of light Rosdan sends through the demon until the darkness tears out of his mouth. The remaining Lowers vanish through the portal before I slump the body against the wall. He or Cass will have to drop it to a mountainside later.

The Uppers fume as they face us, but when Braxis dematerializes, he reappears by his portal at the opposite end of the hall.

"Next time, Chazaqiel," he calls. He nods. "Armaros."

Ros smirks and flips him off.

Once he steps through his portal, we turn to the last demon standing.

Zagan holds up his hands in surrender. "Fair enough. I'm a patient demon, and I can wait. But remember, you can't hide forever, and—"

The amulet illuminates in Rosdan's hand at the same time his head whips over his shoulder. I teleport without checking to confirm Tweedle Dick has reemerged from his portal behind us. Only a fireball catches me in the side at the last instant, searing straight through my shirt and skin.

I land on my back in the living room. "Fuuuck."

Nyx screams from the door where her face is pressed, her snoopy ass trying to watch through the peephole. I wince, pushing myself up to sit against the couch as Nyx runs across the room. She dives at me, clearly missing the massive fucking scorch wound.

I choke out, "Baby, wait," while she scrambles onto me and throws her arms around my neck. My forehead drops to her shoulder. "You are fucking killing me right now, woman."

She sits back fast, covering her mouth when she looks down. "Oh."

I cough out a painful laugh because she's fucking perfect. Then I rest my head back on the couch, and she moves my shirt up, so she can flatten her palms against my chest.

"You'll be thirty by next month if you keep healing me at this rate." I reach out to push the hair off her face, and she turns into my palm, her melty eyes connecting with mine when she shrugs.

"Not like this life has to last me much longer anyway. You'll get your light back soon"—she straightens her shoulders and presses her hands into me—"and then I'll unbind you and reset."

Her lids fall closed, and the hum shivers over my skin. It's the first time Nyx has said she would unbind me from Abaddon. That, after we reverse the light from the blade, she'll willingly die. For me.

My heart starts beating faster, and I've never been surer of anything in my existence.

I can't let her.

TWENTY-EIGHT

CHAZ

If I wondered about Zagan's cutoff comment from last week in the hallway—before his cheap shot at me with a fireball—I'm guessing it probably would have gone something like this: *But remember, you can't hide forever, and there are plenty of ways I can be a fucking prick in the meantime.*

They hit Rosdan first. He couldn't tell if they were after him or his charges or just there to make a point, but it was five Lowers all at once. I had a pack of them outside my window a few nights back—Zagan in the background with his blue flame. Cass dealt with an Upper stalking him and Hannah through their building's parking lot until he lost his patience and chased her off. She seemed like an independent contractor though. Another Upper ready to take over Donny's crown.

With the attacks spread out over all three of us now, Rosdan has drastically cut down on his time here. He spends more time with the triplets and follows his other two charges anytime they leave the house. Even though the kid sits in a classroom all day and Mark stays in his cushy executive office—both protected by blocker bags. Not that I blame him. So far, none of the demons have realized my unprotected charges live five feet away from me, but I still stare at the palm stone like my eternity depends on it. And if my light returns—so that I'll still have one—it will.

"You need help?" Nyx asks, coming into the bedroom.

I've been researching all day and stockpiling any spells that show promise. A little while ago, I activated the blade with Nephilim blood and cast every one. All worthless.

She sprawls out on the bed beside me. I move my books over, sliding one under the pillow in case she's figured out how to read a dead language in the past few hours. Since I've decided I fucking love this woman, I've branched out my search beyond the Dimming Blade. If I'm unbound from Abaddon, it won't be by her. I'll find a spell or track down another Descended—anything other than letting her die.

"I'm good." I scrub my hands over my face.

She crawls onto my lap, and I lean against the headboard. "You've been in here for twelve hours."

"The fuck?" Sure enough, it's after eight when I check my phone. "Sorry, baby. You eat?"

"Mmhmm," she says, laying her head on my chest.

I have zero plans on moving first, and I hold her on one side while watching the palm stone in my other hand. Kai's working toward a deadline while Avery empties the dishwasher. Riveting stuff. I'm about to switch to her brother again when she drops a fork in the basin and reaches for it. Then she screams, jumping back.

"Fuck," I say, jolting upright and knocking Nyx off me. "Avery just sliced her arm open."

"What?" She scrambles off the bed as I dash out of the room.

"She caught the tip of a knife." I've listened to her bitch at Kai to quit leaving knives sticking up countless times. Christ, if I lose my eternity over a household chore, I'll be so pissed off.

Not caring about demons, I rush across the hall and pound on the twins' door. "Aves, open up."

"Chaz?" she cries from the other side. A second later, she answers in tears, panicked, with her hand clamped over a dish towel.

I hit an invisible wall with my next step. "No, no, no. Aves, I need you to listen to me."

She nods, and I start to tell her where in the kitchen the blocker bag is when I remember she'll only deactivate it for Cass or Rosdan. I teleport to my bedroom for my phone, but before I call Ros, I hear Nyx. Across the hall.

"It's okay," she says as I blink to the twins' door again.

"Nyx."

But she's already inside—safe. For the moment. She stands in the living room where I can see her and picks a crystal out of the bag. Then, I'm in the apartment, and the amulet around my neck glows as I cup Avery's face in my hands.

"We're going to help you." I try to smile as her cheeks warm, and she falls under the light's effect. "You won't try to run or make any noise, okay?"

She nods, and I hitch an arm around Nyx and teleport them to my living room. I head straight back and *suggest* Kai stay chill, too, and then all four of us are in my apartment. Kai immediately sits on the couch without a word like I told him to.

Nyx carefully peels the bloody towel back. "She probably needs stitches."

I call Rosdan, but it goes to voicemail after several rings.

Avery's paling—not a fan of blood in the first place.

After an unsuccessful call to Cass, I blow out a breath. "I'm going to have to portal her to the ER."

"Wait." Nyx shakes her head and backs Avery to the couch, prompting her to sit down, and then she turns to me. "All stitches do is hold the skin together until it heals."

My eyes dart to my bleeding charge and then return to Nyx, and I huff out a shocked laugh. "Fuck, I love you." I smash my lips to hers and lower to my knees beside Avery.

After a second, Nyx steps around me. She throws a leg over Avery and scoots up her thighs. Under different circumstances, incredibly hot.

I toss the dish towel onto the cushions and hold the wound closed while Nyx sacrifices a month of life to keep my charge safe. Her lashes brush her cheeks, her lips slightly parted. Magic happens right in front of me, but all I see is her.

Once the scar forms, her eyes flutter open, and she turns her head. "What?"

I shake my head. "I just like looking at you."

She smiles. "You fucking better."

We clean Avery up, and then I teleport her and Kai across the hall. I use the amulet to make them forget everything that happened in the past ten minutes. Since the spell will kick me out when I reengage the blocker bag, I also tell them not to touch the velvet pouch on the table. Cass or Ros can put it away later.

I leave Avery's room, already thinking about Nyx's head on my chest again while I read. As I go to shut the twins' open apartment door, I see her across the hall through mine. It only takes her eyes landing on me and then shifting to something behind me. I whip around with the amulet, its light slamming into the demon before her flame touches me. She staggers backward, and I snatch up the crystal and toss it in the bag. It forces us out of the apartment, and we pop up outside the building in the grass.

The location change disorients her long enough that I can teleport into my apartment. I land, and the first thing I scan for is Nyx. And once again, she's across the hall.

I throw my hands in the air and flash to my doorway. "What the hell are you doing?"

"You left it open!" She grabs the twins' doorknob.

I reach for her, jerking her over the threshold just as the Upper appears. The door slams, and with everyone in their safe place, my forehead falls forward against the wood. I draw in a deep breath, feeling Nyx's arms come around me, her head resting on my back.

"I meant it," I say.

A few beats of silence has me thinking she doesn't know what I'm talking about, but then she slips around to get between me and the door. I move enough to give her room and run my hands up her neck. She hangs on to the front of my shirt, staring up at me.

"Say it again."

I trace her bottom lip with my thumb. "I love you, Nyx."

Her eyes close, and she sighs. "I love you too, Chazaqiel." She waits a second and then smiles, looking at me again. "But I've got a few lives on you."

"Yeah, well, you had a head start." I bring my mouth to hers and mumble, "I'll catch up somewhere between here and eternity."

DARKENED SOUL

The attacks only grow stronger over the next few days. More calculated.

The Uppers begin coordinating, and I'm starting to get the impression they give less of a shit about *who* kills me as long as *someone* takes me out while I'm bound to Abaddon. The dude collects enemies for a hobby.

Their strategy depends on my brothers turning on me. Threaten the Nephilim, so Cass and Rosdan have to pick—their charges and eternities or me. I have no illusions about how it would go down if that happened. I'd choose Kai and Avery over them too.

But the demons have to get to a Nephilim first.

"Hannah's on Thanksgiving break," Cass says, pulling her to his side. "We'll stay inside our apartment or drop straight to your charges' place."

Rosdan sighs through the speaker of my phone. "Alistair's on break as well. I'm going to suggest Mark take his vacation early this year, and then the entire house is going on lockdown. Family time galore."

I nod, and Cass leans forward with his bullshit radar engaged.

"We're getting this figured out." He lifts an eyebrow when I don't immediately respond. "If you think I'm letting any of us get taken out because of something Donny pulled, maybe you *should* be wiped from existence."

Hannah shoves his shoulder, and one side of his mouth turns up.

"You're a dick," I say.

"And you're an asshole," Rosdan chimes in. "I'll be there later after I get everyone settled in here."

The second Cass and Hannah leave, the amulet powers down. I swear, it's like my fucking pet at this point. A living, breathing thing I've bonded and formed a connection with. Its power increases every time I use it—nowhere near as strong as Samy had it at, but he knew a shit-ton more spells. Each power bump also intensifies the ache of the darkness, though, so it can level off anytime now as far as I'm concerned.

When Nyx comes out of the bedroom, she beelines for me on the couch. She still hides when Cass comes over. She claims she'll stop once he quits glaring at her. I hate to break it to her, but that's just my brother's face.

We only get an hour before Rosdan calls so I can let him in. Unlike Cass, he has fully warmed up to Nyx.

With him on knife duty in the living room, Nyx is occupied with yet another one of his quizzes on The Descended. I take advantage and sneak off to flip through the last book that might help unbind me from Abaddon. I've hit so many dead ends that I'm starting to wonder if Nyx has any idea what she's talking about. Binding of life essence or force or the soul seems outside anything The Fallen have run across in our time on Earth. Everything is wiped out each time the Abyss opens to cleanse the Earth in preparation of a new creation, so if a spell like this existed prior to the last reset, we'd have no way of knowing.

"Shit." I close the back cover, no further ahead than when I started.

After I set the book under the bed to avoid nosy women finding it, I teleport to the sink in the bathroom. I splash water on my face, trying to wake up after numbing my mind. As I dry off, Nyx's voice floats in through the cracked open door.

"Can I ask you something?" She sounds serious, and since when does she ask Rosdan shit instead of the other way around?

"Sure," he says.

I hang the towel and step closer to the door.

"The darkness will leave when Chaz gets his light back, right?"

"If not then, it should once he's unbound. From what I can tell, the darkness is trapped inside of him because of the bond with Abaddon. It stays in his body even if blasted with light from the amulet. In a true demon, the darkness wouldn't stick around."

Ros and I are on the same page with that one. Usually, the darkness is forced into a mortal by a demon, or in rare circumstances, it swoops in on its own as a mortal's dying. By catching the soul before it leaves the body, the darkness can extinguish it and take over, postponing death in a way. Flood a host with enough light to overpower the dark, and you banish it. The shadows inside of me can't seem to escape, though, and my soul seems intact, like it can't quite get the foothold needed either. In my body, but not a part of me. It's as if the darkness were leasing with an option to buy.

"I check on his life force sometimes," she says. "Each time, I have to push through more darkness to get to what's him. He can teleport farther, and I bet his portals would cover more distance, too, if he tried."

She must not have noticed yet that I can control the shadows, direct them where to go. I clench my fist, feeling them beneath the surface.

Rosdan stays quiet for a few seconds. "The light left a void inside of him. If the darkness is coming from Abaddon, it might split more evenly between them over time. Or he's getting a better handle on the powers, so you're sensing it more."

"Yeah," she says, and I hear the fake smile. "Maybe."

Later, Rosdan is about to take off to do a quick check on his charges.

"I'll be back in a bit. I've tracked down a few viable spells I need to try."

I nod, not offering more. I haven't said anything to him or Nyx since I came out after their little chat. Honestly, I'm fucking sick of being the topic.

Once he drops, I head to the kitchen. Nyx is sitting on the counter as I take care of the bag.

"You okay?" she asks.

"Great." I throw the pouch into the cupboard and slam it shut. "I have a legion of upper-level demons after me, my brothers are chancing an eternity of their souls sitting outside the gates, and you're having conversations with Ros about the darkness." I stop in front of her and lean on the counter, my hands on either side of her. "Do you want me to use the amulet more?"

She shakes her head. "No, of course not. It hurts you."

"I'll hurt then. If it stops you from worrying, I'll fucking suffer."

Nyx tugs on the pockets of my jeans until I move closer, pushing between her knees. I sigh and hang my head down to her shoulder.

"I can't stay locked up in here much longer." I glide my hands up the outside of her thighs. "Not with everyone in danger because of me."

She rolls her shoulder, so I straighten up. "It won't be much longer."

"You have no idea how long this could take. And the demons won't let up for the holidays or because Rosdan's charge runs out of vacation time. Every minute I sit on my ass in here, a charge is closer to losing their life. Cass could end up losing Hannah forever. I could lose you."

Every attack, I grow closer to losing my shit. So much of it has to do with her. The need to protect her burrows deeper anytime she's in danger.

I owe Cassannah a million apologies because I fucking get it now. All the way down to my darkened soul.

"You just need to hold on a little longer," she says. "Please?"

The concern on her face feels like another blade slipping between my ribs. Stealing everything left inside of me until I'm down to a shell. But I want her to have it all.

I curl my fingers under her chin and tip it up, so I can kiss her. "When this is all over, I'm giving you eternity, Nyx. I need you to remember that, no matter what happens. We're a given."

She smiles and drapes her arms over my shoulders, and I lock her into memory when she says, "Can't wait."

The sun is skimming the horizon by the time Rosdan gets back, and I shift Nyx from my lap to the couch. I let him in and then plant a kiss on top of her head.

"I'm going for a quick shower."

Ros is already on the floor with the dagger, and I slap him on the shoulder on my way past. I lock the bathroom door and scratch my jaw, staring into the mirror for a second. Then I teleport to the bedroom.

I ease the door shut, careful not to make any noise, and grab the stack of books off the dresser. While I'm shoving them in a back corner of the closet, I notice the picture sticking out of a box on the other side. It serves as a decoy to the mystic shit compartment underneath. A few old photos and artifacts I sell for extra cash. The picture peeking up is of my brothers and me years ago. The one Nyx tried to sneak out of here and back in. Like my existence hasn't revolved around watching longer than she's been alive.

I take it without looking and adjust the lid before moving the box to the floor. Over the past few weeks, my stockpile of Nephilim blood has diminished, but I have enough left for one spell.

All I need is one.

Bringing the vial with me, I leave the letter I wrote earlier on my pillow and set the frame with the photo of Nyx and her sister on the now-empty dresser. I tuck the group shot in the corner, giving them both a last look, more time spent on one face than the others. She's what I'm looking at when I close my eyes, the image of her still on the back of my eyelids, and when they open, I'm in the parking lot.

I promised Nyx forever. I'll give her forever. Ours just might not start right away.

Twenty-Nine

NYX

The longer Chaz is in the shower, the worse I feel about him hearing me with Rosdan earlier. I couldn't give two shits about the darkness inside of him. Even if it stays after his light returns, I'll take any version of him. Including the hollow one that's been appearing the last few days.

"Your charges are safe?" I ask Rosdan.

He glances up from the note he's been scribbling out for whatever spell he's about to try. "Between the level of security they have for humans and what I have for demons, they're more secure than Area 51."

Rosdan reaches for one of the vials of blood he grabbed from the closet earlier. I look past him to the dark hallway. The soft whine of pipes comes from a different apartment, but I keep listening for the door.

With the blade on the table, Rosdan tips the vial. The blood drips onto the steel, and it flares to life. The brightness burns my eyes, this entire side of the living room bathed in white. I squint to see Rosdan as he picks the weapon off the table. He stares right at it, not bothered in the least.

"How can you look at that?" I ask after a minute.

Rosdan scrunches his face. "The blade?"

I nod. "I've never seen it activated before, but—" I hold out a hand to block the mini sun.

He studies me before his eyes return to the table and then shoot back to me. "Nyx, what do you see when you look at it?"

"Blinding light?" It starts to dim, and I lower my hand.

His eyes dart again, almost frantic before they stop, unfocused on the air in front of him. "You see…" Rosdan lets the dagger clatter onto the table. "Oh shit, you see divinity."

I sit back as he suddenly three-sixties off the floor and into the center of the room, holding his arms out.

"What do you see?"

"Is this a trick question?" I ask because, right now, I see an angel on the verge of losing it.

He strides toward me and swoops down onto one knee in front of me. "You said you can sense life force if you focus on it. What do you sense when you look at me?"

I narrow my eyes at him before I close them and concentrate on finding the essence inside of him. "White light mostly. Warmth."

"Is it the same as what you sense from Chaz?"

Still searching him, I tilt my head. "You're … more, if that makes sense?" I blink my eyes open, meeting his. "All the way in the center, you're the same, but the rest—"

"It's like the blade," he says, pushing to his feet. "Holy fuck. The rest is like the blade." He walks off, pulling at the back of his hair. "Two things differentiate an angel from mortals—their immortal soul and divine light. But the light is what *makes* us immortal. It's why Chaz is mortal right now, and he looks different because you're not seeing his light."

I glance around the room before landing on the weapon. I focus, seeking out the energy, and then the white light appears. "Turn it on." I wave my hand at the table and stand beside him. "Activate it or whatever."

Rosdan grabs the last vial from the table and twists the lid. I squint as he starts to tip it, bracing for the brightness, but I still have to look away when the blood drips onto the blade. It throws me off at first because I can't sense life—just the overwhelming light. I let my eyes fall closed, wading through the sensations, and then I feel something familiar. A soothing heat that's crept over my skin more than once.

"Chaz," I whisper.

I latch on, trying to keep it separate from the rest. The longer I concentrate, the more distinct it becomes, and I slowly gain control. I drag his light toward me. My nails bite into my palms, each breath a struggle while all of me goes into keeping ahold of it.

"Oh my God." Rosdan shifts beside me as the light clears the steel.

I fight to bring it further into the room, but I can't handle it anymore. The second I release Chaz's light, it retreats into the weapon. Every muscle aches, and my head pounds. None of it matters though.

Ros throws his arms in the air and laughs until he turns to me. "Whoa, sweetheart." He slides an arm around my waist, keeping me upright.

"Get Chaz," I tell him after a second.

Even though I'm exhausted, I want nothing more than to rip his light out of that stupid weapon and push it as far into him as possible. I steady myself and shove on Rosdan's arm to prove I'm capable of standing.

He grins and grabs my face, kissing my forehead before he goes to bang on the bathroom door.

The light is still blinding me, so I go to the bedroom to wait. Without any lights, the throbbing in my head eases. I'd crawl straight into bed, but if Chaz finds me there, he'll make me rest first.

I turn on the bedside lamp. As I bring up my knee to sit on the mattress, I notice the closet is open. The books are gone from the dresser, with the picture of Nyla and me in their place. The one of Chaz and his brothers is in the corner of the frame. A chill rushes through me as Rosdan's knocking stops, and I look down at the bed.

He comes up behind me, stopping the second he sees me picking up the envelope from the pillow. "No he fucking didn't." Rosdan runs out.

I haven't even lifted the flap yet when he breaks through the bathroom door. His footsteps approach again, and I hand him the letter. One side is for him and Cass, the other side for me.

"Did you read yours?" Rosdan asks, an unfamiliar edge to his tone.

"Only the beginning."

I know you'll forgive me eventually—even if it takes the next century. And I swear, we'll both still fucking be here in a century.

Within minutes, Cass and Hannah appear in the living room. Rosdan has read the letter at least five times, always offering it to me when he finishes. I shake my head each time, too furious to even see Chaz's handwriting.

"So…" Cass paces through the living room. "That asshole left me his charges, and you"—he gestures to me on the couch as he passes—"his fucking girlfriend."

"Yep," Rosdan says, skimming the letter again. But then he looks up, an apology on his face. "Well, he didn't *leave* me Nyx. He demanded I keep her safe, or he'll blade me."

I turn away and bite my lips together until the tightness in my throat disappears.

"And we're supposed to…" Cass waits for Rosdan to find the exact wording on the paper.

"Go bust his ass out when we finally jailbreak his divinity."

Cass stops and leans against the far wall, lowering his head. "I can't believe he fucking went to Abaddon. We were *handling* this."

"We knew he wouldn't bury his head for long, Kasdaye." Rosdan lets the letter flutter to the coffee table. "I'm surprised we kept him here for as long as we did."

I swipe a rogue tear, hoping no one noticed, but Hannah scoots down the cushion. She doesn't say anything. Just stays beside me. At least one person can stay and not teleport out of the bathroom to go turn themselves over to Abaddon.

"He won't hurt him," Cass says, and I look up. His head is back against the wall, his eyes on me. They're softer than usual and not glaring a hole through me for once. "He'll keep him locked up, but as long as they're connected, Donny will assure Chaz doesn't even catch a fucking cold."

I force a small smile and nod, but inside, it feels like I'm standing beside Nyla's bed. Only this time, I didn't get a goodbye. I got a letter and a shitty apartment.

Rosdan shakes his head, scanning the room. "I just can't believe he'd willingly go back to the cage."

"Cage?" I ask.

Rosdan winces. "He never mentioned Donny and the cage?"

I shake my head, sitting forward. I knew Chaz hated Abaddon, but since he never gave me a reason, I decided it was because of the demon's ridiculous vendetta against him.

Cass sighs from where he's propped against the wall. "The only other time Abaddon successfully pulled off a revenge plan, he imprisoned Chaz in a cage."

"What?" Hannah says, looking to Rosdan for confirmation.

"Before we were sent to Earth, we…" He rubs the back of his neck. "It never should have happened."

Cass crosses the room and picks up the letter. "Donny was going to keep him in there until he found the Dimming Blade. But we found him first. It took us almost two hundred years, and then we had to get him *out*. Abaddon had that thing spelled to shit, and if it wasn't for Samy's amulet, he'd probably still be in there."

No wonder he felt suffocated, being stuck in here for so long. Not that a cage could possibly be any better, even with the questionable carpet in the hallway.

I'm staring at the dagger on the table, and when I look up, both of the angels are staring at me. "What?"

Rosdan's eyes shift to the side to Cass. "We know how to get his light back to him…"

"And after the desert disaster, I made sure he gave me a few vials' worth of blood, so we could track him." Cass tips his head as if weighing a decision.

My mouth dries as I realize what they're saying, and I bolt off the couch. "Let's go. If we get the blade close enough, I can get the light into him."

Hannah's at my side, and once Cass's attention moves to her, everything about him is conflicted. After a second, he shakes his head. "*In theory*, we know how to get his light back to him. We have no idea if it'll actually work."

"Right," Rosdan says, his line of sight following his brother's. "And if we get in there and it doesn't work, we're all-out fucked. I won't have easy access to my powers, and we can't risk Hannah being there in danger just so you can use yours."

They both deflate a little, and I see them switching courses.

"No." I pick up the blade, wrapping my hand around the handle. But unlike last time, I'm on the right end of the tip. "It will work. It's no different than passing life from me into him. Let me show you."

Cass and Rosdan backpedal when I step forward.

"Not on any one of your fucking lives," Cass says, extending his arm all the way out so he can take the knife from my hand without his body being anywhere near it. "We're trying to fix the problem, not multiply it."

Rosdan's watching me when I look over.

"You saw me bring the light out, Armaros. You know this will work."

The room falls silent for a few beats, his eyes sweeping over to Cass again.

Then he licks his lips and nods. "Fuck it. Stab me."

THIRTY

CHAZ

The Lower follows behind me like a puppy on his leash as I step out of the portal. I stop to close it, and he messes with the light-infused chain around his neck, so I give it a tug—harder than if he were truly a puppy and not a being of Hell. His hands fall away. Such a good boy.

I snagged three different demons outside the apartment building before I caught one stalking around on behalf of Donny. He'd brought the chain for me, so one tackle and a quick spell later, and he was staring up from the ground at the glowing amulet in my hand. Without a word from me, he was promising to show me straight to the Upper.

"The desert?" I say, looking around. "What is his deal?"

The sunset still burns the sky while I look around the scrubby desert floor with a few rock formations towering nearby along with a cliff. My Lower points toward one of them. Seconds later, Abaddon teleports in front of the boulder. Along with five grungy demons.

"You agreed to let me go," the one next to me says.

I unwrap the chain, and he teleports out with two of Donny's lackeys following after him. Chances are, they'll take each other out, ridding the world of a few more nuisances.

The other four figures stay in place, lasered in on me. As I stride toward them, the Lowers ease backward, smart enough to understand that they're the only ones who stand to get hurt.

"What?" I say. "No smart-ass comment or *Chazaqiel*?"

Donny shrugs. "Guess I'm done with the game."

I'd really like it if these assholes would quit referring to my existence as a fucking game, but that's a subject for another time. I throw the chain at his feet. He looks down at the links on top of his loafer and moves his foot, so they clank to the ground.

"Uppers keep coming for me in order to take you out. It's annoying. So, time for a deal."

"You want to make a deal with *me*?" His slimy smirk curls the corners of his mouth. "Don't disappoint me, pretty boy."

I cross my arms, letting him know what comes next isn't up for negotiation. "Leave Kasdaye and Armaros alone. Don't go near any of the Nephilim—mine included."

"So many demands, Chazaqiel. What do I get?"

"Me." I look him straight in the eye, not wanting him to know I'm a fucking nervous wreck inside. "I'll go in the cage."

His face hardens. "Do not test me, Watcher."

The very thought of losing Nyx, even for a little while, is an anchor threatening to drag me down. Living without my light the past few weeks, while excruciating, has been bearable. The torture of the darkness trying to escape the amulet is tolerable. But knowing I won't touch her, stare at those eyes, or hear her voice for decades … that's slowly tearing apart my soul. I need to buy my brothers more time though. A real chance to figure out my light. And with Abaddon, the greatest currency is me.

"I'm not," I tell him. "I'll walk in on my own and close the door behind me. Hell, I'll even click that mystical padlock shut to save your fingers the trouble."

Either he's suddenly developed a poker face or he thinks it's bullshit. He folds one arm over his chest, propping his elbow on it and rubbing his chin. "You want something else."

I nod, steeling my expression. "Nyx lives her life. My brothers will protect her, and when she dies *naturally*, she'll unbind us. Then you can do what you wish with me."

"Why?" Abaddon cocks his head to the side. "After all this time, why would you give yourself up to me?"

Because I'm banking on the last part being a lie. Cass and Ros will figure out the blade and break me out long before Nyx dies. Once I'm immortal again, no Upper will even try to touch me. We'll lock Abaddon up until Nyx unbinds us, and then I'll switch to Cass's plan—banishing the darkness from this asshole once and for all.

Or shit goes sideways, and I'll die in the same cage that held me for two centuries, taking the demon down with me. Either way, Nyx stays alive and safe. I'll chance my existence for that. I'd risk everyone's. Now, tomorrow, forever. Sign me up for an apocalypse as long as she's untouched at the end.

But in response to his question, I lift a shoulder and let it fall. "Love will kill us all." Then I add, "Remember that, Baddo. This is a learning moment."

"Right." He points a finger in the air, drawing loops. "I'm jotting it down now."

I smile, shaking my head. "Just think, we'll get decades of this banter."

He looks like he has more sass left to give, but then his head whips to the right. At the same time, my pocket heats—and glows.

Shit.

I slap a hand over the light, and with Donny's attention elsewhere, he misses it. A Lower flanking him notices though. Shadows flow from his hands until I flick up my flame by my side. His eyes move to Abaddon and then back to me. Then his shadows suck back in, and he teleports out.

Huh. That was easy. I was expecting to go all stealth and kill him without alerting everyone to the powerful amulet I'm attempting to smuggle into the cage with me. Before I get too far on the optimistic track, I check to see what has the others so distracted.

And the train fucking explodes.

An army of Lowers is gawking at us from the top of a cliff. I squint at the two figures off to the side and force out a laugh when I make out Braxis and Zagan.

Great.

The douche twins have finally worked out their issues.

Right on time to fuck up my plan.

THIRTY-ONE

NYX

"We really doing this?" Cass asks, standing in front of Rosdan.

He has his arm on his brother's shoulder, the illuminated blade between them. Since we couldn't find any more vials of Nephilim blood, Cass slid the dagger through Hannah's partially closed fist, dripping hers onto the metal to activate it. Much more than a vial's worth. It only took me a few seconds to heal her. She's standing on the other side of them, looking nearly as worried as Rosdan.

His eyes keep bouncing from Cass to me, a little more panicked every time. "What's the worst that can happen?" He blows out a hard breath like he's amping himself up. "I live out a mortal life and then poof out of existence?"

Cass nods and laughs, but there's no humor in the room. "Yeah, brother. That's exactly what could happen."

Rosdan looks over at me. "I trust her—*fuck*!"

The blade plunges deep, and he grabs on to Cass's arm. Cass aimed between the ribs, the same place as Chaz's scar, but with a little more precision to avoid hitting anything vital. I missed this part with Chaz. The absolute torture crossing Rosdan's face as he reaches for his side where his brother buried the point. His light flows out of him, and it's as if the life dies out too. His color fades, his eyes dulling.

When Cass pulls back, Rosdan grunts and drops to his knees.

The pain radiating from him is so much, I snatch the handle out of Cass's grasp and lower down beside him. I focus, finding the energy I felt earlier inside of Rosdan. The exhaustion returns as I slowly bring his light out of the steel. It only needs to travel a few inches to Rosdan's chest. I throw the dagger off to the side, and once the light touches him, he hauls in a deep breath like he was suffocating without it.

"Shit," he says, nearly panting. Then he lunges at me, tackling me to the floor in a hug. "Thank you. Fuck." He jumps up, still breathlessly cursing, and lifts me to my feet.

I get an approving nod from Cass, and he reaches for the weapon.

"Wait." Rosdan shakes his head, his hands flexing. "Something's not right."

Terrified I somehow screwed it up, I tense. "You can't feel your light?"

"No," he says, looking up, and then his palms start glowing. "I *can* feel it. *All* of it."

He disappears from beside me, and a few seconds later, Cass fishes his phone out of his pocket.

"What?" he answers. His eyes widen as Rosdan drops in from where he left, and they both lower their phones.

"They're all safe." Rosdan combs a hand through his hair, visibly shaken. "Alistair and the triplets are asleep, and Mark's watching a nature documentary." The room falls silent until he says, "I have my powers back, no Nephilim required."

Cass flips the blade around, handing it to Rosdan. "Stab me— no." He swivels around to Hannah. "You do it. I'll go ballistic on Ros."

"Hell no," she says.

He cocks a brow at her. After a second, she tosses me a concerned glance and grabs the hilt. Cass pulls up his shirt and tugs her forward by the wrist, lining up the point for her. His hand stays on her as he nods, his nostrils flaring.

She thrusts forward.

His jaw muscles work below the skin, but the only sound he makes is rough breaths, his focus always on Hannah. Just like with

Rosdan, he grows peaked as the light leaves him. He moves Hannah's hand back and grips the handle, rotating to me.

I take it and am about to close my eyes.

"Hold the fuck on." He turns and yanks Hannah toward him, his mouth colliding with hers.

Rosdan sighs from beside me. "Jesus Christ."

When they break apart, Cass shrugs. "You're still better than the light."

She laughs, and he holds his arms out.

"Let me have it," he says to me.

I've only sensed his light once, but I locate it rather quickly. I reverse the process, giving him back his divinity, and his palms spark.

He smiles, and I think I've finally redeemed myself.

"You ready?" he asks Rosdan.

Rosdan snorts. "To ruin Abaddon's day? Always."

Cass drops Hannah across the hall with the twins, and I tighten my hold on the Dimming Blade. "Will I be able to get to Chaz if he's already in the cage?"

Rosdan quits inspecting the already-fading scar on his side. "You're not coming with, Nyx. We'll get him and bring him back here."

I open my mouth to argue, but Cass reappears.

"I've got Chaz's blood at my apartment. We can figure out where he is from there."

"But—"

Rosdan cuts me off with a shake of his head. One I've gotten before from Chaz, and I know I'll have the same results, so I don't bother trying.

"Don't forget the blocker bag when we leave," Rosdan says, and I nod, heading toward the kitchen.

But when they disappear from the living room, I stop.

I wait a few seconds to make sure they aren't coming back before I grab my phone from the table. With the blade in one hand, I scroll through my contacts until I reach *NEVER ANSWER*.

And I'm not going to, but I will call.

"About damn time, love," Hex says when he picks up. "Finally come to your senses?"

"Can a demon track another demon?" I ask, unsurprised that he clearly already had my number. "Say I needed to find Abaddon, would any asshole Upper be able to help me?"

A deep sigh comes through the speaker. "Under normal circumstances, no. But this one might have a few tricks up his sleeve."

"Can you find me?"

The question barely finishes before he appears, stepping through a portal in front of me.

He holds the phone away from his ear and smirks, spotting the active blade and then looking up. "We're going to save your dark angel then?"

THIRTY-TWO

CHAZ

Ten minutes. The demons chill on the cliff for ten damn minutes without moving a muscle. If not for the Uppers, Abaddon and I would have portaled out and continued our conversation elsewhere, but they would only track us. So, we enter into one of those notorious demon standoffs. Each side waiting to see who can last longer. It's almost as if they were compensating for something.

Finally, our friends teleport into a loose formation in front of us.

Abaddon's already shuffled against the boulder when he hisses out a command. "Get him to the cage."

When the three Lowers move toward me, I bring the amulet out from my pocket. It still emits light as I hook it around my neck, sending them retreating. Abaddon realizes my smuggling scheme, and more of him than usual beams red. We don't get a chance to talk it out before the opposing team launches the first round of fireballs. Whether we like it or not, Abaddon and I are each other's only option for survival at this point.

"Stay behind me, facing the other way," I tell him, stuffing the necklace down the collar of my shirt.

Surprisingly, he listens and then spouts an order of his own. "Keep inside the ring."

Before I ask, he blinks to the side of the boulder. He takes a knee, lowering the blue flame in his hand, and the ground ignites on contact. It races away from him and curves to form a massive circle around us, burning demons on its trip to the other side of the boulder, where it stops.

The fucking theatrics never end with him, but at least this one benefits me.

All the demons fit inside the ring with us. After the initial shock wears off, the unburned Lowers resume their sad attempts at an organized attack. I easily teleport out of the way of one fireball and duck to miss another. The amulet roars to life, crackling around my neck. With the crystal against my chest, the light surges down my arm, and a bolt shoots out of my hand. *God, I've missed that.* The demon I aimed at crashes into another one, and it strikes them both.

Even with close to forty of them, I fall into a rhythm, anticipating their repetitive moves—pitch a fireball, teleport here. Fireball, teleport back. At this point, I could lob light over my shoulder and still land it. If threatened, they scramble or misfire at each other, doing the job for me.

"No strategy." I catch one with a streak of light, careening him into a group. "This is why you guys never win."

Abaddon snarls behind me. "We are at a slight disadvantage, given you can't die. Well, you couldn't," he adds, a whole lot of smugness to his tone, considering he's fighting for his own life right now.

I alternate between shadows and light, slowly making headway. The farther back in the line we get, the smarter they are, and keeping up becomes a little more of a challenge. When I glance over my shoulder, Abaddon's drifted across the circle from me.

"Donny, what the—"

He zeroes in on something behind me, and I jerk around to Braxis barreling toward me. Divine light strikes the Upper square in the chest, flinging him in the opposite direction. Except the light wasn't from me, and it sure as hell wasn't from Donny.

I smile, even before lightning flashes overhead—twice—and then my bright-as-fuck brothers dive down, white wings spread. Their impact blows back a cluster of Lowers. They fold in their wings and drop, one appearing on each side of me.

"Screw you," Cass says, raising his glowing palms. "Leaving me *more* Nephilim."

Rosdan brings his up as well. "You're officially prohibited from making fucking plans from here on out."

"Not like you followed it anyway," I shoot back.

We all arc bolts at the frontline of demons before Cass tilts his head toward me and cocks an eyebrow. "The hell we didn't."

The fuck they did. Unless…

I aim my shocked-as-hell look at Rosdan, but before he can confirm, Abaddon teleports in behind me. Not wanting to spoil the surprise, Ros only gives a slight nod. They've figured out how to reverse the blade. I'll have my light again. Although the immense relief coursing through me has less to do with what I'll get back than what I won't have to lose.

"Why are they retreating?" Abaddon hisses.

The Lowers are falling back to the fiery edge with Braxis and Zagan. Tension floats between the four of us while we try to figure out the play. I see it first and point to a spot near the Uppers.

"There," I say.

An open portal, just inside the flames.

"Another one." Rosdan juts his chin to the opposite side of them, the air rippling from more than heat.

Abaddon curses and adds five feet of space between us and him. "They're trading out."

As he finishes, Lowers begin filing into the second portal, and new ones funnel out of the other one. They're switching the injured for fresh ones, and Cass groans as they advance.

Zagan leads the charge this time. He blinks in front of us, his army of dark following him. Rosdan and Cass meet them head-on while I hit the periphery. So much of the Lowers' defense relies on sensing divinity that I skirt the edges nearly undetected until the crystal kicks on, and by then, I've already struck. My brothers and I fight the way we have since our beginning. We know each other's moves and seamlessly assist in banishing darkness.

As we're warring our way through the horde of rats, Braxis targets Abaddon. I teleport to Donny, grabbing him by the collar to bring him back over with us, but he shoves me off. Rather than bother with saving his life—which goes against everything I stand for anyway—I move to what's threatening him.

Once I pop up in front of Braxis, the amulet discharges stronger than ever. The energy and heat surge from my palms and trap the Upper in divinity, not giving him a chance to escape. His black pupils spread while the darkness searches for a reprieve. With all the power coursing through me, the static is almost more than my own shadows can bear.

Finally, I have to teleport away, so I can breathe. Rosdan immediately drops to where I was with Cass right behind him, both of them clasping on to Braxis's already-wilting shoulders. They bombard the demon with light, and in only a few seconds, his head tips back, and the darkness pours out of him.

His lifeless body collapses between them, and then everyone branches off again like we didn't just take out one of the more powerful Uppers in existence. Zagan's fallen behind the protection of what's left of his army, either calculating his next attack or an exit strategy. The count of Lowers covering the ground outnumbers those still fighting, so I'll bet he jumps on the latter.

My control over the amulet seems to have increased, and I impale demons with lightning while hovering ever closer to Abaddon. Partly so he doesn't get himself killed, but mostly, I'll need to snag him as soon as Zagan retreats. Our roles reversed when I found out I was getting my light back. He just doesn't know it yet. But if he figures it out, he'll bolt, and Donny the Destroyer is nearly impossible to find down in the pits.

Out of the corner of my eye, I catch a new source of darkness. I rotate toward the rock formation, ready to light up a demon until my heart thrashes in my chest. Nyx smiles when I look up. She's holding the Dimming Blade—my light in her perfect fucking hands. But I'm more stuck on the hands, the legs, the face I expected not to see for decades.

I'm not even paying attention to the arm Hex has around her when I blink onto the boulder next to her. My mouth covers hers before she even realizes I'm there, kissing her like it's already been a lifetime. Fuck, I wouldn't have lasted in that godforsaken cage without this.

Since we're still technically in a battle over my life, I break away from her. Hex hasn't moved his arm from around her yet, and I'm about to explain why he should when I'm blindsided. And not with a fireball or a flame, but fucking Donny himself, using his body like a battering ram to knock me off the rock.

We crash to the ground inside the burning circle. I blink to the center with him right behind me, and a guttural sound rips through me as I stalk toward him. A Lower gets between us, and I toss him into Cass's line of fire. Donny barely moves more than his arm to clench another around the throat—with the same look he had while his grip tightened around mine.

He lets the body fall once I reach him, and I step right into his face, but he refuses to back down as the two of us seethe at each other, almost nose to nose.

I've wanted to look him in the eye while he dies since I got out of his fucking cage. Now, we're finally here after all this time, and I won't lay a finger on him. Other than to shove him into the same barred prison I called home for centuries.

After one last crack of lightning, the air stills, except for the crackle of flames surrounding us. The fighting has stopped, and Zagan and whatever Lowers remained are gone. Leaving only one last order of business to take care of before I get my light and life with Nyx.

Donny's minions appear at his sides, and I sense Cass and Rosdan drop in behind me. I step backward, falling into line with them. Cass shakes his head when the Upper stretches his hand. The three demons flanking him give the three of us a scan before they share a silent exchange. Their self-preservation kicks in, and once they teleport, it's just us and the Demon of Destruction.

I notice the spelled chain piled nearby, and Abaddon's throat jumps in a hard swallow when I move toward it. Throwing a look over my shoulder, I catch a glimpse of Hex teleporting himself and Nyx down in front of the boulder. As I pick up the links, she starts for me.

"Shit," I say. "One of you might have to deal with Abaddon."

Cass shakes his head but surprisingly smiles. I make a mental note to ask what the hell they did to their charges to have their powers for so long, but right now, I have a woman with a blade to tend to. Cass steps toward me for the chain, but when I look behind him, it falls from my hand. The metal clinks, hitting the ground, and Cass's head jerks to what Rosdan and I are already staring at—everything back to shit in an instant.

Nyx isn't running toward me anymore. She's not running at all.

I hold out a hand and take a slow step. "What the *fuck*?"

Hex grins from behind her, his arm across her chest. "Small change of plans," he says, clutching the Dimming Blade. "I'm going to need you to kill Abaddon."

She struggles to get away from him, but he only holds her tighter against his chest.

"I will," I say. "The next time Nyx dies, she'll unbind us. I'll even invite you to the banishing."

"Now, I'm afraid." Hex slides backward, dragging her farther away from me. "See, if it's *my* plan that kills him, then I'm responsible for his death, and his title transfers to me."

Donny teleports closer to me, his flame out. "You ungrateful—"

Cass cuts him off with, "And if we don't?" He and Rosdan are facing each other with their sides to me, and I see his hand flexing, ready to strike the demon down if given a chance. "If we decide to stick to our plan, are you going to kill her?"

"Never. Well, never again," Hex corrects. "If you refuse, then I disappear"—he tilts his head to talk to me—"with your girl and your light."

As long as I'm mortal, the Uppers will come for me—for my brothers' charges and Kai and Avery. It wouldn't even do me any good to go in the cage. Not to mention, Nyx would be condemned to two lifetimes of being held by him.

"We'll track him," Rosdan says.

"He won't hurt her," Cass adds. "She'll be safe until we find them."

But while my brothers are looking at me, I'm tracing every inch of Nyx's face. Her eyes fill with tears, and her fingers pry at Hex's forearm.

She starts shaking her head when I rub at the chain around my neck. "Chaz!"

It might take longer than a century for her to forgive me for this, especially if I'm not around to beg, but my thumb catches, and I pull the amulet from under my shirt.

"Don't you fucking dare," Cass barks at the same time as Rosdan says, "Brother…"

Nyx is fighting even harder against the demon's hold and cries out. Like what happens next is even a choice—our messy ending. Just not the one either of us expected.

"Chazaqiel," Abaddon says from beside me, his voice cracking.

I roll my head toward him and shrug with my hands. "What did I tell you, Donny?" My fist tightens around the crystal, heating by the second. Samy always did have a thing for self-sacrifice. It burns a brand into my palm as I look back and smile at Nyx. "Love will kill us all."

"Wait—"

That's all Abaddon gets out before the amulet detonates.

The flash of divinity illuminates the night sky with the two of us at the center. For every second of calm and peace the white light brings me, the darkness inside screams. Shadows flood out of the demon beside me, his head thrown back. They scratch and claw around my chest with both of us dropping to our knees at the same time.

But it's not Donny I'm watching. I'm not sure if it's because we're within the light, but I see everything on the outside perfectly. My brothers' shocked faces, Hex with the dagger by his side. And then her.

A part of me has always been mildly curious about what it would be like to die. To be a mortal and have your soul leave the body and float up to the beyond or whatever, not quite sure what comes next. The bright-light bit I buy—wanting to go toward it even if it means leaving everything else behind. For as long as I've been deprived of the divine light, if it were to shine on me again, like they claim, I would have expected my incorporeal ass to sprint toward it—until recently. Now, I realize I was a fucking idiot for ever wondering. Screw the light, the afterlife, my eternity, all of it. None of it matters at this moment.

Dying fucking hurts. And I'm not talking about the physical pain.

The real torment is the last of my soul feeling ripped apart— courtesy of the look on her face as she watches it happen. But if I could have picked the last thing I wanted to see, it still would have been her. It would always be her.

THIRTY-THREE

NYX

The last of the light hasn't even faded yet when I break away from Hex. Tripping over demon corpses, I fall more than once as I struggle to get to Chaz. And then I collapse to the ground for an entirely different reason.

"No, no, no." I say it so many times, like a word can undo any of the mayhem from the past thirty seconds.

I kneel beside him, pushing his shoulder and arm over and over, begging him to move. But he stays perfectly still, not a scratch on him. With each shove, the amulet shifts on his chest, its crystal split in two. Abaddon lies feet away, his body burned and no darkness inside him anymore. No life.

"Fuck!" Cass shouts from behind me, and then Rosdan appears at my side.

My breaths come fast as I glance up at him. Everything spins—my head, the world.

"Is he…"

"Dead," I choke out. Tears spill down my cheeks, but I swallow them back. "He's dead." My voice is stronger the second time. More resolute.

I sniff and swipe under my eyes, forcing measured breaths to calm myself. Then I knock the amulet away, pushing up his shirt, and I place my hands flat on his chest.

Here's another thing about death: it's not over until it's over. I just have to start before he finishes.

Blowing out one more exhale, I focus deep inside myself. Somewhere under the skin and muscle and all the rest of the junk is what really separates us from death. And I grab on to it with everything I have, dragging it from where it should reside and putting it where I need it to be. Inside of him. Not a month or a year. All of it.

A chill starts in my hands and feet, slowly creeping its way to the center. I feel the life draining from me, my heart pounding harder but slower. Each breath grows longer and less effective while my muscles ache and tire. After a few seconds, I can't hold myself up anymore.

Rosdan grabs for me when I sag onto Chaz's chest, yet he doesn't move me, leaving his hands on my back. He lets me die, so his brother can live.

Like it was always supposed to be in the end.

Even with my eyes closed, blackness bleeds in. The void is so much darker as my lungs draw in their last breath. My life force fully abandons my body, leaving me empty and so cold. But it doesn't matter. Because when my heart stops, I feel the first thud of his beneath my cheek.

A moment of relief before the pull takes me all the way under, and then I'm in the basement with Hex helping me off the floor. Abaddon's across the room, blocking Chaz until he stumbles back. I see us in the desert, experience the glares and scowls, relive the realization that the darkness was inside him. The bar, the trailer, all the days in the apartment together. And the nights. I witness Nyla die all over again, Chaz comforting me. Then the demon attack and Rosdan with the blade, and suddenly, we're back to the explosion of light.

After feeling the death over again, I'm over my body, which is draped across Chaz's.

I see the energy inside him—my life.

"Nyx." My name's garbled, not underwater but distorted all the same as it drifts from the physical world into the spiritual.

Chaz blinks awake and then jerks upright at the sight of my body. "Fuck, baby." He cradles me in his lap and looks up to Rosdan. "How long has she been gone?"

Long enough. I already feel the tether between my body and soul weakening.

Before I run out of time, I seek out Hex—but not for the cold and harsh essence inside him. I want the fading white light in his hand. Other than being hell-bent on making Abaddon pay, I don't know how I could have missed seeing the light in the dagger last time—unless Nephilim blood keeps it active longer.

But now, all I see is the energy. Even at a distance, I sense Chaz's divinity in the mix of warmth within the blade. I draw it toward me, easing away from the rest and then coaxing it out of the steel.

"Holy. Shit," Rosdan says, and I know he sees it.

I can't check though. All my focus stays with the light. While Cass's and Rosdan's almost felt magnetized to them, Chaz's seems less steady, as if it wants to scatter in several different directions. Still, I keep forcing it closer to him. Inch by inch.

Once his light reaches a certain point, it glides through the air with almost no effort on my part, wanting to return, like it recognizes him. He inhales deeply as it crosses into his chest, spreading through him until his essence radiates as brightly as his brothers'. No more void.

My angel is glowing.

I feel myself slip and quickly fall into my body before losing hold. Reentering is different this time. My soul settles as it should, but I know it won't happen again. The next time I die, I won't come back. And I've accepted it by the time the heat of Chaz's skin reaches me, and my lungs breathe in air filled with him.

When I open my eyes, every muscle in his face relaxes at once, his eyes glistening. I throw my arms around his neck as he buries his face in mine. My cheek presses to his shoulder, and I grasp him all the tighter, seeing Hex on top of the boulder. The fire highlights his smile, and he takes a slight bow, the Dimming Blade still in his hand when he steps through a portal and disappears.

Cass hits his knees, slapping a hand on Chaz's shoulder while he scans my face. "Thank you." His mouth turns up on one side. "Now, I'm going to hunt down your ex."

He drops from there with Rosdan giving me a quick smirk and following. But Hex is long gone and won't resurface anytime soon.

"Damn it, Nyx." Chaz pulls back and grips my face between his hot palms, crushing his mouth to mine. "That was my fucking moment," he says, still kissing me. "I was saving you."

I melt into him, placing a palm to his chest where his heart hammers, and I can sense the life in him.

After a second, his lips leave mine. "Shit."

Gripping my chin, he turns my face away. His fingers skim around, and as he sweeps my hair away from the back of my neck, I brace for what I already know. He traces down a wavy line but not the ring of the Ouroboros.

"My tattoo's gone," I whisper.

His face grows serious as he nods. "I'm so sorry, Nyx."

I smile, grazing my nails over the stubble of his jaw. "I'm not. Not even a little." I kiss him before I sit back and run my hand over his cheeks and then his forehead, pushing his hair back. "You're so warm now. Is that a light thing?"

He nods. "Apparently, it's a full-time gig now. Why? Are you disappointed? Because, if you're worried about not getting off on the darkness anymore…" A chill works its way through my jeans as his thumb rubs over my leg. "Seems a few of the shadows weren't quite ready to let go yet."

"Doesn't it hurt?"

"No, baby. What fucking hurt was thinking I might lose you." He lets out a long breath, searching my face. "I love you, Nyx. I have no idea how I survived any of my existence without you, but I'm not doing it again for a single second of my eternity."

I feel his words in my soul, becoming a part of me—like I always knew he was supposed to be. While it might be the start of my last life, it gets to be my second one with him. And so far, it's already everything I've wanted throughout all of them.

THIRTY-FOUR

CHAZ

It's only been a week since the Demon Massacre of the Mojave—which, without our powers, would have been a bitch to clean up. After I sacrificed myself to save the woman I loved, only for her to out-sacrifice me by dragging my ass back from death, one would think a vacation was in order. But Watcher duty doesn't afford much time off, so I'm following Avery home from the daycare.

Life's already back to normal with the twins, no one any the wiser. At the beginning of their apartment lockdown, Rosdan and Cass took care of bosses and professors and anyone else who might take issue with them essentially disappearing, so it was a smooth transition.

While the light might always be pumping through my veins now that Nyx shoved it back in, everything inside me flows Avery at the moment. I watch her park under the lamppost outside the apartment building, and I flex my hands. Heat cascades down my arms and into my palms, the ever-constant cool in the tips from the shadows. But I sense the difference between the usual divinity and what's coming from her.

Once my charge gathers her bags, she climbs out with her hand buried in her purse. I wait for her to get to the sidewalk before I step around the corner.

"Hey, Aves," I call, hitting the lock on my key fob.

My car beeps from a few spaces away, and she slows down.

She brings her hand out of the bag when she sees me, letting go of the pepper spray, and she adjusts the strap. "Do you usually get home now?"

I shake my head, crossing her path to her opposite side. "Early night." Then I add, "Lucky you."

We walk toward the building together, and she rolls her eyes, never noticing the dude with the switchblade retreating in the direction he came from. Inside, I usher her onto the elevator and hit the button for our floor.

As the doors close, she glances over. "So, what exactly is it you do?"

"Life insurance," I say, willing her not to push for specifics.

But she does.

"I know that, but do you file the claims or sell it or—"

I turn toward her fast, the glow breaking through my skin as I cup her face. "You know exactly what I do, Aves," I tell her, my voice butter and her eyes softening. "And you think it's boring, so you never ask about it."

She nods. "Most of what you do is boring."

Smiling, I nod back. "Incredibly. You won't remember this conversation."

I let go of her, and she blinks out of her daze as we reach our floor.

"You and Nyx should stop by later," she says on our way down the hall. "We could watch something—no horror."

"You sure?" I ask. "I know how much you love that shit."

After a little suggestion, the twins think the chick Kai dated was Corey, who looks nothing like Nyx. Helpful in keeping movie night and Chinese from being incredibly awkward.

We go our separate ways at our apartment doors. I flip the lock on mine and set my keys on the counter as I head to the bedroom. Nyx has successfully taken over half my dresser since I won't let her use the closet. Right now, it's occupied.

I open the door and squat beside the UV light set over Samy's amulet. The crystal might be broken, but with a little Nephilim blood and TLC, it should repair itself over time. I hover my hand over the top of it, emitting light for the crystal to absorb until it glows on its own.

Once I finish feeding my pet rock, I seal it back up. Then I drop to the lake behind the farmhouse.

Nyx is already on the dock, staring out at the water, and I walk up behind her and slide my arms around her. We've done the lake thing the past few days since she scattered Nyla's ashes. But while she's here for the ripples reflecting the colors of twilight, I come for an entirely different view.

"I'm thinking about calling a realtor," she says after a minute.

She sinks further into my chest, resting her head on my arm, and I lean down to kiss her temple.

"Or we could hang on to it for a little while. I'm about over the shitty-apartment scene, and it would be nice to have more room."

She cranes her neck to see me. "For what? When you crack and move Kai and Avery in with us?"

I make a face and shake my head. "Fuck no. For when you decide you want this in miniature form."

Nyx spins all the way around in my arms, eyebrow raised. "Are you asking me to create a Nephilim-Descended hybrid with you?"

"Not even a little," I say fast.

Jesus. What a disaster that would be. Lydia would self-destruct. Not to mention, I rather like this version of creation. I'd hate to be the reason it got a reboot.

I tuck her hair back. "I was planning on a more basic human-Descended model."

Nyx stills, not breathing or blinking until she whispers, "But that would mean…"

We haven't talked about what happens now that I have my light. I'm immortal again. No aging. No dying. As far as I'm concerned, that only leaves one option—I ask to become human. A request I never considered until recently, but if it means spending my forever with her, I'll fucking beg on my knees.

I tip my chin down to bring my face closer to hers. "I've been in the light, Nyx. I've felt the darkness inside of me. Hell, I've experienced them both at the same time. None of it compares to you. None of it ever will."

She smiles, and I skim my nose along hers as I move my hands to either side of her face.

"You're going to marry me," I tell her with no light coming from my palms.

She nods. "I am."

I nod back, rubbing my thumb to catch a tear. "And we're going to live a mortal life together, die, and then I'm going to fucking love you for eternity."

"Yes," she says. "To all of it, Chazaqiel."

"Good." My mouth turns up. "Because it was going to get weird if we weren't on the same page about this."

EPILOGUE

ROSDAN

A rap version of "Jingle Bells" blares from the speakers in the living room, tinsel hangs off tinsel in the doorways, and Cass murder-glares at anyone who even looks like they might not be having a jolly time. Must be Christmas. Our second one of the year, thanks to Hannah insisting we celebrate in July too.

"Jesus," Chaz says, stepping beside me. "We need to end Cass because I cannot keep wearing these fucking sweaters."

My eyes dip to the angels on his chest, playing soccer with a halo, and I sip from the cup that was forced into my hand to hide a smile. As I swallow whiskey with a dash of nog, I tip my cup toward Kai on the couch. "Explain to me again why your charges are here."

"Kelley insisted I not leave them alone for the holidays." He shrugs and spins, backing farther into the room until he sinks down on the sofa. "Easier to play along than upset Cassannah, brother."

I nod. "Yeah, I'm sure it is. Speaking of, where's the other half of Naz?"

He flips me off, and I get a shove from behind as Nyx comes through the door.

"You're supposed to be the tolerable one," she says.

When she sits on the couch beside him, Chaz hauls her into his lap and kisses her cheek. It's weird as shit to witness, like seeing a unicorn in a petting zoo—which were real until the last reset on creation. For whatever reason, they didn't make it back into the fold.

I finish off my whiskey, and when I turn for the kitchen, a five-three blonde hits my chest. I catch Avery by the waist with my free hand before she stumbles, and she grabs on to my arm. She finds her balance and peeks up at me, her cheeks flushing.

"I'm sorry," she says, releasing her grip. "I usually let a guy buy me a drink before I throw myself at him."

One side of my mouth perks up, and without missing a beat, I offer her my empty cup. "We'll just do things a little backward."

She laughs. "I guess we will."

Instead of letting go, my fingers curl around her hip, and she tips her chin the rest of the way up. She has no idea most of this has happened already. And she proves it a second later.

"It's Rosdan, right?"

I nod, my smile tight as my hand falls away. "Ros."

My name means nothing to her, though, and she taps the rim of my cup, stepping around me. "Thanks for the drink."

"Anytime," I say, turning with her.

She crosses to the couch. Despite the leggings with Santa's face splattered all over them, my eyes stay glued to her ass until Chaz cuts off my view.

I worry he's caught me checking out his charge, but he stops in front of me and knocks his empty cup against mine. "I need to be drunk before Kelley wants to karaoke or some shit."

"Very drunk."

"Did the lights just flicker?" Nyx asks from behind him. "Did they flash or something?"

He looks over his shoulder. "Probably. The breakers can only handle a few thousand twinkly bulbs at a time."

Not an untrue statement. With the amount of decorations plugged in, we're lucky the Kelley family house hasn't caught on fire. According to Cass, Hannah's dad nearly electrocuted himself annually. Not that I felt much sympathy over him juggling two charges—one now, and he fucking lives with her. Same with Chaz and his two across the hall. I have five, three of them not even potty-trained yet, meaning I have plenty of time left on Earth before any chance of going home.

Chaz's head is just coming around again as a hand slaps my back and jerks me through the doorway by the shirt.

"The fuck?" I say, spinning around to Cass.

Since Nyx gave us back our light, I could stand balls out in a snowstorm and stay warm, but seeing the panic on Cass's face as he backs across the kitchen to Hannah chills me down to my fucking soul.

Chaz steps beside me. "Shit, what now?"

The tension radiates off him as we exchange a look. Neither of us is used to Cass being alarmed over anything other than the safety of the woman at his side.

"I don't know." Cass shakes his head. "She was just getting something off the fucking shelf, and—"

"What the fuck happened?" I ask.

"She fell off the counter. I went to catch her, but then … shit." He drags a hand through his hair and gestures to Hannah. "Just show them, baby."

She hesitates for a second until Cass gives her a nod.

And then she drops from one side of the kitchen to another.

"Oh—holy shit," I say as Cass drops right behind her.

He snakes an arm around her, giving us a *what the actual fuck* look. But even if Chaz or I had the slightest idea of what the actual fuck that fucking was, we wouldn't have time to report before the room stills. All three of us sense darkness—and not from Chaz. Cass moves Hannah behind him, and Chaz and I cover the door. My phone vibrates in my pocket, but I stay focused on the dark corner where a shadow shifts by the table.

"I come in peace." A hand appears first, palm out, as if fending us off, followed by a black loafer and then the rest of his fucking suit.

My palms glow at the sight of the Upper, but Chaz's all-out spark.

"We might have a problem," Hex says, bringing the Dimming Blade from behind his back—the handle first and then the broken-off blade.

ACKNOWLEDGMENTS

To my readers, thank you, thank you, thank you for following me on this journey. Whether you're new to me or have been on the train since the beginning, you've taken a chance on my words at one time or another, and that means the world to me.

LB, I seriously have no idea what I did to deserve you. And, yes, I'm purposely leaving it vague, so no one knows whether I mean that in a good or bad way. WE were meant to be. Thank you for riding shotgun on Chaz's fuckboi transformation. I'm glad he won your heart.

A huge thanks to my beta readers—Emmily, Callie, and Joe. The time you took to read, comment, joke, and help me shape the story is forever appreciated. I know, Callie. Chaz is your future ex-husband. Chill.

Jovana, my editor, my word-slaying queen. You never fail to catch the details and make the story shine. And Christina, I swear I haven't sold my soul to anyone. What happened before my birth, though, I can't be sure. All the hearts.

Murphy Rae, as always, you created magic. You're the best. Thank you.

Christine from Wildfire, for keeping me on track and being a sounding board when needed.

Joey, you guitar-playing, math-writing, Always Sunny-watching nerd. I hope you know how grateful I am for you every damn day. I appreciate you. I love you. To the rest of the fam, you're pretty cool, too.

All the Cool Kids, ARC readers, bloggers, and bookstagrammers—you're the real MVPs. The tireless support you show authors and the indie community is incredible. I appreciate you and everything you do to share what you love. You're all such beautiful people.

xx
CG

About The Author

CG Blaine writes unapologetically messy and emotional romance novels. She loves her characters complicated, the connections intense, and rip-your-heart-out feels.

She is obsessed with her vicious cat and aggressively cute bunny. Her favorite stories hit with the hurt and then apologize oh-so well.

Never miss a thing!
Join my reader group: CG's Cool Kids
Instagram: @cgblaine
Facebook Author Page: @cgblaineauthor
Website: cgblaine.com

Be sure to stay in the loop and sign up for CG's newsletter. You'll also snag a **FREE** short story.

Sign up at https://www.cgblaine.com